ALSO BY KATE McMURRAY

Whitman Street Cat Café Series
Like Cats and Dogs
What the Cat Dragged In

WHAT THE CAT DRAGGED IN

Kate McMurray

sourcebooks
casablanca

Published by Sourcebooks Casablanca, an imprint of Sourcebooks
P.O. Box 4410, Naperville, Illinois 60567-4410
(630) 961-3900
sourcebooks.com

Library of Congress Cataloging-in-Publication Data

Names: McMurray, Kate, author.
Title: What the cat dragged in / Kate McMurray.
Description: Naperville, Illinois: Sourcebooks Casablanca, [2022] |
  Series: Whitman Street Cat Café; 2 |
Identifiers: LCCN 2021028412 (print) | LCCN 2021028413 (ebook)
Subjects: GSAFD: Love stories.

Printed and bound in Canada.
MBP 10 9 8 7 6 5 4 3 2 1

CHAPTER 1

PAIGE HAD STOPPED LISTENING TWO minutes ago, choosing instead to focus on the bowl of green curry in front of her. It was excellent, mildly spicy with a rich coconut flavor, and she wanted to pick up the whole bowl and drink it, but instead, she took dainty sips as her date went on about...something. When Paige had checked out, he was talking about some band he'd seen at BAM last weekend.

This had to stop. Well, the food was good, but this was the third time this month she'd gone on a date with a guy she had zero in common with. This one was twenty-eight, had some unfulfilling office job to pay for his passion—which seemed to be avant-garde sculpture made with found objects, though he'd made zero money from this—and he lived in an apartment over an ice cream parlor with two roommates. He had such a "Down with the Man" attitude that Paige was afraid to admit she'd once worked for a bank.

"So what do you do?" he asked. His name was Trevor, and despite his age, he had a full Tom Selleck mustache just like Paige's father. Never a fan of facial hair, Paige had resigned herself to beards because it seemed like 75 percent of the men her age in Brooklyn had them, but mustaches?

She sighed. "I'm the events manager at the Whitman Street Cat Café."

"Oh, that's cool! I've walked by that place a bunch of times but never gone in. It's right up the block from the Petrified Cow Skull."

"The what now?"

"It's a punk bar. They have live music on Fridays and Saturdays. You should come check it out with me sometime. Friday is indie night, kind of an open mic night for punk bands, but you sometimes see some really great undiscovered bands."

Undiscovered punk bands sounded like a lot of loud noise. Paige had been game for that kind of thing ten years ago, but she was staring down her thirtieth birthday. At this point in her life, she preferred a good cocktail and friendly company to live music. Of the bars on Whitman Street, she much preferred Pop, a martini bar down the street from the Cat Café where they played music at a level low enough that she could have a conversation with her friends without raising her voice. She said, "What other bars do you like on Whitman Street?"

"Oh, there's that German place, Lautemusik. I hesitate to call it a *biergarten*, because there's no real garden element to it. They don't even have an outside seating area."

Given that the place was literally called "loud music," if Paige remembered her German correctly, she suspected she and Trevor would not see eye to eye on this, so she asked, "What about Pop?"

"That place? So dull. I'd much rather hear live music. I heard this great band last week at the Way Station on Washington. You know, that nerd bar? They have live music on Saturdays, and once a month this alt-rock band plays, and they are amazing. They're called…"

Paige concentrated on her food as she half-listened to the rest of his story. She liked music but didn't share Trevor's passion for hearing it live. She tried to change the subject a handful of times, but Trevor spent the time between when she signaled the waiter for the check and when he asked, "Is it cool if we go Dutch?" talking about some other band that played something he referred to as "punk bluegrass." When she mentioned that the last concert she'd been to had been at the Barclays Center, Trevor said, "Ugh, how could you even set foot in that place? It's *so* mainstream," and Paige knew they would never be seeing each other again. Anytime Trevor disdained something as dull or mainstream, Paige realized *she* was dull and mainstream. She was fine with that, but Trevor clearly wasn't.

After they each paid their half of the bill, they walked outside. "My place is a few blocks from here, if you wanna…" Trevor said with a wink.

"I need to get home. I'm opening the Cat Café tomorrow. But this was fun."

She waited for his departing figure to disappear around a corner before she set off for home on foot. She spent the entire walk home telling herself she was done with dating for a while, although she said this after every bad date. She joked with her friends that she had to kiss some frogs before she met her prince, but New York City seemed to be all frogs lately. So maybe it was time to give it a rest, at least for a little while. Paige's friend Lauren had told her several times that love would find her when she stopped looking, which was basically what had happened to Lauren, so there might be some truth to it.

But Paige was tired of being single, too. Surely there was some single man in this city with whom she would be compatible? How hard could he be to find?

———————

Landing a job at a high-powered corporate law firm was not all it was cracked up to be.

At eight o'clock, Mr. Provost's paralegal carried a stack of files into Josh's office. Josh glanced outside. He had an office, at least. The internship he'd finished at Davis, Cash, and Lee the summer between his second and third years had ensured that he'd been offered a good job at a great salary upon graduating from law school and passing the bar, which he'd done last summer. Josh certainly couldn't complain on that front; his salary was adding a lot of padding to his bank account right now. Unfortunately, he never got to spend any of it because he spent every waking hour at this very desk.

"Mr. Provost wants a summary of the Donaldson depositions before he has to be in court at ten on Thursday."

"Yeah, no problem. I'll just squeeze that in between the Appleton case and the O'Dwyer paperwork."

The paralegal winced and left the office.

Josh sighed and gazed out the window. His office faced Sixth

Avenue, about three blocks south of Rockefeller Center. He could see roving bands of tourists walking up and down the street, the lights on the signs of the bodegas and souvenir stores and clothing shops and grab-and-go lunch spots across the street. He'd been so absorbed in what he'd been working on that day that he hadn't noticed the sun setting.

New York City had a lot of lawyers, but it also had a lot of ex-lawyers, and Josh was starting to understand why.

When he finally left the office close to midnight, he took advantage of the company car service account and got a ride home. His apartment was in a massive high-rise in Downtown Brooklyn, and given that he'd started work at DCL about a week after he'd moved to the city, he hadn't had time to decorate or, well, furnish the apartment yet, despite living there for almost six months. The bed, the old sofa, and the kitchen stuff had come from his apartment in Georgetown, but most of his books were still in boxes, his refrigerator was empty except for energy drinks and an expired bottle of milk, and the desk he intended to set up was still packed in a long, slim box, waiting to be assembled.

On the way into the building, he stopped to say hello to Bill, the doorman. He'd picked this building because it was about eight blocks down Whitman Street from the Cat Café where his sister worked and had an upstairs apartment. When he'd signed the lease, he had a vision of popping down there on weekends to say hi and hang out. He spent his weekends now mostly sleeping or working.

Something had to give. Josh was fucking tired.

As he brushed his teeth, he thought idly about Megan and

what she might be up to now. Was she just as busy at her new firm in Chicago? Although he still felt a pang in his chest whenever he thought of her, maybe it was just as well that they'd broken up. Working a schedule like this, he'd never see her anyway.

He finished the summary of the Donaldson deposition and brought it to Greg Provost the next morning. Provost was a bit of a snake, but he was a partner in the firm, a widely respected attorney, and Josh's boss. He spent the bulk of his time defending the firm's corporate clients against accusations of fraud and other financial crimes. Since Josh had spent the better part of the last twelve hours reading through depositions, he felt confident concluding that the fraud charge in this particular case was bullshit. So he handed over the summary and was getting ready to leave again when Provost gestured toward an empty chair and said, "Have a seat."

Provost had a corner office on the fifty-fourth story of the sleek high-rise the law firm occupied. He wore expensive suits and worked reasonable hours and Josh had to remind himself that paying his dues now was how he would eventually get to this place. He took a deep breath and waited for Provost to speak. Provost asked for an assessment of what he'd put together, so Josh gave him the bottom line.

Provost smiled. "Good work. I had a hunch, but I'm glad the rest of the evidence bears that out. Hopefully this stays out of court." Provost set Josh's summary aside. "You got that done rather quickly. I only gave that to Allison last night."

"I worked quite late."

"And I appreciate that. You show a lot of promise, Mr.

Harlow. I want to give you some additional help on the Appleton case. Let's get another associate on it and a couple of paralegals. Would that help?"

"Yes, sir. That would be a huge help."

"Great. Hopefully that will free up time for one of the firm's other initiatives."

Oh, great. Just when Josh could almost taste free time, Provost was going to pull him into something else. He knew he had no right to complain; based on all the venting that went on in the private Facebook group for his law school class, his classmates were all going through the same thing right now. This was paying his dues and being rewarded handsomely for it. But at the same time...he missed sleep. And reading novels and watching garbage television and eating home cooked meals. He missed going for runs in the park and going on dates and having art on the walls of his apartment.

"All right," he said.

"We at Davis, Cash, and Lee believe that giving back to the community is something every employee should be a part of. As such, we ask all of our associates to volunteer for something."

Right, of course. Someone had mentioned this to Josh when he interviewed for the job. The associates had to volunteer a set number of hours per quarter. Most of the partners just donated money to good causes, which could be translated into volunteer hours via some elaborate equation. Josh nodded to seem game.

"I'm not picky about what you volunteer for, although my assistant Jane has a list she keeps of organizations we've done work for in the past if you want some suggestions. I only ask it be a long-term project and not just a charity event that takes place once a year."

"No problem. My sister works with a lot of animal shelters. She probably knows of some good volunteer opportunities."

The words were out of Josh's mouth before he realized what he was saying, although it was true that his sister Lauren managed a cat café that did a lot of work with local animal shelters in Brooklyn. It was the path of least resistance—if he asked Lauren, he could find a project easily and wouldn't have to waste a lot of time researching it.

"Splendid!" said Provost. "Jane's got a form for you to fill out."

Josh arrived back at his own office fifteen minutes later with a form to fill out recording his volunteer hours. He added it to the mound of paper on his desk and wondered if all law firms killed this many trees.

CHAPTER 2

AS PAIGE WIPED DOWN THE tables after the Whitman Street Cat Café's monthly book club meeting, she heard the bell ring. Startled, she dropped the cleaning cloth, and as she bent to pick it up, she heard her friend and boss, Lauren, who'd been cleaning up front, hit the buzzer to let in whoever was at the door. Paige set the cloth aside and left the cat room to investigate.

Mitch walked in. Mitch was an old friend of Lauren's who ran an organization that captured and spayed feral cats.

"Hi, sorry I'm so late," he said to Lauren with a bashful nod toward Paige. Paige didn't like to assume, but she was fairly certain Mitch had a crush on her. He was a nice enough guy, but a good fifteen years older than Paige and really not her type.

"It's fine, Paige and I were just cleaning up after book club. You have flyers for me?"

"Yeah." Mitch carried a medium-size box to the table closest to the counter and put it down. He opened it to show rows of brochures. "A buddy of mine just opened a copy shop in my neighborhood. He let me print these in color for free."

Lauren took one out and looked it over. "Wow, these are nice."

Sadie, the feline café manager, hopped up on the table and sniffed the box. Occasionally, Mitch brought by boxes that had cats or kittens in them, and Sadie was clearly deeply skeptical of this box.

"Not everything needs to be inspected by you," Lauren said.

Sadie meowed in response.

Paige walked over. "Are these for the next rescue night?"

"Yes," said Mitch. "We heard from the mayor's office that there's been something of a cat population explosion in certain Brooklyn neighborhoods, so we're trying to hold these events more often. I updated the brochure to show we're meeting every other week instead of once a month for now. Our next one is next Thursday. You should come."

It was an idle invitation, one Mitch made every time he saw her, but Paige had been meaning to say yes one of these days. As the Cat Café's events manager, she'd made it a point to get to know all of the animal rescue organizations in the region, because many of them worked with the Café to help cats find forever homes. Paige periodically volunteered at a no-kill shelter in Park Slope, but she hadn't done a shift with Mitch's group yet. She was free next Thursday—she was certainly done trying to fill her off hours by dating guys she had no future with—so maybe it was time.

"If I decided to help out next week," Paige said, "what would happen exactly? Because I'm a little worried about a feral cat scratching my eyes out."

Rather than laugh, which Paige had expected, Mitch nodded gravely. "These cats can be dangerous. Some are more skittish than aggressive, but some bite. All volunteers work in groups of two or three, and we recommend wearing long sleeves and pants, heavy clothing if possible. I know it's summer, but better safe than sorry. We provide gloves and will do a workshop on how to trap the cats safely before we get to work. We're usually out there a couple of hours. Sound good?"

"Yeah, that seems reasonable." Still a little scary. The cats at the Café could get hostile if they got riled up enough, and they were all tame, domesticated cats. Paige was a little afraid of the feral ones.

"Cool. We meet in front of the Brooklyn Museum, on the Botanic Garden side. The regulars usually congregate near the subway entrance. Do you know it?"

"Yes. Sounds good. I'll try to make it next week. I've been meaning to, but schedule conflicts." Paige shrugged in a "what can you do" way.

"You should come, too, Lauren," said Mitch.

"Not next week, unfortunately. Caleb has a few days off in a row, so we're taking a little vacation. His cousin has a place upstate. We're gonna bring the dog and savor the peace and quiet in the woods. I've been looking forward to this for a month, so I will not be canceling it. Sorry, Mitch."

"Hey, I get it. Spend quality time with your husband." Mitch glanced at his watch. "I just wanted to drop these off. I didn't mean to keep you from closing. I'll get out of your hair. But I hope to see you next Thursday, Paige!"

"Yeah, okay. I'll be there."

Josh could walk to Lauren's place from his Downtown Brooklyn high-rise easily enough. So the first evening that he actually made it to Brooklyn in time for dinner, he'd texted Lauren, thinking he'd get a cup of coffee and pet some cats, and she invited him to dinner.

Now he sat at a small table off the kitchen in Lauren and Caleb's apartment, three people crammed onto a table that was really only big enough for two.

"Good to see that law firm hasn't killed you yet," said Lauren's husband, Caleb, as he poured wine for everyone.

"It's a near thing," said Josh. "I still haven't decorated my apartment. I miss sports. I miss reading novels and watching shitty television. I miss sex. And bless you for the home cooking, because I've been living off takeout, and it's nice to eat something on a plate instead of out of a plastic container." He surveyed his plate. A nicely seared steak was nestled next to a scoop of rice pilaf and a garlicky vegetable medley. "I didn't know you could cook like this, Lauren."

"Caleb helped. And by helped, I mean he did most of it."

"One of our wedding gifts was a certificate for some cooking classes with a chef one of Lauren's friends knows," said Caleb. "Lauren was busy, so I took the classes."

"Well, that explains a lot." Josh cut off a piece of steak. It melted on his tongue. "Man, that's good. Money well spent on those classes."

Caleb chuckled. "Lauren cooked the rice."

"I boiled the water," Lauren said.

"You did it very well, honey," said Caleb, reaching over to rub her arm.

"Better than Mom," said Josh.

Lauren rolled her eyes. "That's not saying much." To Caleb, she added, "You're still new here. Mom is not the best cook."

"The chicken she made the last time we visited was good," said Caleb.

"She's not here," said Josh. "You don't have to be nice."

"Also, that totally came from a store," said Lauren.

"Ah, that checks out." Josh ate a few more bites and said, "Well, anyway. How's business?"

"Good. Diane, the Café's owner, is still resisting my plan to hire our own pastry chef, and there's some nonsense with the health department we still have to negotiate to do that, but I think if I find the right person, she'll have to hire them."

"Fond as I am of cat hair in my pastries, that seems like something you should be careful about," said Josh.

"Yeah, yeah. I am very careful."

"What's going on with the health department?"

Lauren sighed. "New York has a bunch of rules about animals and food service. This slimy real estate developer guy who has been buying up buildings in the neighborhood tried to shut us down last year by ratting us out to the health department. We were in compliance, so nothing happened." She narrowed her eyes. "Are you trying to lawyer me?"

"Hey, I was just curious. Don't you bring in all your food from outside vendors? Would hiring a pastry chef put you out of compliance?"

"No. Not if we rearrange some things in the Cat Café. There's a way to do it."

"Uh-huh."

"We have our own lawyer, by the way."

"Okay, okay."

An alarm went off on Lauren's phone. "Hang on, I gotta call Paige."

"Paige?" Josh asked.

As Lauren held the phone to her ear, Caleb explained, "Lauren's friend. She must have had a date tonight. This is the fake emergency call in case Paige needs to bail."

"Huh. I thought they only did that on TV."

"Paige doesn't have…the best judgment. I don't know if she only dates guys who are all wrong for her or if she hasn't quite learned that men are not exactly at their most truthful when filling out their online dating profiles. Either way, she goes on a lot of bad dates."

"Yikes."

"Don't get me wrong, Paige is great. One of the sweetest, nicest people you'll ever meet. She was one of Lauren's bridesmaids at the wedding, actually."

Josh frowned. He had missed the wedding and was still upset about it. He'd flown to Chicago two days before to interview at one of the big law firms there, figuring he and Megan could save their relationship if he moved with her, even though he had the job at DCL waiting for him in New York. Not only had he completely bombed in the interview and not gotten the job, but a massive storm had blown through the Midwest and grounded a bunch of flights, and Josh couldn't get anywhere near the East Coast until the day after the wedding. So he'd missed his own sister's wedding and had not gotten the job or the girl in the end.

Caleb shrugged. "She's smart and together most of the time. Just not when it comes to her love life."

Lauren put her phone on the table. "No fake emergency needed. He stood her up."

"Wow," said Caleb.

Josh laughed, a little surprised at all this. He and Lauren had always been close, but many years of living in different cities meant they weren't up to date with each other's friends or personal lives. This was also quite different from life at the law firm, but in a refreshing way. Nice to talk about friends' misguided dating decisions instead of depositions and briefs. "Anyway, you were saying about the pastry chef?"

Lauren waved her hand. "It's all boring work stuff. Not important. How's the job going?"

Josh would rather have gossiped about strangers than talk about work, but he said, "It's pretty interesting. I only wish I didn't keep getting stuck at the office after hours to get everything done. On the other hand, I just made a huge student loan payment. So silver lining."

"Oof," said Lauren.

"But actually, there is something you can help me with. My boss is urging all the associates to do some kind of volunteer work, because DCL gives back to the community." Josh added some sarcasm, which made Lauren chuckle. "You work with a lot of animal rescue organizations, right? Can you think of any opportunities?"

Lauren nodded. "My friend Mitch runs an organization that traps, neuters, and returns feral cats. He's doing an event next

Thursday. He dropped off brochures at the Café yesterday. I can email you the details."

"Isn't that dangerous?"

"It can be, but he trains everyone before he puts them to work."

"Have you ever done it?"

Lauren shook her head.

"I did events like that a few times when I lived in Boston," said Caleb. "A lot of it is setting up traps and waiting around for the cats to walk into them."

"Well, that doesn't sound too hard."

"Then I'm one of the vets who actually neuters them and has to deal with them when they come out of anesthesia. So you have the easy job."

Caleb's tone was light, but Josh took his point. "Fair enough."

"The feral cats don't usually bite too hard," said Lauren with a twinkle in her eye.

"Gee, thanks."

CHAPTER 3

"THESE MAY LOOK LIKE CUTE, sweet, ordinary house cats, but they are tiny killers," said Mitch. He stood before a crowd of about fifteen people near a Statue of Liberty replica in the parking lot behind the Brooklyn Museum. He'd already explained that a feral colony lived back here. They hid during the day, but came out to hunt at night, which is why Paige was now standing here, bundled up in jeans and a hoodie, as the evening grew increasingly cold and dark.

Mitch held up a trap, which basically looked like a cage with a door on it. "I'm going to put you in teams of two, and your job is to lure cats into the traps. Then carry the traps over to the van. Nina here—wave to everyone, Nina—she's got a little scanner that she's going to use to scan each cat. The ones we've already neutered have been implanted with a microchip between their shoulders. If the cat has already been fixed, we'll let him go at the end of the night. The rest we'll load into the van and take to the Whitman Street Veterinary Clinic to be fixed, then Nina and I will bring them back after they've recovered."

"Sure, yeah, just lure wild cats into the traps," said a bearded guy in flannel off to the side. "No problem."

Mitch laughed, clearly impervious to the sarcasm. "Mostly we put the traps out with the doors open and wait for a cat to go in. When one does, close and latch the door. You can lure the cats in with tasty treats. There are cans of cat food piled up in the back of the van. I recommend the fish ones, they're stinkier. You might even make a little trail of food to draw them out of the bushes over there. If a cat seems interested but won't go in, throw a towel over the top. If it looks dark and hidden, the cats feel safer. There are towels in the back of the van, too."

Everyone nodded.

"Do *not*," Mitch said, "try to catch any of these guys with your hands. They *will* bite, and you can get not just rabies but a few other kinds of infections. You can use your bodies to try to guide them over toward the traps, but for the most part, we're setting the traps and waiting." He glanced back toward the van. "We just got a few new traps, and some have spring doors, so when the cats step on a pedal, the door will swing shut and trap the cat. In that case, you can keep a safe distance and keep an eye out."

"Aren't we wasting time coming to the same spot you've already caught a bunch of cats?" asked a woman with an Afro.

"Good question, but no. New cats join the colony all the time, and this is the largest colony in Brooklyn. The only way to control the population is to spay and neuter as many of these guys as possible. And some of them might be strays or cats that escaped or were abandoned. But there's no way to know, really, since domesticated cats are freaked out by strangers with traps, too, so assume all cats are feral until proven otherwise."

"What have I gotten myself into?" said the guy standing next to Paige.

She glanced at him. He was a good-looking guy. Dark brown hair, a strong jawline, a dusting of freckles across his nose. He looked like he was about thirty. He had an average build, a little on the thin side.

"There are, uh, fourteen of you, I think." Mitch pointed to each person and silently moved his lips while counting. "Yeah, fourteen. Everyone find a partner."

Paige turned to the cute guy. "Hey, wanna be partners?"

He turned and gave her a once-over. "Yeah, sure. I'm Josh."

"I'm Paige. And...you look weirdly familiar. Have we met before?" Because it was a little uncanny. Paige felt almost certain she'd seen this guy's face before, but couldn't place it any context.

"I don't see how. I've only been living in New York City for, like, a month, and I work crazy hours. But I have one of those faces, I guess. You're not the first stranger to ask if they know me from somewhere."

"Everyone come get supplies at the van!" said Mitch. "I've got gloves for everyone, too. Hopefully that'll keep you from getting bitten."

"You ready for this?" Josh asked.

"Not really. I'm still pretty convinced one of these cats will scratch my eyes out."

Josh chuckled. "I'll try to keep you safe."

Mitch gave each pair two traps—which were surprisingly not

very heavy—two pairs of gloves, and a couple of cans of cat food to start. Josh suggested watching Mitch and a few of the veterans set up their traps before they attempted their own.

As they set up their own traps, Josh said, "So I've never done anything like this before. I'm gleaning you haven't either."

"No. I'm an event planner. I like cats and all, but this type of thing is all new. But I run into Mitch at work sometimes, and he's been trying to convince me to try this for like a year."

"That's a better motive than me. I'm here because my boss makes all of his employees do volunteer work. My sister knows Mitch, so she recommended I try this."

"Interesting. What do you do?"

"Oh, I'm an evil corporate lawyer. The volunteer work is to mitigate some of the evil."

Paige laughed. "Well, at least you're upfront about that."

They both stepped back from the traps. Following the lead of the more seasoned volunteers, they stood a few feet behind the traps and looked around.

"Corporate law, huh?"

Josh shrugged. "Yep. I work in litigation."

"Isn't that, like, *especially* evil?" Then Paige thought better of it. "Sorry. We just met, and I don't actually really know anything about law firms."

Josh laughed. "It's fine. You're not wrong. Well, not evil, per se. But the firm represents some, uh, less nice people."

There was a metallic jingle followed by a feline howl that interrupted the underbaked joke Paige was about to make about lawyers. Probably for the best.

"I think we got one," said Josh. He approached the closed trap carefully. Paige walked up behind him and gazed into the trap.

A very angry black-and-white cat was indeed inside. He hissed at Josh, which made Josh jump back and bump into Paige. She grabbed his waist to keep from falling and was startled both by how strong and hard his body was and by how good he smelled.

Hoo boy.

She cleared her throat and backed off. Her heart raced as she realized what was happening. They'd caught a cat! Paige cautiously leaned down to get a better look at the little guy in the trap. Josh stood near her, close enough that she could still feel the heat from his body.

"Not sure I can carry a crate full of angry cat by myself," Josh said, sizing up the trap. "I think if you grab the handle on the far end, I'll take this side, and we'll carry it over to Mitch. Deal?"

"It's worth a shot."

The cat fought ferociously, jumping around the trap and snarling while Josh and Paige carried it over to the van. The walk was only about ten feet, but Paige was terrified she'd drop the trap and injure the cat. She wished the cat would calm down, but he was pretty mad about getting stuck in the trap. Mitch smiled as they approached, which was unnerving. "Got a live one, eh?" Mitch said.

Paige was happy to be relieved of the trap. Mitch took it from her and put it on the floor of the van. "I got it from here. Take this new trap."

And so Paige and Josh set up another trap. Once it was ready,

Josh sat on a curb made by a little island in the parking lot, so Paige sat beside him. Her heart still felt a little fluttery, but Josh's presence was reassuring.

She really liked this guy. He was charming and handsome. Paige liked how his hair fell over his eyes, liked his strong body, liked the way he moved as he helped her set up the traps. His voice had a nice cadence to it. He licked his lips and she thought about what it might be like to kiss them. Which was crazy, because she never just went for it like this on a first date, and they weren't even on a date!

"You have any pets?" Josh asked.

"I do have a cat. She's a lot nicer than that guy was. She doesn't much like going in her carrier, but usually I can lure her in there with treats. I really thought that cat would get out and kill us."

Josh glanced back toward the van. "Yeah. My heart is still pounding, actually." Then he shook his head. "Was that a bad thing to admit? Do you think less of me now?"

"Nope. These feral cats are scary."

"Oh, good."

His honesty was something else, too. Many other guys would have tried to be all macho, but Josh seemed to have no trouble admitting that cat had scared him. That was endearing.

A cute guy who was smart and had a real job and seemed genuine? He was a real diamond in the rough. Paige wasn't normally very aggressive with men, but she felt like she had to do something to make the most of the universe putting Josh in her path. Maybe she could invite him for a drink or to her place or...

But that was all so forward. Not at all like her. On the other hand, whatever she'd been doing with men hadn't been working. She wanted Josh. Why shouldn't she go for it?

"Well, what now?" he asked.

"I guess we wait."

———————

That first cat must have been an outlier, because no other cats even approached the traps while Paige and Josh sat there. Some of the other volunteers floated over to chat as the hour wore on. Mitch suggested changing out the lure in the trap to a smellier brand of cat food, so they tried that. A few of the other pairs snagged cats, but Paige and Josh stood between two empty traps while nothing happened.

Which wasn't a hardship. Josh was enjoying spending time with Paige. She was friendly and funny and kept the conversation moving when Josh felt like he was running out of things to talk about. She was gorgeous, too. Long, wavy blond hair pulled back into a ponytail, revealing a heart-shaped face and plump pink lips. Even in just a hoodie and jeans, she looked beautiful, the sort of woman who could pull off a burlap sack and make it look like high fashion. Her laugh was angelic. This was a woman he wanted to get to know better. He was about to ask her a question when Mitch announced that they were gonna start shutting down for the night within the next ten minutes.

"Time really flies when nothing's happening," Josh said.

Paige laughed—wow, that laugh hit him right in the gut—and said, "Sure does. I'm almost sad this is ending. It's been fun not trapping cats with you tonight."

"Yeah, same. Although, we could go get a drink or something now. If you know anywhere in the neighborhood, I mean." Josh tried to give her his best suggestive face. "The night doesn't have to end here."

She raised an eyebrow. "Are you…propositioning me?"

Josh smiled and tried to play it off like she'd inferred too much. "Hey, I just asked for a drink. I don't know the neighborhood, but there's gotta be a bar up one of those streets on the other side of Eastern Parkway. And after that, who knows? Do you *want* me to proposition you?"

Paige surprised Josh by grinning instead of looking offended. "We'll see. And you're in luck, because I live in Prospect Heights and know the neighborhood pretty well. There's a really cute little bar on Washington. Fancy bespoke cocktails, so a little on the pricey side, but they've got an excellent whisky selection."

Josh mock swooned. "Ah, a woman after my own heart."

They helped pack everything back into the van. Now that Josh had developed a tendre for the fair Paige, he bristled a little at how effusive Mitch was as he thanked Paige for coming to help tonight, but Mitch was a big friendly guy and seemed to be effusive with everyone, so Josh let it go.

Paige draped her purse over her shoulder and turned to Josh. "You still want that drink?"

"Lead the way."

They walked around the museum, and Paige led Josh across Eastern Parkway to Washington Avenue. Crossing the huge street felt harrowing, and they were both a little breathless after basically running when the light changed.

"I've lived here for a couple of years, and I go to the museum all the time, but crossing Eastern Parkway always freaks me out a little," said Paige. "I feel like some of these drivers think yielding for pedestrians is more of a suggestion than a law."

Without thinking about it, Josh reached over and rubbed her arm. "So. Where do we get that drink?"

She smiled and said, "I know just the place."

They walked a couple of blocks and came to a dimly lit storefront with a sign that said *Trespasser's Alley* over the door. He followed her inside.

They snagged a table by the window. Josh felt underdressed; before coming to the rescue event, he'd put on old jeans and a Georgetown sweatshirt to stay warm and free of cat scratches, but this seemed like a classy place. Still, the waitress seemed unfazed as she handed each of them a menu—a piece of paper nailed to a plank of wood, of all the weird, pretentious things—and placed tiny glasses of water on the table.

Josh looked at the menu and then realized there was a leatherbound booklet on the table, which turned out to be the full listing of available alcohol. His favorite whisky was indeed listed, so when the waitress came back, he ordered one neat. Paige ordered one of the cocktails from the menu.

"This is nice," Josh observed.

"Yeah, I like this bar. It's quiet enough that I can hear you talking. Some of the small plates are good, too. I like the stuffed olives."

"Ooh, let's order those when the waitress comes back."

Paige laughed. "All right. I guess I am a little hungry. I ate before I went to the museum, but trapping cats builds up an appetite." She took off her hoodie, revealing a plain pink T-shirt that hugged her body nicely.

She really was quite pretty. Josh liked her smile and the way it reached her eyes and made her whole face light up. He liked the way little tendrils of hair had escaped her ponytail and were framing her face in a way that made her look a little ruffled and unpolished. He liked the way she talked with her hands when she was explaining something. He'd be happy to sit back and listen to her talk for hours, stopping only to make the kinds of jokes that would get her to smile at him again.

When the waitress returned, Josh ordered stuffed olives and an interesting-sounding asparagus dish. This bar only had small plates, but none of the usual pub menu mozzarella stick fare. Josh appreciated that; a quiet bar, good whisky, and a pretty girl, and he was feeling quite content.

"That was fun, but I feel a little schlubby," Josh said.

Paige gave him a once-over, her gaze settling on his chest for a moment long enough to indicate she was interested. She covered it by blinking a couple of times. "You look good to me. I take it you went to Georgetown?"

"For law school, yeah."

"I feel a little silly that we just stood around some traps for an hour and only caught one cat when we weren't really paying attention."

"The group got six cats in all tonight. Mitch said that was pretty good. I'll take it."

"I saw an article in the *Times* that the feral cat population in the neighborhoods just south of here is exploding, so there will always be a need for this kind of work. And at least Mitch is doing this humanely. In some states, people are allowed to shoot the cats."

"He said he'll take the trapped cats to the vet clinic now, right?"

"Yeah, the Whitman Street Veterinary Clinic. Downtown Brooklyn, kinda near the courthouses. Do you know it?"

"Yeah, my sister lives over there. I basically know the stretch between my apartment building and my sister's place and that's all I've got figured out as far as Brooklyn is concerned."

Paige smiled. "Where did you live before moving here?"

"DC. I just graduated from law school... Well, it feels like five minutes ago, but it was last year, and I moved here six months ago. I had my job lined up when I graduated. All I had to do was pass the bar." That had turned out to be somewhat harrowing, and he'd spent the whole last month of school trying to finish his course work while furiously studying for the New York, Illinois, and DC bar exams. He'd passed all three on the first try, barely. But his employer didn't care about his score, only that he'd passed.

"Why New York?" Paige asked.

He shrugged. "Some of the best law firms in the world. Plus, I wanted to be close to my sister. I guess I could have moved back to Ohio if I wanted to be around the rest of my family, but the paycheck was hard to turn down."

"Hey, I worked for ANP Bank for ten years. I don't judge."

"Wow, really?" For some reason, when she'd mentioned she was an event planner, he'd pictured her throwing weddings and bar mitzvahs, not corporate meetings for a huge multinational bank. Even though her tone was self-deprecating, he was impressed.

"Yeah." She leaned across the table, a little closer to Josh, and spoke softly. "When I finished college, I wanted a solid paying job but didn't know what I wanted to do when I grew up, so I applied to be the assistant to ANP's corporate event planner. Turned out, I was really good at that job and they promoted me pretty quickly. Then I got to travel. I lived in London for a couple of years, then Dubai for a year, and we did events in Tokyo, Bangkok, and all over Europe. It was great until I got really homesick and tired of the pace of that life and decided to move home and do something with lower stakes. So I still plan events, but for hipsters in Brooklyn, not billionaire bankers."

"I admire that." Josh leaned close, too. The bar wasn't especially loud, but he liked being near her. "I mean, I figured I'd get my corporate shill experience in now, and make enough to pay off my student loans, then I'd go do something more personally fulfilling."

"Like what?"

"Not sure yet. I could go work for a nonprofit. The ACLU. Public service. When I started law school, I thought I wanted to be a prosecutor. My focus was actually in criminal law, but then I got this internship... It's kind of a long story." Josh shook his head. He knew complaining about having such a great job made him look like a dick, so he didn't bother. He smiled at her instead. "I'm really grateful to have gotten this opportunity. This first job as an associate is a lot, though. I see why New York has just as many former lawyers as lawyers."

"Yeah. I know a lot of former lawyers. Two of them are librarians, actually. One works in IT. That first year of corporate hackdom burns you out, I guess."

"They make you pay your dues to earn that overstuffed salary, that's for sure." Josh sighed. "On a scale of one to asshole, how bad do I sound?"

Paige laughed. "You're doing fine. I still like you. Not an asshole."

Well, that was good news. He grinned. "Awesome."

Their gazes met. Josh didn't think he imagined the electric zip between them.

The waitress delivered their snacks. The stuffed olives were indeed very good. The asparagus had a cheese on it that Josh couldn't identify, but it paired well with the whisky.

As they ate and chatted, Josh started to contemplate how he could get this woman home and into his bed. He didn't have much hope for a relationship beyond tonight, especially since he'd be chained to his desk all weekend to make up for taking tonight off. But he liked Paige a lot and was crazy attracted to her, and he got the impression the feeling was mutual. He'd have to go back to the law firm in the morning, but he wasn't ready to let Paige go yet.

"Can I just say, it's so nice talking to a mature adult man," said Paige.

"Yeah?" Josh laughed, not believing he qualified for that description. "Do you talk to a lot of men-children?"

"The last few guys I've gone out with would have balked at the drink prices here and then talked to me about artisanal pickles and indie rock bands for half an hour. Not that there's anything wrong with those things, but the men in the Brooklyn dating pool and I have not been working out much lately."

"Sorry to hear that. Except not, because I'm enjoying your company and happy to hear that you're single."

She smiled. "I'm enjoying your company, too."

"I was just thinking, I'm sad to even think about going back to work tomorrow, because I'd love for tonight to keep going."

The way her smile widened told Josh all he needed to know. "Yeah?" She raised an eyebrow.

"You live in the neighborhood, you said?"

"Yeah. Closer to Barclays, so a couple of stops on the subway."

"Oh, me, too. Other side of Flatbush. In one of the new high-rises. It's a pretty cool building. Very modern, lots of amenities."

"Interesting." She reached across the table and ran a finger along his knuckles. The gesture left tingles in its wake. "Are you suggesting I come see it?"

"I am. You wanna?"

"I can't believe I'm going to say this, but I totally do. You wanna go now?"

Josh laughed, admiring her boldness. "I sure do. But you should know before anything happens that I'm a month into a very demanding job and barely have time to bathe these days, so I'm not sure I'm exactly grade A relationship material."

"That's fine. I'm just glad you're not living off a trust fund so you can make beer in your bedroom. That was true of a guy I went out with last week."

"Where do you find these guys?"

Paige shrugged. "Tinder."

"Oof. Well, I mean, I'm game for whatever you are. Just know that if I don't call next week, it's because I have died after the pile of paper on my desk at work finally tipped over and killed me."

"I'm kind of just rolling with things here. Let's not talk about it too much."

Josh laughed, delighted. "Okay, then. Let's get out of here."

CHAPTER 4

JOSH'S BUILDING *WAS* PRETTY SPECTACULAR. A doorman sat at a marble counter in the cavernous lobby; Josh waved at him as he took Paige's elbow and steered her toward the elevator bank. There were eight elevators in all.

"How many floors does this place have?"

"Thirty-six, although the third floor is the gym and the pool and the top floor is a lounge, so there aren't any apartments on either of those. And there's laundry and storage in the basement."

"Wow. There's a pool?"

"Now it feels like I'm showing off. Am I showing off?"

"You're making me wonder about your salary at the corporate shill firm."

Josh chuckled. "I got a good deal because the developer is a client at my law firm. And I promise you will be less impressed when you see my actual apartment."

Paige smiled. "I moved a couple of years ago into a new building on Pacific that is really nice. But we only have a doorman on weekdays and the 'gym' is two treadmills in a tiny dark room in the basement. I can't get over that this building has a pool. I'm so jealous."

"Please understand that I'm selling my soul for it. I read a brief today about a client who I'm pretty sure belongs in jail. White-collar crime, though, so they'll send him to Danbury and he'll be out in six months, but still." He sighed. "You don't want to have sex with me anymore, do you?"

"Promise to keep volunteering and donate some of your exorbitant salary to charity and sex is still on the table."

"That's generous of you."

Paige grinned. The elevator was taking its sweet time, so she took advantage of the opportunity to look at Josh now that they were actually under good lighting. He had surprisingly long eyelashes for a guy, and they drew Paige's gaze right to his eyes. He smiled at her, and those eyes sparkled. He shot her a little half-smile and rocked on his heels.

"It just occurred to me that we've only seen each other in the dark," he said. "And, well, gosh, you're pretty."

Paige smiled at him. "Thanks. You're not so bad yourself."

She leaned against the wall next to the elevator. Josh stepped closer and put one hand near her head. He stared at her for a long moment and then met her gaze. He lowered his eyelids.

Paige's heart sped up as she sensed that he was about to kiss her. She lifted her chin and rose on her toes to get closer to his face. He smiled faintly and then closed the distance between them, his lips gently pressing against hers.

She hooked a hand behind his head and pulled him a little

closer to deepen the kiss. He sighed and rested against her, and it was like they might melt together from the heat of this simple kiss.

Then the elevator dinged.

"We'll get the next one," Josh mumbled against Paige's lips. He flailed a bit but managed to press the elevator button as the one next to them closed.

Paige giggled and kissed him again.

Josh pulled back slightly. "Probably making out in the elevator bay is not the *best* idea."

"I hope that next elevator gets here quickly." Paige shot Josh what she hoped was a meaningful look.

He returned her heated gaze. "Let me see if I can work my magic." He pressed the button again.

They stared at each other for a long moment.

Finally, mercifully, the elevator doors opened.

They rode the elevator to the twenty-first floor and Josh led Paige down a brightly lit hall to his apartment. He'd spent the entire subway ride trying to downplay her expectations, so she had been picturing the standard twenty-something bachelor pad: few decorations, hand-me-down furniture, the faint but unmistakable odor of old sweaty socks, and everything dusty or dingy. But no, Josh's apartment was clean and neat, if sparse. The front door opened to a wide hallway. Josh led Paige through to an open-plan kitchen and living room. The kitchen counter sparkled like it had never been used. A big leather sofa sat across from a wall-mounted TV. There were several bookcases and a small table shoved to the side, which seemed to be the place Josh dropped his mail, and even that was sorted into neat stacks. There were still unpacked boxes, granted, but the apartment looked like an adult lived here, and not a college student.

"You want a drink, or…?" Josh hooked his thumb toward the fridge.

Paige didn't want to break the tension that had started building in the elevator bay, worried she'd lose her nerve. She scrunched her face into what she hoped was a seductive look and said, "Maybe you should show me the bedroom."

Josh grinned. "I love how you think. The bedroom is right this way."

The bed was a mattress and box spring on a cheap metal frame, and it was unmade, but there was no way Josh would have anticipated having a woman here tonight. A closet door was ajar, and there was a plain dark dresser in the corner and a matching nightstand next to the bed, but that was really it as far as furniture went. This room would look nice if the bed had a headboard, or if there was a rug or some art on the walls.

"See?" said Josh. "I told you."

"It's not that bad. Believe me, I've seen worse." Paige sighed, hearing what she'd just said. How many men's bedrooms must she have seen to make such a comparison? "Wow, you must think I'm the biggest slut."

"I don't. At all."

"I feel like I've spent half the night talking about all the terrible men I've dated."

"Yes, but I came out better by comparison, no? And you're here with me now. I feel pretty lucky."

Paige crossed the room and put her hands on Josh's shoulders.

The more they talked, the more she fretted about what she was doing. So, she pressed her lips against his. He opened his mouth and moaned softly, like a man who had finally gotten a glass of water after crossing the desert. He tasted like whisky, and his lips were warm and promising. Kissing was enough of a distraction to lessen the fluttering of Paige's nerves. She decided to stop worrying and throw herself into this.

"You feel lucky?" she said. "You're about to get lucky."

He burst into laughter but didn't let go of his clutch on her waist. "That was a corny line."

Paige laughed with him. "I just heard it."

"It was amazing." Josh kissed her. "You're awesome. Please say more cheesy things while we have sex."

"Are you joking?"

"No. Sex should be fun. We should be able to laugh. Don't you think so?"

"Totally. All right. I'll try to think of sexy puns."

"Or not. I don't want you to invest mental energy on sex jokes if your focus is, uh, being pulled elsewhere. Do what feels natural. As long as we're having fun."

Paige smiled. "We're having a lot of fun. Kissing you is fun."

"Kissing *you* is fun. I can think of some things that will be even *more* fun."

"Mmm, I agree. Because I'm guessing based on all this…" Paige ran her hands over Josh's chest. "…you're hiding a pretty great body under this sweatshirt."

"You haven't caught me in my sexiest clothes today, it's true."

"I bet you look great in a suit."

"I look amazing in a suit. I look even more amazing wearing nothing at all."

Paige couldn't wait to verify that, but she decided to play a little coy and raised an eyebrow. "Awfully confident of you."

"I bet you look the *best* wearing nothing at all. In fact, I think we should test that theory."

"Interesting. And how do you propose we do that?"

"Uh, duh. Take off your clothes."

Paige laughed. She unzipped her hoodie and cocked her hip.

Josh wolf whistled at her. "Oh, yeah. Take it off."

She continued to giggle as she took off her hoodie. She winked at Josh and then pulled her T-shirt off over her head. She'd put on a very plain bra that day, just white and simple, but Josh nodded and said, "That's what I'm talking about."

"Quid pro quo, my friend. Take off that sweatshirt."

He whipped his sweatshirt off over his head. "Is this a trade-off? If I take off something, will you take off something?"

"I accept these terms."

Without breaking eye contact, Josh undid his belt and pulled it through the loops of his jeans. Paige toed off her sneakers. Josh took off the white T-shirt he'd had under the sweatshirt, and he did indeed have a strong chest. Not super muscular, but Josh probably made use of that gym on the third floor in his downtime. Paige looked her fill before she pulled off her socks. Josh pulled off his own socks and gestured for her to go next. She undid her jeans and pulled them down, so he did the same.

"Not fair," he said. "You've got more clothes left than I do."

Paige couldn't help but stare at the bulge in his black briefs.

And now that those briefs were his only remaining clothing, she realized that he in fact had a pretty great body, and she couldn't wait to touch him everywhere. So she reached behind her and undid her bra, then slid it down her arms. Josh stared, which was gratifying.

Then he blinked and said, "Very nice." He took off his briefs. So Paige took off her panties.

"I...uh," said Josh. "It seems we've run out of clothing."

"What are you gonna do about that?"

One second, Josh was drinking in the amazing sight of Paige's beautiful body, and the next he was rolling around on his bed with her, kissing her with everything he had.

He hadn't been with anyone since Megan, which hadn't really been *that* long in the scheme of things, but the excitement level in his body was akin to the first few times he'd ever fooled around with a girl. Paige was gorgeous and fun and smart and he liked her a lot.

He tried to slow things down a little. He cupped her cheek and kissed her, then ran a hand down her front, pausing to feel her left breast in the palm of his hand. It felt perfect there, her skin soft and warm, her nipple hard.

Paige ran her hands through his hair, then moved her hands down his neck, his back. Josh kissed his way down her neck and placed a series of kisses across her collarbone. She arched her back, pressing her chest against his, and he worried he'd combust, he was so turned on.

"Do you have…?" Paige asked before moaning because he'd slid a finger between her legs.

"Top drawer of the nightstand." He was eternally grateful he hadn't thrown those condoms out when he'd moved.

"Good," she said. "God, I want you."

Josh took the hint. He reached for the nightstand and pulled a condom out. It took some maneuvering, but he managed to get it on. She shot him a seductive look and then lay on the bed with her legs parted, so he crawled between them. He kissed her hard, licking into her mouth, running his tongue along her teeth, along her tongue.

He hesitated a little. He was so revved up, he worried he'd come too fast, but Paige guided him inside her and he went along with her. He groaned as he pushed forward; she was slick and warm and squeezed him in the very best way.

He met her gaze as he started to move inside her. Her eyelids were lowered, but she looked back at him and there was a moment when he thought, *Yeah, this, all the time, forever.* But he shook it off; he knew this was likely a one-night stand. But he pushed that aside and lost himself in her instead. He focused on how amazing being with her made him feel, how his heart raced and his skin tingled and he especially loved the way she ran her nails down his back, not applying pressure but implying that she could.

She groaned when he got his hand between them and pressed his thumb against her clit. He was going to come very fast and he wanted her there with him. He rubbed little circles and she moaned and threw her head back. Then she cursed and practically vibrated around him when she came. He was lost after that, pumping inside her until he hit his release in one vibrant explosion. He clutched at her shoulders and murmured her name as he came.

A few minutes later, they lay beside each other, both still out of breath.

"That was almost too fast," he said.

"I came pretty hard if you didn't notice."

"This is like the opening volley. The dress rehearsal where we work out our jitters. We absolutely have to do it again so I can do it right next time."

Paige laughed. "All right. I'll look forward to that, then. Not that you did it wrong this time. That was very, very right."

Josh turned on his side to face her. "I have to get up pretty early tomorrow, but I want you to spend the night."

"Are you sure?"

"Yeah. Spending time with you has been the most fun I've had since I moved to New York City, and I don't want that to end yet."

Paige frowned briefly, probably remembering this would just be tonight. Practically, Josh couldn't see this having any sort of longevity. Oh, he would love nothing better, but given his work schedule... Or maybe they could date casually for a bit, and when his schedule calmed down, they could...

He was getting ahead of himself.

She smiled now. "I am pretty sleepy. I guess it couldn't hurt to squeeze in a power nap so that I'm ready when you, how did you put it? Do it right?"

He grinned. "That's the spirit! Come here."

She smiled and let him fold her into his arms. She settled her head on his shoulder. "I mean, it went so fast I didn't have time to come up with any sexy puns."

"Glad I made you forget."

"It was pretty *hard*. You'd be pretty *cocky* if you thought you could come up with better puns than me."

Josh laughed even though he thought the jokes were corny. He hugged her as he did.

"I could keep going," she said.

"I'm good." He yawned. "And apparently a little sleepy as well. That power nap sounds good."

"Nighty night, pretty boy. See you in a few hours when we do this the right way."

Josh was pretty sure he fell asleep with a smile on his face.

CHAPTER 5

WHEN JOSH WOKE UP, HIS right arm was pins and needles. When he tried to pick it up, he couldn't, and after a brief moment of worry over sleep paralysis, he realized that Paige was lying on top of it. And, well, for that, he'd willingly sacrifice his arm.

He'd always thought watching someone sleep was a little creepy, but Paige was so beautiful he couldn't help himself. Her lips were slightly parted, her hair was splayed across his pillow, and he admired the way her bare shoulder peeked out from under the covers. And then, because he didn't want to seem creepy if she woke up, he closed his eyes and tried to go back to sleep.

He had started to drift off when he felt her stir. When he opened his eyes, she was looking back at him.

"Hi," he said.

"Hi. It seems to be morning."

He rolled back and looked at his alarm clock. It was 5:00. "Barely."

"I didn't really mean to spend the night."

He reached over and ran his fingers through her hair. "I'm not sad you did. I asked you to, remember?"

"See? Don't be cute, because then I'll feel bad about not seeing you again."

"Who says you won't see me again?"

"Be real, Josh. We talked about this. One night, remember?"

"Yeah." Although the prospect of this being it was tremendously disappointing. "I know. And that's best. But we get along great, I think you're amazing, and the sex was fantastic. Is it really going to be just the one night?"

Paige bit her lip. "What about your job? You said you live at your office."

"Yeah, but I could...work around my schedule."

"I deserve more than a periodic late-night booty call."

He sighed. He flopped onto his back and gently pulled his arm out from under her. "You're right, you do. I just hate the idea of us never seeing each other again."

Paige rolled over and placed a hand on Josh's chest. "I know. The idea stinks, in fact."

Josh smiled. He wasn't sure if he could have said it better. They had woken up around three in the morning, and the sex had been long and languorous and amazing and not the speedy dance of the overly hormonal teenager, and that was something Josh would think about on lonely nights when he couldn't sleep. "It does stink. I can't...that is, there are limits to how much time I have right now, and I can't give you much, but this can't really be it. We're too good together."

Paige nodded. "Tell you what. Next time you get a night off, give me a call."

"All right, deal." Josh leaned up and kissed her. He loved how soft her lips were. He lifted his hand and wove his fingers through her hair, which even when disheveled was silky and smooth.

Paige pulled away gently. "That kiss was a very persuasive argument."

"I'll stay here in this bed forever if I can keep you."

Paige laughed. "No, no. We have lives to get to. But I can stay here a little while longer."

Josh smiled and kissed her. Probably whatever was happening here was doomed, but he was going to enjoy it as much as possible. Maybe he couldn't do a relationship right now, but he could do *this*, whatever this was. And in a few months or a year when the insanity of being a first-year associate at the law firm began to wane, who knew? There were a lot of possibilities. He looked forward to exploring them.

Paige smiled down at him and nudged her hips against his. "So…you wanna?"

He put his arms around her. "I've never heard a sexier half-hearted come-on."

She raised her eyebrow.

"I wanna," he said.

―――――――

When Paige was able to breathe normally again, she turned and looked at Josh, who was still panting.

"So that was awesome," he said breathlessly. "Again."

"It was." She let her head sink into the pillow. What was she doing? She really liked Josh, but this had no future. And still, three times in one night and they were in bed together despite the sun rising in the sky. To say the night had blown up all her expectations was an understatement. It was so unlike her to seize an opportunity like this without overthinking it until she chickened out, and yet she'd gone for it with Josh and it had been better than she ever would have hoped for. She was just as reluctant to leave as he seemed to be to let her. She wanted to keep seeing him if time allowed. Maybe it was time to take the dang apps off her phone and spend more time in the real world if more guys like Josh lived in Brooklyn. Or she could just…wait for Josh's schedule to be less nutty.

But first, nature called.

"Mind if I use your bathroom?"

"Knock yourself out. Do you remember where it is? Go through the kitchen back toward the front door. Bathroom is the first door on the right."

Paige pulled on her shirt and panties and found the bathroom again without issue. This room at least looked lived in. A shelving unit opposite the sink held a surprising array of skin and hair products and a few neatly folded towels. A coffee mug on the edge of the sink held a toothbrush and a razor—that was the sort of improvisation one employed when one had not yet finished shopping to furnish one's new apartment, and Paige found it endearing—and a red terry cloth robe hung from a hook on the back of the door. She peeked in the shower and spotted a bottle of dandruff shampoo, so maybe he was human after all.

After she finished in the bathroom, she took a moment to look around the rest of the apartment.

Really, this guy was too good to be true. He was hot, he was easy

to talk to, he had a real job and a nice, if sparsely decorated, apartment. The sex had been amazing. He had no obvious flaws, which
meant he had to have a few hidden ones. And he read books, clearly;
an industrial wood and metal bookcase was stuffed full of more
books than really fit, with some of them wedged above the other
books. There was a whole row of law books and textbooks on the
bottom, then some sci-fi novels, then a shelf with some framed family
photos. One of Josh with his arm thrown around some woman. Well,
wouldn't it be just perfect if he had a girlfriend? Or at least an ex he
was still hung up on? That would certainly be a big flaw.

Paige took a closer look at the photo. Based on the posing, it
could be just a friend. A friend who…well, a friend who looked
a lot like Lauren. Paige picked up the photo. It *was* Lauren. Paige
had seen Lauren wear that same shirt to the Café a few times. Had
Josh dated Lauren? Were they friends? What was this?

She took the photo into the bedroom and said, "How do
you know Lauren?" She held up the photo to show who she was
talking about.

"Lauren? My sister?"

"Your sister?" Paige turned the photo around and looked at it.
There was definitely a family resemblance. Lauren's features were
softer and Josh's more angular, but their hair was nearly the same
color and they both had freckles. "Lauren Harlow is your sister."

"Yes. Hello, woman I just had sex with. My name is Josh
Harlow. I'm a twenty-eight-year-old lawyer. I have an older sister
who was loud and bossy when we were kids. I like piña coladas
and long walks on the beach. What else did you need to know?"

"Wait, you're the brother who couldn't come to the wedding?"

"Yeah, I got stuck in Chicago. Long story. Why does it matter?"

"Well, I mean, not to put too fine a point on it, but Lauren is one of my best friends and also my boss."

"Your boss?"

"I'm the events manager at the Whitman Street Cat Café."

"Oh." Josh frowned. "Wow, okay. Didn't see that coming. Awkward."

"Oh god, oh god, oh god."

"Why are you acting like this is a huge problem?"

"Because you're Lauren's *brother*."

Josh pushed himself up so that he was sitting upright on the bed. The bedding pooled at his waist. "Why are you treating this like a crisis? Neither of us did anything wrong."

Paige couldn't articulate why, but something here felt very wrong. "How am I supposed to tell one of my closest friends that I slept with her brother?"

"You...don't."

Paige narrowed her eyes. That was interesting. "I don't?"

"Don't tell her. Why does she need to know?"

Paige turned that over in her head. She supposed she didn't *need* to tell Lauren. But if she didn't, then last night would remain in this apartment. "So...this was just one night. One secret night that we never tell anyone about."

Josh shrugged, and his nonchalance was a little infuriating. "Sure," he said. "I mean, I'd love to see you again. I meant everything I said. But this doesn't have to be anything more than what it is right now if you don't want it to be."

If it were just one night, then they wouldn't be seeing each other again, and although Paige wouldn't want to have to explain this relationship to Lauren, it still made her sad. But Paige couldn't imagine any way to make this work. "Oh. Okay."

"I mean, I don't know about you, but I kind of make it a policy to never talk about my sex life with my sister. Lauren and I are pretty close, but not that close."

"I mean, I don't tell her *everything*." Paige felt heat come to her face. Feeling embarrassed or out of control put her in exactly the place she did not want to be.

In her work life, she was always so on top of things. Give her a big event with many moving parts and she excelled. Why was her love life such a damned mess? She finally met a guy who matched her in ambition and intelligence, a guy she really liked and could see going on more than one date with, and he was her best friend/ boss's brother. Wasn't that just perfect?

Josh frowned, looking sleepily confused. "You're still freaking out. Why?"

Paige stood at the foot of Josh's bed and watched him rub his eyes. He was gorgeous in the morning, his hair disheveled, his bare chest shown to its best advantage in the morning light streaming through the window, his sheets draped haphazardly over his lap. He'd been very clear about what his schedule meant, and she didn't *think* she needed more than one night...but she did. She wanted more. But how could she possibly keep dating her best friend's brother? That was a recipe for drama Paige did not need.

She sighed. "Maybe I should go."

"You don't have to." Josh looked over at his bedside table,

and his eyes went wide when he saw the clock. "Oh, yeah you do. When did it get to be so late?"

"It's six in the morning."

"And I have to be at my desk before my boss gets in at eight. I mean. I've got some Cheerios in the kitchen, and you can shower if you want before you go home, but I gotta get ready. Uh. I'm gonna shower, I guess. Feel free to make coffee." Josh scrambled out of bed and walked across the apartment naked.

Paige got dressed, found her bag, and paused in the kitchen as she waited for the shower to go on. Once she was confident the noise from the water would mask her movements, she slipped out of the apartment.

CHAPTER 6

AS PAIGE SAT BESIDE EVAN at Pop, Evan looked up from his phone and said, "Where's Lauren?"

"She's closing. Told me to go ahead so you wouldn't wait here all alone too long." Paige made a faux sympathetic pouty face.

Evan pocketed his phone and smiled. Paige reflected on how much she valued these friendships. She'd met Lauren shortly after moving back to the city after her time working overseas. As a way to meet people, Paige joined a book club that met at a bar in the Village once a month, which was where she'd met Lauren and Evan. The book club was run by a woman named Eileen who had a literature degree and a lot of pretention, but the books they read were, if not always Paige's favorite things to read, good for discussion. The three of them, and sometimes Lauren's friend Lindsay from college, got in the habit of sticking around after the discussion ended to have another drink or three, and that had cemented their friendship.

She did one annual meeting for the bank in New York and finally decided she'd had enough. She had squirreled away enough money to coast for a bit while she figured out what to do next, but as soon as she mentioned this to Lauren, Lauren had insisted Paige come work at the Café.

Paige hadn't had a single regret—until now. Although Paige's salary was now a small fraction of what it had been at the bank, Paige had more creative freedom at her job than she'd ever had. Plus, the work was *fun*. She loved working with her friends and loved the challenge of putting on events that attracted people to the Café. It was a joy to get up and go to work each day.

But now she started to wonder if working for her friend was really one of the smarter decisions she'd made in her life. Working alongside people she loved and respected was great, but once that all seeped into her personal life, things had the potential to get messy.

Evan didn't work at the Café; he was a freelance graphic designer. He did the odd design job for the Café sometimes, like designs for T-shirts or the logo on the website. And their other friend Lindsay was a food writer, although even she had helped out the Café by connecting Lauren with some of their human food vendors. So it really was a family affair. And Paige did consider this group of people her family, but sleeping with Lauren's brother put this into some other strange territory. Her mind was still reeling from it.

"Actually," Paige said to Evan, "before Lauren gets here, I... have a problem."

Evan leaned forward. "That sounds promising. Something you can't tell Lauren about? Did something happen at the Café?"

"No, nothing like that. Far worse."

"Tell me."

"Do you know Lauren's brother Josh?"

"Not well. We've met a couple of times."

"So, I had never met him until two nights ago."

"Oh, did you meet at that feral cat thing? Lauren mentioned you might both be there and wondered if you'd run into each other."

"Well, we *did* meet."

"That sounds ominous. Is he a dick?"

"No. He's a pretty great guy, actually. But, uh, we had a one-night stand."

"You...oh." Evan frowned. "Wow. Normally I'd be all *get it, girl*, but I don't know what to do with that. I mean, he's cute. But he's Lauren's brother."

"I *know*. Thing is, I didn't know he was Lauren's brother until the next morning. I just thought he was a cute guy named Josh who was fun and flirty and easy to get along with. I really *liked* him. I was kind of looking for his flaws the morning after because he almost seemed too perfect. And of course, he was."

Evan tilted his head. "Hmm, okay. It's not like he lied, because he didn't know you knew Lauren, did he?"

"No, I don't see how."

"You could also just...not tell Lauren."

Paige sighed. "That's what Josh said."

"And it might not be a big deal. Lauren might not even care."

"Well, I wondered about that, but then... Do you remember what happened at the wedding?"

Evan frowned. "A lot of things happened at the wedding."

"Lauren and the other bridesmaids and I got ready at Lauren's apartment, so we were all there when she got a call from Josh saying he couldn't make it. He was supposed to land at LaGuardia that morning because he was coming back from somewhere, but his flight had gotten delayed so much that he wasn't going to make it back in time for the wedding. And Lauren was devastated at first. Josh was supposed to be a groomsman."

"Yes, I remember that."

"But then she got pissed. I totally forgot about her being upset about that until after I left Josh's apartment, but Lauren went on this huge rant about Josh's girlfriend and how she was stomping on his heart and how the only reason he went to Chicago at all was a futile last-ditch effort to save the relationship."

"Sure, okay. It's coming back to me. What's your point?"

"Lauren is protective of her brother. She was furious with his ex. I don't want to be on the other side of that wrath."

Evan frowned. "Yeah, Lauren really didn't like her. I do remember that. But she loves you. Why would it go that way?"

"Maybe it will be fine, but...it's so much potential for drama. And I'm tired of drama in my love life. I just want a nice guy and a drama-free relationship."

"Well, *I* won't tell Lauren." Evan mimed zipping his lips. "And sex is, you know, a private thing. You're not obligated to tell Lauren anything. Remember how she dated Caleb for all those weeks without telling us?"

Paige stewed on that for a moment.

"And, you know, being related to Lauren isn't actually a character flaw," said Evan.

"But it's weird, right? I mean, he's my friend's brother. And said friend is also my boss. It's too complicated."

"But you like him."

Paige decided to ignore that. "Besides which, he's a new lawyer at some big firm, so he's working insane hours and doesn't have much free time. That's not really an equation that equals a good, lasting relationship."

"Yeah, Lauren mentioned he pretty much lived at the office. She's only seen him twice since he moved here, and they live, like, eight blocks from each other."

"Not to mention, if we break up, Lauren will totally side with Josh. Blood is thicker than friendship."

Evan frowned. "I guess."

"So, see? It's hopeless."

"All right. So don't call him, and we keep this from Lauren, and we all move on with our lives. Is that what you want?"

Was it? No, not really. She wanted to see Josh again and she wanted to see where the relationship could go and she wanted him not to be Lauren's brother. She sighed. "I guess so."

Lauren arrived then. Evan mimed zipping his lips again when Lauren wasn't looking, but she quickly spotted them and walked over to the table. She slid into the booth with a smile. "Caleb is doing the overnight shift and wanted me to pass on that he misses you all but also would not be interfering with, in his words, *girl talk*."

Evan laughed. "We're all grateful for that, but last I checked, I'm not a girl."

"Yeah, he got a little hung up on that point, too, and preemptively apologized."

"Well, like any good husband, he seems to have given you permission to talk about him behind his back, so...any hot goss?"

Lauren shook her head. "No, not really. Same old, same old. The most heated conversation we had this week involved him wanting to buy a new chair for the living room and then us disagreeing where to buy it."

"Wow. What happened to you guys? Your fights used to make armed conflict look like mild disagreement."

Lauren frowned. "What, you mean back when he was still kind of a dick and we fought all the time? Yeah, we've mostly moved past that. Although the fight over where to buy the chair did lead to us having sex on the old chair, so..." Lauren shrugged.

"Whatever makes you happy," said Evan. "So, since we're all here and Lauren is a boring married lady now, I have an important love life update."

Paige looked at the table, suddenly nervous Evan was about to betray her, but then she realized she was being self-centered. Evan probably intended to update them on his own love life.

Which he did. "So, Pablo and that guy with the beard and the glasses who hangs out at the bookstore all the time are definitely a couple." Pablo was Evan's longtime crush who worked at the bookstore a few doors down from the Cat Café. For a long time, Pablo's sexuality and relationship status had been an open question, allowing Evan to live in hope.

"Bummer," said Lauren. "How can you tell?"

"I bought a book the other day and Pablo introduced the guy as his boyfriend, Chris."

"That *is* damning evidence," said Lauren.

"Should I feel guilty for approaching him about an event I want to do at the Café?" Paige asked.

"No, it's fine," said Evan. "I'm the one being a drama queen. He was never really mine. I'd be surprised if he knows my name and doesn't think of me as the needy guy with good hair."

Paige looked up at Evan's light brown hair, which he'd arranged into a bit of a pompadour today. He did have good hair, but she said, "Okay" with a little sarcasm in her voice.

"You're basically singing 'On My Own' like a teenage girl in a high school talent show now," said Lauren.

"Was that your update?" Paige asked.

"No, actually. I merely intended to illustrate that since the love of my life is off the market, I have decided to move on. Darius called the other day. We're going out tomorrow night."

"Darius?" asked Lauren. "Control-freak Darius? Unceremoniously-dumped-you-the-day-before-he-was-supposed-to-meet-your-parents Darius? That guy?"

"He dumped you right before meeting your parents?" said Paige "That's cold."

Evan sighed. "He apologized for that. He has an extra ticket to some Broadway show and wanted me to go."

"You were the fourteenth person he called," said Paige. "I've been on *that* date before."

"Well, be that as it may, he says he missed me and wants to make it up to me, and also this show is supposed to be really good. It's a musical based on some obscure nineteenth-century novel."

"Sounds thrilling," said Lauren.

"I hear your tone, but the *Times* critic gave it a glowing

review, and he doesn't like anything lately. Besides, what can one date hurt? If Darius is still terrible, at least I get to see a Broadway show for free."

"Fair," said Paige.

They talked about musicals for a few minutes and Paige ordered a second martini. When it arrived and Paige took her first sip, Lauren asked, "So, Paige, what happened at Mitch's volunteer thing the other night?"

And...now it was complicated. Paige hated holding things back from her friend, but she said, "It was good. Not the most active. My partner and I only caught one cat."

"Still, that's something. Did I tell you, my brother Josh went, too? Did you run into him?"

Paige's stomach flopped. "Uh, yeah, we met."

Paige could see Evan smiling from behind his martini glass as he sipped and glanced at Lauren. Paige kicked him under the table. That just made him grin wider.

"Did something happen?" Lauren asked looking between Evan and Paige.

"No. Evan's being stupid. I just... I told Evan I thought Josh was cute. But he's your brother, so it's off the table." Paige hoped for a hole to open beneath her to fall through.

"Yeah. How weird would that be?" said Lauren. "Can you even imagine? So gross."

"It could be like a Chandler and Monica and Ross thing," said Evan.

Lauren rolled her eyes. "Not everything in life relates back to *Friends*."

"You say that, but I just rewatched the whole series, and I'm pretty sure it does," said Evan. "Or that's a sign I need to get out more."

"Probably that," said Paige. She looked at Lauren. "It would be weird, I guess."

"*So* weird. I mean, he's…Josh. I doubt he's a virgin, but I try not to think about him in that context."

"Right, of course," said Paige.

"And he *just* got his heart broken. Can you imagine being with someone for almost three years and living with them for one and planning a future together, and then all of a sudden, she's like, 'Just kidding, I'm moving to Chicago'? I mean, I know it's hard to get a job right out of law school, but she thought her career was more important than Josh." Lauren shook her head. "He was devastated. She really did a number on him. He was planning to propose, and she up and left him."

Paige didn't know what to say; she hadn't known Josh's previous relationship was that serious. He hadn't acted heartbroken when they'd been out, but past relationships hadn't come up much either.

She really didn't know him well at all, did she? Was she really thinking about pursuing a relationship? Well, no.

Lauren went on, "And, like, if you guys dated and something went wrong with you two? No, let's not even think about it."

"Yup. Putting that whole idea away," said Paige. And she supposed she had her answer. She liked Josh, but it was just one of those things. Not meant to be. Time to move on.

Although, if he lived in New York, they were bound to run

into each other again, weren't they? Lauren would likely invite him to parties or whatever. So if they dated for a bit and broke up, they'd still have to see each other. That wasn't ideal. Or maybe that job really would keep him in his office and that wouldn't be an issue.

She took a sip of her drink and hoped that this would be the end of all of it. Good thing she hadn't deleted those apps off her phone after all.

———

If Josh was reading the brief correctly, his client was indeed guilty of fraud.

Bobby Giardino owned a small chain of shops that sold doors and windows. They'd been airing commercials about some new shatterproof material that they demonstrated by having one of Giardino's sons whack a window with a big rubber mallet. A woman was suing after a bad storm shattered one of her windows made of this material. Her lawyer had put together an impressive series of documents that showed Giardino's claims about the windows being shatterproof were bunk, and that the window shown in the commercial had a pane made of a different, more expensive material. If this case ever saw the inside of a courtroom, Giardino would lose for sure.

But Josh had to somehow prove Giardino was not at fault for that window shattering.

Not all of his clients were the good guys.

Josh had once wanted to be a prosecutor who would put

people like this out of business or in jail. He'd lucked into an internship at DCL between his second and third year of law school and had liked the job so much, he'd reconsidered his career path. Working with Provost on litigation would give him courtroom experience, after all, and he could prevent the good guys from going to jail or being subjected to frivolous lawsuits. And although a few of Provost's clients were innocent of wrong-doing, Josh was quickly learning that very few lawsuits were actually frivolous.

An image of Paige came unbidden into his mind. They'd talked some that night about taking the well-paying job to pay down debt and get one's feet wet before pursuing one's passion, and Josh still had decades of his career before him. He did not need to spend the rest of his life defending the unscrupulous Bobby Giardinos of the world.

He guessed whatever had happened with Paige was over. That was a shame, because she'd been so great, but on the other hand, it was closing in on eight at night on a Monday and here he still was in the office.

His phone rang and he grabbed it without looking at the caller ID, so he was a little surprised when the caller turned out to be Lauren.

"Oh, hey," he said. "Was not expecting you."

"I tried your cell first, but since you didn't answer I figured you'd be at work."

Josh's cell phone was sitting on the corner of his desk. He picked it up and found that the battery had died while he'd been focused on something else. Then he got nervous, because calling the office line seemed like a lot of work to get ahold of him. "Is everything okay?"

"Yeah, everything's fine. I just wanted to get in touch with you before the week got too crazy and I forgot."

"Oh. Okay. You could have texted."

"And you would have ignored it like you ignore all my texts unless I ask you a direct question."

"I don't ignore them. I'm just...busy, and not everything seems to require an answer. I mean, I got that article you sent me about the best takeout restaurants in Midtown. I didn't think you needed a response. I did try the falafel place from the article today, though. It was pretty tasty."

She let out the long-suffering sigh of the older sister. "How was the feral cat event?"

And there was Paige in his head again. Best not to mention that, though. "Educational. A little scary. That Mitch guy is intense."

Lauren laughed. "Yeah, I know. Any of the cats bite you?"

"You'd like that, wouldn't you?"

"A little."

"No such luck. The group trapped a few cats, a couple of which had already been tagged. But I actually had a good time."

"Did you run into my friend Paige? She was there that night, too. She mentioned you'd met."

Oof. Had he run into her? She'd vanished while he'd been in the shower the morning after, which he supposed he deserved. He'd been a little aloof when she'd started flipping out about him being related to Lauren. He didn't really see the problem.

He supposed it might get awkward if they started dating and something went awry, but it was just one night of very good sex, not a marriage proposal.

"Uh, yeah. I met her. She seems great."

"She is."

Then Josh remembered something from the night he'd had dinner with Lauren and Caleb. "Wait, is Paige the one with questionable taste in men who you had to rescue from a bad date the other night?"

"Yeah, that's her. She has every other part of her life together, but her love life is a hot mess. I guess we can't all be perfect."

"Perfect?"

"I love Paige, I do. She's gorgeous and put together. She's had a ton of career success because she's really good at what she does. I mean, she only works for me because she hated working in corporate America, which, who can blame her? She's also one of the nicest people I've ever known, so I can't even resent her for those things. She deserves a great guy. Not sure why she thinks she'll find him on a dating app."

"Stranger things have happened. I've heard it's hard to meet people in this city even if you're not a person who works all the time. Plenty of great people use dating apps. Just because *you* are happily married now—"

"Yeah, yeah. Whatever. It's just that…"

Josh had to fight to listen to Lauren, because the facts clicked into place. Paige *worked* for Lauren. They were friends *and* Paige was the events manager at the Cat Café that Lauren managed. He'd known that intellectually, but listening to Lauren talk about

Paige made him truly understand. Wow, had Josh stumbled in it. No wonder Paige had vanished from his apartment once she figured out who he was.

As a way to test the water, Josh said, "I liked her."

"Yeah?"

"I mean, would it really be that weird if I asked her out?"

"What about Megan?"

"What about her? We broke up six months ago. Or seven, I don't know. A while ago." And Josh really did not want to talk about Megan. She'd hardly popped into his head at all in the last few days, which felt like a sign he was finally moving on. Although he couldn't even hear her name without acid boiling up in his throat, so maybe he wasn't that over her.

"Paige is a good person. She deserves more than a rebound, that's all."

Josh could sense Lauren's disapproval and decided not to push it. "It was just a hypothetical question. As you've noticed since you called me on my office line, I pretty much live here."

"All right," said Lauren, her tone indicating she knew something he didn't. "I'm actually calling because Paige is doing this fundraiser cocktail party thing at the Cat Café next week. I wondered if you wanted to come or if you could talk your law firm into a big donation. I mean, in the spirit of 'giving back to the community' or whatever."

"Sure, I can run that by my boss. What are you raising funds for?"

"There's a no-kill shelter in Park Slope that had part of its facility damaged in that bad storm a few weeks ago. So we're helping them out by raising some money for the repairs. And Paige wants part of whatever we raise to do some youth programming at the café."

"Okay. I think I can sell that. Or hell, I'll donate. It's not like I have time to spend any of my hard-earned money, except on rent and takeout." Then what Lauren had just said sank in. "Wait, youth programming?"

"Paige read about a cat café in San Francisco that does crafts with cats or something. I'm letting her run with it. Anyway, if you can get out of jail long enough to come by, it's next Tuesday evening at the Cat Café."

"I'll try. No promises. I had to work all weekend to make up for taking off for the feral cat thing."

"How does that make sense? A whole weekend in exchange for one night?"

"It... I don't know. Stuff piles up around here. Time is a flat circle."

"How many of your colleagues burn out before the end of the first year?"

"I don't know, but I'm guessing a lot. I figure if I can just hold on until the end of my first year, it will get better. Maybe. Hopefully. I mean, they'll have a whole new group of naive associates to torture by then."

"Well, I hope I see you Tuesday, but I understand if you can't make it. I can promise cute cats and an open bar if that entices you at all."

"That does sound appealing." Plus Paige would be there. He hadn't decided what to do with that, and the smart thing would be to let her go, but he wanted to see her. He'd figure it out when he got there.

"Cool. Well, try not to kill yourself at work. I'll let you get back to it. Love you, Josh."

"Love you too, Sis. I'll really try for Tuesday. If work doesn't kill me first."

CHAPTER 7

PAIGE EYED THE BAR THEY'D set up in the corner. She really wanted a glass of wine, but she had to do a presentation in order to persuade the guests tonight to part with some money, and she wanted her wits about her. Monique, who usually worked the counter in the café, stood ready to take donations and was chatting with Pablo from the bookstore. Caleb had an arm thrown casually around Lauren as they talked with Diane, who owned the building and the Cat Café. Victor, one of the baristas, was trying to keep the cats from wandering out of the room. They currently had a dozen cats living at the café, and one of Paige's other jobs was to figure out where she'd put the adoption forms in case anyone who came tonight fell in love with one of the cats. Although the obvious objective of the Cat Café was to provide patrons with a place to pet cats and sip coffee, the *real* objective was to charm potential cat owners into adopting one of the café's cats.

There were maybe fifteen guests milling around the party. Paige found the forms under a cat on one of the big sofas, which seemed about right. She was about to bring the forms to Monique when Diane walked up.

"So, talk to me about your programming plans," said Diane. "Lauren said you want to do events for kids."

"Yes. I have two ideas. First, I read about another cat café that does arts and crafts with kids and cats early on weekend mornings. We're usually slow here then, so I thought that could be a good way to get some customers in. I called the owner of that cat café and she gave me some solid ideas for crafts."

Diane bobbed her head. "I like it. You should talk to the ladies at Stitches up the block." Stitches was a yarn and craft store a few doors down from the Cat Café.

"That is a great idea. I hadn't gotten as far as sourcing materials yet, but maybe they have some leftover or remaindered stuff, or...oh, what if we made craft kits for the kids to take home and Stitches could sell them here?"

"See, there you go. You're so quick with the ideas once you get going. And I think that kind of coordination between businesses on this block is exactly what this community needs."

Figuring out how to pull together the small business on the block had been one of Paige's pet projects. She'd invited everyone from the block to this party, although she didn't see any of the women who worked at Stitches. She made a mental note to follow up with them later. Then she said, "And since you mention it, I want to do a program with Stories to have kids read to the cats maybe one day a week."

"You... Kids read to the cats?" Diane tilted her head.

"Yeah. This is a program some shelters have been doing. They bring kids in to read to the cats. This helps the kids develop their reading skills and their confidence with reading, because a cat may judge a kid in their cat-like way, but he's never going to tell a kid he's reading poorly. And, actually, the program benefits the cats too because it helps them socialize and get some attention. I found a journal article about it, and there's plenty of evidence that the program is good for both the kids and the cats. The article had all these ridiculously cute photos of cats snuggling with kids while they read."

"Wow." Diane smiled. "I never would have thought about that, but that sounds like a great program. When can we start that?"

"As soon as we get the word out. Well, I'm still working out the details with Stories. I'm hoping to corner Pablo tonight to see what we can work out. I was hoping they'd lend us books, but the Stories owner doesn't seem too keen to loan books to an event that involves both kids *and* animals. So we may have to buy them. Hence setting aside some of the money we raise tonight for kids programming."

"Don't worry about it. You want some extra money to buy books, give me a jingle. It's a fantastic idea and I want to support it."

"Wow. Thanks, Diane."

"Oh, and who's that? I haven't seen him around the neighborhood."

Paige followed Diane's gaze, and her heart fell to her stomach. "Uh, that's Josh. Lauren's brother." What on earth was he doing here? Paige's heart began to pound. He must have known Paige would be here, even if Lauren asked him to come. Wasn't he supposed to be working?

He looked around. His gaze landed on Paige's and their eyes met for a long moment, but then he turned and walked over to Lauren.

"Oh," said Diane. "So something happened there."

"Oh, no. Is it that obvious? Because Lauren doesn't know Josh and I have done more than say hello to each other."

"Not completely obvious, but something happened to your face just then to make me think something was up."

"It's nothing, really. We both volunteered for Mitch's feral cat trapping program a couple of weeks ago and met there."

"But you made a connection."

"Even if that were true, he's Lauren's brother. First of all, I like this job. And second, Lauren's my friend. It's all too weird and complicated."

"Ah, I see. You know, my friend Carol married her best friend's sister."

That felt like the opening to one of Diane's long stories. Paige liked Diane even while finding her kind of pushy, but she did not have time for a story right now, not when she had to get ready to do this presentation. "I'm sure that kind of thing works out all the time, but I don't know. I'm very good at messing up romantic relationships."

"Right, so I hear."

Paige could sense that Diane wasn't taking her seriously. "What I meant was, I'm twenty-eight and still single, so it's not like you could call any of my relationships a success."

Diane laughed. "Oh, sweetheart. You will make some man very happy someday. Maybe even that man. He's coming this way."

Paige sighed. Diane liked to take a motherly role with everyone at the Cat Café, even though technically they were her employees. And Josh was indeed headed right for her.

"I appreciate that, Diane," she said. "I'll, uh, talk to the party guests. Please enjoy the event."

Diane winked and walked away. Josh approached tentatively. "Did I interrupt?"

"No, you're fine. Um, hi. How are you?"

He smiled. "Hello. Ah, can we talk for a few minutes?"

Paige looked around. The room was filling. She was supposed to give her presentation about the children's programming in about twenty minutes, and one of her roles here was to circulate and make sure everyone was having a good time. "Uh, I guess. But I'm kind of running this shindig, so a couple of minutes is all I can give you."

"Then I'll keep it short. I know what we said, and I know this situation is complicated, but… I have not been able to stop thinking about you."

There. Short, direct, to the point.

Josh knew saying anything was probably stupid, but it was also stupid to let the opportunity pass him by. Sure, she was Lauren's friend and employee, which complicated things. He didn't have an abundance of free time either. But his desire to even just have a conversation with Paige overrode those things. Perhaps it was lust-driven, but...they'd had fun that night. He wanted more of that, too.

Paige frowned at him. "I can't have this conversation right now."

"I wasn't looking for anything, and I'm not even trying to pressure you. But I had a great time and I think you're awesome and I don't see why we should throw that away. Okay, so you know my sister. What's the big deal?"

She stared at him, astonished. Maybe angry. "The big deal? This is a messy, complicated situation. First of all, I really like this job. Second, Lauren is one of my best friends in the world. What happens if something goes south with you and me?"

"But what if it doesn't? What if things work out? What if they go...north?"

"Go north?" Paige laughed softly and shook her head. "I just... In this situation, the risk is all on me. I'm the one who stands to lose. I love Lauren like a sister, but she's your actual sister and blood trumps friendship."

"Not always."

"Maybe not always, but you and Lauren are close. She talks about you all the time. I'm sure if you didn't work such crazy hours, I would have met you much sooner than two weeks ago. Trust me, if something goes wrong, I lose. Have you ever been friends with a couple who broke up and had to choose sides?"

Josh was busy trying to form a counterargument—*Such a lawyerly thing to do,* he thought with a suppressed sigh—but he paused to answer her questions. "Yeah, a couple of my law school classmates. That was…oof." That *had* been a bad scene, but it was nothing compared to how everything had fallen apart when Megan and Josh had broken up. It was a good thing their law school classmates were spread across the country now; it had made it easier for their friends not to pick sides. Josh was still a little resentful over some of the friends Megan had kept in the breakup. "It's messy. So, fine, point taken."

"So, if you and I dated, maybe it would be really great for a while, but if we broke up, trust me, Lauren would choose you. The risk is all mine in this equation, and I don't like that."

"Okay, I hear you. And you're right. Lauren is my sister. And she's been looking out for me my whole life. If she had to pick between us, I'd probably win. But at the same time, I'm not asking you to marry me. I just…want to take you out some time. Get to know you. Have a glass of wine and a meal. That's all."

Something rubbed against Josh's leg then. He looked down and saw a little gray cat snugging up against his shin.

"That's Mr. Darcy," said Paige. "Lauren let me name the most recent group of cats we brought in, so I named them all after Austen characters. The orange cat on the sofa is Mr. Willoughby. The tuxedo over there is Lizzy Bennet."

"Cute. Although that doesn't mean a lot to me. I think I read *Pride and Prejudice* in high school, but I don't remember it."

Paige gasped. "Have you not even seen the movies?"

He shrugged. "I've seen *Clueless*. That's based on some Austen novel, isn't it?"

"We're going to move on past your lack of culture and get back to the point, which is—"

"Which is that we get along well and can talk about anything and one date won't kill you."

"When will you have time for such a date?"

"I don't know. Next week maybe. I'll make time. If I have to work every weekend until July, it'll be worth it."

She sighed. "I hate that you're right. I've thought about you a lot, too, it just seems like the potential for disaster here is very high." She looked around the room. "I have to get back to the party, but okay. One date. And nothing over the top. Just, like, dinner or something. Conversation. Maybe some wine. But that's it."

"All right, I hear you. I will plan a perfectly boring date with you. Then we just...take it from there."

"I... Okay. I'll do it."

Josh's heart soared, but he wondered for a moment if he'd worn her down. "You, uh, do actually want to go on a date with me, right? You're not just saying you will so I'll go away."

"Josh. Half the problem here is that I don't want to stop talking to you right now, but I have to because I have to persuade some of the high rollers who just walked in here to drop some money on my programming ideas."

Josh couldn't help but smile at that. "So you *do* like me."

"More than I should. Don't look so cocky." She took a deep breath and looked at the stack of papers in her hands. "The gray suit over there is an executive of a local community bank and he has very deep pockets. He could probably pay to fix the Park Slope shelter with the change in those pockets, but I'm going to have to really turn on the charm to get even a fraction of that out of him."

"Oh, that reminds me." Josh reached into his pocket. "Courtesy of my firm."

He handed Paige the check and watched as her eyes went wide with astonishment. "Holy cow. Are you kidding me with this?"

"No. Lauren told me about the shelter and the youth programming you want to do, and I pitched my boss this as part of my whole 'giving back to the community' thing. He got the firm to cut a check right away. Which honestly is probably pretty good for my karma. Some of my current clients are not nice people."

"Sorry to hear that but not sorry your boss got the firm to part with this much money. This alone is almost two-thirds of our goal."

"I'm happy to help. Really."

"Take this to Monique. She's the one with the clipboard by the door. She's handling the actual money."

"All right. I'll do that. And I'll call you about the date. I'll find some dull restaurant in Manhattan. No candlelight or tablecloths or anything romantic. Mediocre food you'll forget as soon as you've eaten it. How's next Thursday?"

She laughed. "Sounds good. Tablecloths are romantic?"

He shrugged. "In certain contexts. Just roll with it."

She nodded and walked away. He watched her for a moment, and then Lauren walked over. "You and Paige seem to have hit it off."

Josh wondered if he should tell Lauren he'd asked out her best friend. It seemed like a bad idea without asking Paige if she was okay going public, something she seemed very reluctant to do. Josh guessed Paige didn't want Lauren to know yet, so he kept his mouth shut. "Yeah. I got my firm to make a pretty generous donation, so I wanted to show her the check." He still had said check in his hand, so he held it up to show Lauren.

"Wow. Your boss really wants to be absolved of some sins."

"Yeah. This kind of law seems to involve a lot of helping terrible rich people keep their money. It's...not exactly what I expected."

"Well, like you keep saying, all you can do right now is ride it out while you figure out what you really want to do."

"Too much *Law & Order* made me want to be a prosecutor, but that would be just as many hours for less than half the pay. Maybe that's shallow, but—"

"Hey, do what you have to do. I'm not judging."

"I do have a staggering amount of student debt to pay off."

"Again, it's cool. You want to sell your soul to a giant corporate law firm, that's your business."

"Right. Thanks for your support."

Lauren grinned. "Did you have to trade in a favor to one of your mafia clients to get the night off?"

"Okay, we don't represent any organized crime families."

"That you know of."

Josh sighed. He would not have been surprised to learn that Greg Provost was secretly a Gambino. But that was all just part of his late-night imaginings. Provost was probably innocent of any criminal activity, but he enjoyed his lavish lifestyle too much to feel morally compromised when he was hired by someone very likely guilty of some financial crime.

A cat hopped up on a table near where Josh stood and reached over to whack his arm.

"Hey!" said Josh. He looked at the cat, a striped orange cat with a white belly. Josh reached over to pet the cat's head and the cat closed his eyes in ecstasy.

"You have a new friend," said Lauren.

"Who is this guy? Does he have a fancy literary name?"

"That is Mr. Knightley."

"Uh-huh. That means nothing to me."

"He's the guy Emma ends up with in *Emma*. Or, put another way, he's Paul Rudd's character from *Clueless*."

"Oh, okay. Well, hello, sir."

The cat meowed in response.

"Anyway, I'm glad you're here," said Lauren. "Stick around for Paige's presentation. I think it will impress you. And give that check to Monique before me worrying about you losing it gives me an aneurism."

"I won't lose it." He pretended to lose his grip on the check but caught it before it fell.

"You're a jerk."

"You are."

"Kids," said Caleb, walking over. "Don't make me turn this party around and go back home."

Josh made a show of rolling his eyes and huffing like he felt put out and then carried the precious check over to Monique. Mr. Knightley the cat followed him, which was cute.

Five minutes later, Paige and Lauren stood on one side of the room. Caleb banged on a wine glass with a fork to get everyone's attention. Josh snagged a beer from the bar and settled in an empty chair to watch Paige's presentation. As soon as he sat, Mr. Knightley hopped up on his lap, so Josh pet the cat.

Paige really was in her element. She put two posters up on one of the walls with Evan's help. She pointed to the one on the left first and explained that their first order of business in this fundraiser was to come up with the thirty thousand dollars the shelter needed to replace the roof on the building and fix the other structural damage incurred during a bad storm a few weeks before.

"All of the animals have been moved to the undamaged side of the building, but having a whole wing be essentially unusable means they have a significantly decreased capacity. We want to make sure there's space for all the orphaned animals in this city, and we're also hoping that some of the programming I have planned for the next few months will inspire more people to adopt cats. There's certainly no shortage of shelter animals in Brooklyn. Our ultimate goal is to find these animals good forever homes."

Paige turned to the other poster and launched into her explanation of the children's programming. Josh wasn't totally sold on Crafts with Cats, but then he'd never been very crafty himself. The literacy program was an amazing idea, though. He had a vague memory of reading an article about a similar program in another city a few years ago, and he'd been impressed by it at the time, too.

Paige's voice projected across the room well. It had a soothing quality to it, and clearly everyone in the room held her in rapt attention. She wrapped up her presentation by explaining where the money raised for the youth programming would go—mostly toward materials like craft supplies and books, but also toward advertising and some administrative tasks—and she also said she was looking for volunteers to facilitate both programs and got a raised hand from a woman who introduced herself as a second-grade teacher who would love to get involved.

Paige never faltered. She never looked nervous. She spoke passionately about her program ideas. She even worked in a plug for the Cat Café, showing off some of the T-shirts and coffee cups that Evan had designed. And Lauren was right, Josh was impressed. When the presentation ended and Paige started working the room, Josh could see how Paige had been so good at her banking job. This fundraiser was probably similar to a lot of bank events, albeit with cheaper booze and a more casual dress code. She ran this whole show like it was the easiest thing in the world, and Josh knew full well it wasn't.

She was everything he wanted in a woman. He definitely needed her in his life.

He started to stand before realizing that the orange cat was still on his lap. "Uh, excuse me, Mr. Knightley, but I can't sit here all night." Mr. Knightley dug his claws harder into Josh's thigh.

Lauren appeared at his side. "So what did you think?"

Josh was a little preoccupied with trying to get this cat off his lap, but he said, "Paige's presentation was great. I feel even better about talking my law firm out of a big chunk of change. Um. How does one extract a cat from one's lap without losing something important?"

"One doesn't."

"Mr. Knightley seems nice, but he hasn't left me alone."

"I think he's chosen you."

"Chosen me?" Josh realized suddenly what she meant. "What? No. Oh, no. I can't get a cat."

"I don't think you're being given a choice."

Mr. Knightley closed his eyes and started purring, while simultaneously sinking his claws more forcefully into Josh's thigh. Josh hissed, as those tiny needle claws sank into his flesh. He tried to lift Mr. Knightley's paws, hoping he hadn't drawn blood.

"But I work a lot." Josh addressed the cat more than Lauren.

"You also live alone. Having a companion would make being home even better. And cats are pretty self-sufficient."

"This is what you do, isn't it? You let unsuspecting people into the Café, where the cats can then choose some poor sap and charm them into taking the cat home."

Lauren grinned, looking a little smug. "That is exactly what I do. So what do you say? Will you take home Mr. Knightley?"

Mr. Knightley looked up at Josh, and his big eyes seemed to say, "Pretty, pretty please!"

Josh knew he was a sucker. He pet Mr. Knightley's head. "I will consider it."

CHAPTER 8

THE CAT CAFÉ WAS STARTING to feel as familiar to Josh as the law student bar he'd hung out at in DC. He walked in Friday night to meet Paige so that she could go with him to a nearby pet store to buy everything he needed for Mr. Knightley. He found her in the cat room doing something on her laptop.

"Hi," she said when he walked in. She smiled brightly. "I'm just finishing up the schedule, I'll be right with you. Have a seat."

"Okay." He sat beside her at the table. A little calico cat lay next to Paige's laptop and looked at Josh as though he were not to be trusted. Josh reached over and pet the cat.

He looked around. He didn't see Lauren, but Monique was at the counter helping customers, and a guy with tattoos on both arms that Josh did not recognize wiped down the unoccupied tables.

"Are you closing tonight?" Josh asked.

"No. Monique and Victor can do it. We're trying a new thing where we stay open later on Fridays, but we haven't been advertising well, so, as you see, it's not exactly bustling. Lauren said it's fine for me to go, and she's right upstairs if these guys need help."

The tattooed guy—Victor, he presumed—went back to the front of the café, effectively leaving Josh and Paige alone. Paige was looking at her laptop, so she didn't see Josh move toward her, cup her cheek, lean close, and kiss her. He lingered there, tasting her, letting her taste him. If he could kiss her all day, all the time, he'd die a happy man.

When he pulled back, she smiled at him. "What was that for?"

"You're pretty."

She giggled. "Okay. Now leave me alone for three minutes so I can finish this."

Josh sat back in his chair and surveyed the room. A couple of the cats were snuggled up with each other on one of the sofas. One of them hopped onto one of the nearby tables and stared at Josh for a second before beginning to groom itself. And the chubby one—Sadie, the café's permanent resident—sashayed over to Josh with her tail in the air.

"I've never seen cats strut around with their tails up straight like that."

Paige looked up. "Oh, yeah. Sadie does that all the time. I saw a documentary about cat behavior that kind of explained it. Apparently, in feral colonies, cats do that when they approach each other in a friendly way. It's a way of showing they come in peace. I don't know if that's true of Sadie. She's not exactly the brightest bulb. But I like to think she walks around wanting to be friends with everyone."

Sadie walked over and sniffed Josh's shoes before rubbing

against his leg. He bent down to pet her and she arched up into his hand. She immediately started purring like a freight train. Then something must have caught her attention across the room because she took off running.

"Cats are so weird."

"Sadie's a bit of an oddball, but she's very sweet." Paige closed her laptop. "Okay. Schedule's done. I'm just gonna grab my bag from the back and we can go."

As Paige walked into the backroom, Josh stood and tried to picture what having one of these little guys in his house was going to be like. Most of the cats in the room were sleeping, although a little black and white cat was going to town on a toy mouse with a neon green feather for a tail.

Paige returned with a smile. It made her whole face light up. She casually draped her bag over her shoulder and held out her hand, so Josh took it and led her out of the café.

"The big pet store two blocks away should have everything you need," she said.

"Yeah. I found it on the map before I walked over here. Is it really across the street from a prison?"

"Well not exactly *across* the street. More like kitty-corner."

Josh laughed. "Downtown Brooklyn is a strange place."

Paige pulled her phone out of her pocket and tapped the screen as they walked. "Look, I made you a list of everything you need." She handed Josh the phone.

It was a lengthy list. Josh marveled again at Paige's type-A tendencies. "Wow, thanks. This is quite a lot of stuff."

"You don't need *all* of it. Some of these things are just

suggestions. See, I color-coded everything. Necessities in green, helpful but not necessary things in yellow, and just for fun stuff in purple."

He found her listmaking endearing and almost leaned over to kiss her again but refrained since they were outside. "Let's go inside," he said, nudging Paige toward the pet store.

Josh seemed overwhelmed as they walked through the pet store. It was a big chain place that carried everything, so she instructed Josh to get a cart.

"A litter box and litter are the first essentials," she said, leading him to that aisle.

The litter box was easy enough, but Josh stared in awe at the selection of kitty litter. "Why are some of these so expensive?"

"Dunno. Various levels of scent-blocking crystals or whatever."

"I'm sure these are all great, but I'm sorry, I'm not paying almost twenty dollars for something my cat pees on."

Paige recommended the brands she bought for Bianca, and they moved onto food, which was even more overwhelming. "You work with Mr. Knightley," Josh said. "Do you know what he eats?"

Paige laughed. "You say that like we're colleagues."

"I'm serious."

"Lauren feeds the café cats this special food she special orders through the vet clinic that is supposed to be easy to digest and free of things cats are commonly allergic to. You don't have to get that fancy. It might take a few tries to find something your cat really likes, because cats can be finicky eaters. But here's what I feed Bianca."

Josh picked out wet and dry food and told Paige to lead on.

"Well, you've got the basics. I'd also recommend getting some kind of scratching post and some toys."

"Okay."

"And to help relieve stress, you can get a pheromone diffuser."

"A what now?"

They turned into the cat toy and treat aisle. "You can buy these diffusers that are like plug-in air fresheners, but they pump out pheromones that only cats can smell. They help calm cats down if they are stressed. And moving into a new home can be quite stressful."

"Really?"

"Yeah. Caleb recommends them to new cat parents because there's some science that shows they really work."

Josh seemed skeptical, but he said, "Well, let's pick out some toys first."

They stood before a display of toy mice in various sizes and colors. But Josh was drawn to a display down the aisle. Paige followed him and saw that there was a display of cat toys that looked like *Star Wars* characters. "Oh my god," Josh said. "Mr. Knightley totally needs this Darth Vader mouse."

"Darth Vader mouse sounds like a German opera."

Josh chuckled and started giddily loading up the cart with pop culture–themed cat toys. Paige picked up a Superman mouse and tossed it at Josh. It hit his head, but he laughed and caught it before it hit the floor. He grabbed a Batman mouse and tossed it back at Paige. She laughed, although it hit her shoulder and then rolled onto the floor. She picked up Batman, but when she moved to drop it in the cart, Josh stopped her by placing his hand on her arm. Then he swooped down and kissed her.

"I hate to be the one who points this out," said Paige, "but we haven't even gone on a second date. And yet you keep stealing kisses."

"We're *planning* to go on a second date, aren't we?"

"Yeah."

"Or *this* is our second date." Josh scrunched up his face. "No, our next official date should be a smidge more romantic than shopping under these glaring fluorescent lights."

"I thought you said no candlelight or tablecloths."

"There's gotta be a happy medium between candlelight and this."

"I mean, we could get completely unromantic dinner after we drop all this stuff off at my place. There's a sandwich shop near my place that makes a mean meatball parm."

Paige hesitated. When Josh had texted her asking for help getting stuff for his new cat, she'd volunteered to help without thinking about it much, but going to dinner seemed to cross a line. Part of her was still freaking out about going out with him at all, although it was hard to deny that they enjoyed each other's company. He was fun to be around, even doing something as mundane as picking out cat litter for his new cat. She liked him, genuinely so. And he obviously liked her as well, if he was pursuing her this hard.

It didn't solve the problem of what Lauren would think, and Paige still worried about that. She wanted to say yes to Josh now. But instead, she said, "Rain check. I actually have a few more errands to run after this. I figured I could help you pick everything up, put you in a cab, and then finish everything else while I'm in this part of the neighborhood."

"All right. We'll do our date next week as planned."

"It's not that I don't want to."

He smiled. "It's all right, Paige. I'm the one imposing on your time now." He pushed the cart forward. "I swear we had cats when I was a kid. I just had no idea how much stuff they needed. I appreciate your taking pity on my lack of cat knowledge. I'm sure you had better things to do tonight."

Ugh. She should embrace this. Josh was a great guy. She hadn't met anyone she liked nearly as much in a few years. Why should she toss this out just because she was worried about how her friend would react? Why *not* go for it?

"I mean, I could get a sandwich," she said. "And finish my errands tomorrow."

"Yeah?"

"Yes. But I'm going home after that. No funny business."

He grinned. "All right. No romance, no funny business. Just two friends who secretly want to jump each other's bones eating totally not romantic and not sexy sandwiches before they part ways for the weekend."

"Jump each other's bones? You think highly of yourself."

"Oh, please. Like you don't want to get on this train." Josh stood back and gestured at himself.

Paige laughed. "Okay, okay. Come on, let's finish up here."

"What can possibly be left? Half the store is in my cart." But he pushed on to the next aisle.

CHAPTER 9

TWO DAYS LATER, JOSH RETURNED to the Cat Café. He didn't see Lauren or Paige when he walked in, so he walked up to the counter. The barista who'd been handling donations at the fundraiser was there, a tall, pretty woman with dark skin. Her name was...Monique.

Josh walked to the counter and said, "Uh, hi, I'm here to pick up Mr. Knightley." He held up the empty cat carrier he'd brought.

Monique smirked. "Yeah, Lauren mentioned. Congratulations on your new friend."

"I feel like I need to make it really clear that he chose me."

"That's usually how this goes."

"That's what Lauren said. I wasn't, like, looking for a cat or anything, though."

"Sure you weren't. I believe you. That's why you're standing there with a cat carrier."

Josh sighed. He'd spent the last few days preparing his apartment. He'd stayed up late one night to finish unpacking the boxes. He'd spent Saturday assembling his desk and then setting up all the stuff he'd bought with Paige. So he was all ready for Mr. Knightley to move in, although he still couldn't believe he was getting a cat. It wasn't the sort of thing he imagined for himself, although he was a teensy bit excited. As he'd set up the litter box and found a good place for the cat bed, he'd imagined having a little furry friend in his apartment and how nice it would be to have a purring cat at his side on the nights he got stuck working late.

He would never admit that to Lauren, though. He didn't want her to get that "I told you so" expression on her face.

"Lauren's in the back," Monique said. "She can help you."

Josh peeked back toward the cat room. He could see through the glass door that Lauren was busy with some customers. "You know, I'm not in a hurry. Can I have a latte?"

Josh hadn't spent any time in this space aside from the fundraiser. It might be nice to have the full cat café experience. He looked around while Monique made his latte. The front part of the café was separated from the cat room by a wall with a glass door, and on this side of the door, there were three café tables and a smattering of chairs set up, but the more comfortable seating was back with the cats. There was a little vestibule in the front, too, likely as extra insurance against the cats getting out.

Josh still couldn't believe he was adopting a cat. He was a total sucker.

"Lauren said you're a lawyer," said Monique.

"Just barely."

"My sister just graduated from law school, too. She works at Weiss & Polk now. Do you know it?"

"I do. I've heard great things. One of my law school classmates works there."

"I never see her anymore. I think she sleeps in her office."

"Yeah, the first year is rough going."

"Anyone else in your family a lawyer?"

"Nope, I'm the first."

"Same for my sister. She is the first one to go to grad school,
even. My poor mother keeps asking her to come over for dinner
and she's canceled almost every time. Mom doesn't quite understand why my sister is working so much. It's almost comforting to
know this first-year experience is nearly universal."

"Yeah. Based on what I've heard from my law school classmates, it is. At least Lauren is my only family here and she seems
to get it, but I won't lie, it's hard. Rewarding work, yes, and I've
learned a ton even though I've only worked at my firm for two
months, but I'm tired."

Monique nodded. "My sister says basically the same thing."

Josh tilted his head toward the backroom. "Is it crowded back
there?"

"A bit. Pretty typical for a weekend. You're here in time for
the post-brunch crowd."

"Post-brunch?"

"The crowd on Sunday afternoons is usually groups of two or
three who just had brunch and want to sit and chat a little longer
over a cup of coffee before heading back home."

"Sure."

"But go on back. There's an adoption form to fill out, and you
might need a couple of people to load Mr. Knightley into the carrier."

"A couple of people? What have I gotten myself into?"

"Have you ever had a cat?"

Josh shrugged. "Sure, we had a couple of cats when I was a kid. I think my mom did most of the wrangling."

Monique patted his shoulder. "This will be fun."

Josh winced and carried his coffee and the cat carrier to the cat room. Lauren and Paige were both there, which could have been awkward, but Josh figured he'd play it cool.

"I expected you later in the day," said Lauren instead of greeting him.

"Well, I'm here now."

She nodded and looked around the room. She didn't need to look hard; Mr. Knightley trotted over and smelled Josh's shoes before rubbing against his shin.

"I'm sorry to say he is your cat," said Lauren, taking the carrier from Josh.

"I got a latte," he said, holding up his cup. "I'm not in a hurry. I thought I could sit for a few minutes and chat with my sister and have the whole cat café experience."

"Sure. Have a seat."

Paige was seated at a table in the corner, looking at a laptop. She looked up and met his gaze. "Hi, Josh."

"Hi. Uh, mind if I sit with you?"

She smiled, which was promising. "Not at all."

"Hey, Lauren?" called Monique from the front of the store.

Lauren sighed and shoved the cat carrier under the table, near Josh's feet. When she left the room, Josh turned to Paige and said, "I came for the cat. I still can't believe Lauren talked me into it."

"Yeah, Lauren told me. She does that to everyone, by the way. All of her friends and most of the employees have cats who were adopted through the café."

"Price of doing business, I guess."

"This is really just a fancy cat shelter that serves coffee."

Josh nodded and sipped his latte. "This is a solid latte. I'm impressed."

"There used to be a great coffee shop across the street, but it closed, I dunno, eighteen months ago? After that, we became the main place for coffee between about Henry Street and the subway. Business basically doubled overnight."

"Wow, okay."

"I mean, we always sold good quality products, especially since this is the sort of place where people tend to sit for a while. But we stepped up our coffee game when we got all the business from the old coffee shop. Also, your brother-in-law is a coffee regular type, and when he mentioned offhand once that the plain old coffee here was a little on the weak side, Lauren spent a month figuring out how we could make a better cup of coffee."

"Coffee regular?"

"That's a New York thing, I guess. Coffee with cream and sugar."

"Ah, okay. Lauren has picked up some New York slang since she moved here, but I hadn't heard that one."

"You didn't sit next to me to talk about coffee."

"True." Josh smiled. "Actually, I'm glad you're here. I was going to call you today. Is Thursday still good for you?"

She clicked around on her laptop. "Yes, I'm still free."

"Perfect. There's an Italian place near my office, if you don't mind coming to Manhattan. Uh, real middle of the road. Not remotely romantic. Like barely a step above meatball subs."

Paige laughed. "I don't mind coming to Manhattan."

"Cool, I'll text you the address."

Mr. Knightley hopped up on the table and stared at Josh. Josh stared back, wondering what he should do. Mr. Knightley lifted his paw and tapped Josh's arm. Josh took this to mean he was supposed to pet the cat, so he did. Mr. Knightley immediately started to purr.

"That cat really likes you," said Paige.

"Yeah, not sure what I did to deserve all this."

"Cats choose people more often than people choose cats. I have an aunt in New Jersey who got a cat recently because one showed up on her back porch one day."

"Well, buddy," Josh said, petting Mr. Knightley's head. "I hope you like sitting around while I do legal work, because that's pretty much my whole life right now." He scratched under Mr. Knightley's chin. "You're just trying to get sprung from this place, aren't you? Are you going to be my friend once I get you home?"

Mr. Knightley kept purring.

"Are you going to be one of those guys who talks in baby speak to their pets?"

"It's possible. Does that make me look cute and charming or like a pathetic loser?"

Paige smiled. "More cute than anything else."

"Then yes. Who's a good boy?"

Mr. Knightley butted his head against Josh's chin.

Josh and Mr. Knightley really were awfully cute together.

He'd ended up hanging around the café until close because Lauren had been so tied up helping customers and her staff that she hadn't had enough time to help Josh get the cat into the carrier. So she and Josh had spent a couple of hours chatting while Josh steadily put more caffeine into his body. She'd enjoyed his company immensely, even if it distracted her from putting together the next month's event schedule. She could finish that tonight, though.

Josh was a great-looking guy; it was true. Now that she knew he and Lauren were related, the resemblance was unmistakable. They had the same coloring, the same eyes, the same freckles, but Josh's features were harder, more masculine. He had an ease about him, too, like nothing really bothered him. Maybe that was true; he seemed to be able to compartmentalize work when he had a day off, and he definitely was not a worrier the way Lauren could be. Paige had enjoyed watching him as he'd lounged in the chair across the table from her, wearing a pair of well-worn jeans and Washington Nationals T-shirt that stretched nicely across his chest.

The Cat Café was closed now, and Josh and Lauren were struggling to wrestle the cat into the carrier. "You want to go home with me so bad, go in the carrier, cat," Josh grumbled.

Paige snuck into the backroom and found the plastic tub full of cat treats she knew Lauren kept there. She grabbed a handful and went back to the cat room. She wedged herself between Josh, Lauren, and the recalcitrant cat and tossed a few into the carrier. Then she made a little trail of treats from the cat to the carrier.

"Did you learn nothing from trapping the ferals?" Paige asked.

Josh looked at her with awe on his face. They all stood back and watched as Mr. Knightley ate the treats and then hopped into the carrier to finish off the rest. Paige swooped forward and closed the flap.

"Well, gee," said Josh.

Mr. Knightley let out a mighty yowl as he realized he'd walked into a trap.

"You need help getting him home?" Lauren asked.

"You think that carrier is secure?"

Josh had bought a model that looked like a duffel bag. It was the sort of thing affluent women carried their purse dogs around in. Paige checked all the zippers and found them to be closed securely. "Yeah, he can't get out of there."

"Then I think I should be okay. I'm gonna call a cab, because I can't imagine hauling ten pounds of angry cat all the way home will be easy, but then I should be fine."

"Okay. I mean, Paige, you can close, right?"

Paige had wanted to volunteer to help Josh, but she didn't want Lauren to ask questions. Maybe she was paranoid. But she said, "Sure, Monique and I can finish here."

"Let me grab my bag," said Lauren. "Then if you're really nice, I'll buy you dinner."

While Lauren was in back closing down her office for the day, Paige said softly, "I'd help, but..."

"No, it's fine. I'll see you Thursday."

Mr. Knightley yowled again.

"Uh, congratulations on your handful," said Paige.

Josh didn't seem to notice and was in fact staring at Paige intently.

"Do I have something on my face?"

Josh shook his head. "No. It's just that you're beautiful and I want to kiss you, but I really don't want to get caught. That was like a whole debate that played out in my head in an instant."

Phew. Paige couldn't help herself and looked at Josh's lips, which looked soft and kissable. Suddenly she really wanted to kiss Josh, too. But then she heard footsteps and said, "Hold that thought. Thursday."

Josh nodded and leaned down to pick up the carrier. He took his phone out of his pocket to pull up a ride share app as Lauren walked out of the back.

"Paige, everything in back is set, but can I bother you to do one last litter box cleanup before you go?"

"Sure, no problem."

"I hate to ask. It's a gross job."

"Lauren, it's fine. Make sure Mr. Knightley settles in at his new home."

"Okay. Well, let's go."

"I've got a car coming," Josh said as he held up his phone.

Lauren said goodbye, and Paige tried to will away the inevitable awkward pause as Josh did the same, but Lauren didn't seem to notice. Paige watched them leave, then went to the backroom to grab the vacuum so she could clean up the cat room.

Monique stuck her head in and said, "Front of house is clean. You need any help back here?"

"Yeah, sure. I'm going to vacuum. If you could put all the cat toys back in the bin, that would be a help."

"Sure, no problem." Monique glanced back toward the front of the café. "Lauren's brother is a cutie, isn't he?"

Paige sighed. "Yeah."

"You like him, don't you? Like, not just in a 'he's a cute guy who spent the afternoon in the Café' way. I saw you guys chatting earlier."

"Maybe. Yes."

"Wow, Lauren will hate that."

That was exactly what Paige was afraid of. "This is why you won't be saying anything about it."

"Of course." Monique mimed zipping her lips.

Paige plugged in the vacuum. "You really think she'll disapprove?"

"You know her better than I do. She always struck me as someone who likes her life ordered in a certain way. You dating her brother threatens to upset that order."

It was a fair point. Paige remained hopeful that Lauren would ultimately be okay with this, but she feared the worse. Nothing she could do about it now. She moved the vacuum to start on the floors. "All right, let's do this."

CHAPTER 10

THURSDAY ROLLED AROUND AND JOSH wore his favorite tie to work in preparation for the date with Paige. He'd made a reservation at the nice Italian restaurant near the office and was conscious of the fact that she'd be seeing him tonight in all his besuited, lawyerly splendor. He hoped she thought he looked great in a suit. He also hoped he could persuade her to go on a second (or third?) date.

But then four o'clock rolled around. Josh had been pretty busy all day, but he'd kept one eye on the clock since lunchtime, as if that would move time forward faster. Mr. Provost appeared in his door, though, and Josh's heart sank because he knew what that meant.

"I'm due in court tomorrow morning at nine," said Provost. "I need to file the brief on the Giardino case before then. Can you finish my draft? I've got all my notes and the partial brief put together on this drive. I just need the language finessed a little. If you can finish the draft, I'll proofread it before I file it in the morning."

"By tomorrow morning?"

Provost handed Josh a thumb drive. "Yes. I should have filed it today, but other things kept coming up, and now I'm up against the clock. I think we're fine as long as I get it in before the end of the week, but we shouldn't delay."

"But I...I had plans tonight, sir."

"I'm sorry that you'll have to cancel them. I'd finish the brief myself but I have to finish preparing for my court appearance tomorrow, plus Mr. Davis just dropped a new client in my lap. Some luxury condo developer. I'm supposed to meet with him Monday, so I'll probably have more to say about that soon, but I have to read the file first."

It was hard to be mad at Provost when he clearly had just as much work on his plate as Josh. They discussed the particulars of what Josh had to do for a few minutes and then Provost, who was clearly stressed, left. Josh let out a breath and counted to ten. His disappointment was profound. He thought about texting Paige, but this felt like the sort of news that merited a phone call.

When she answered and confirmed that the café was dead and she had a few minutes to talk, he said, "I'm so sorry, but work emergency. I'm going to have to cancel. I feel terrible."

"Oh, that's okay."

"No, it's not okay. I've been looking forward to this all week, and my boss literally just handed me a thumb drive and told me I have to write a brief by the morning, which really means it has to get done tonight, and it's going to take me at least an hour just to read through his notes and get up to speed on the case before I can even...well. You don't need the details. But I'll be stuck here until the wee hours of the morning, probably. I'm so sorry, Paige. I will make it up to you as soon as I can."

"No, really, it's okay. I forgive you. Although we should reschedule as soon as you're able. Maybe this weekend?"

"Yeah, maybe. I should have known better than to try to schedule something on a weeknight. I think I'm free Sunday afternoon? But I can't even count on that right now."

"Well, give me a call when you're able. And I'm sorry, too, for what it's worth. I was really looking forward to tonight. I got dressed up and everything."

"Ugh, don't tell me that. Now I'll be picturing what you look like instead of focusing on this brief, which…" He plugged the thumb drive into his computer. "Oh, right, the fraud case. Misleading ads about windows."

"Sounds scintillating."

"I'm really sorry."

"Me, too. But you'll make it up to me, so it's fine. I gotta get back to work, but we'll talk soon, yeah?"

"Yes, definitely. I'll call you this weekend either way."

After he put his phone down, Josh leaned back in his chair and closed his eyes for a long moment. Losing out on a date was a dumb reason to contemplate quitting his job, and yet…

He pushed it aside and got back to work.

And then, like a miracle, a few hours later, Paige appeared at his doorway.

"Are you a mirage?" he asked.

She looked around his office. "Although there is a decided lack of color here, this hardly looks like a desert."

"Why are you here?"

She held up two plastic bags. "I brought dinner. Have you eaten?"

"Uh, no. I forgot, in fact." His stomach grumbled. "A beautiful woman bringing me food must be some kind of dream. I must have fallen asleep on my keyboard."

"I'm very real. I'll pinch you, if it helps."

Josh knew he would like that too much. He shook his head. "How did you even get in here?"

"Security is really loose in this building. I just had to tell the guy in the lobby that I was coming to see you and he let me right in. Then I was really charming to a receptionist on the seventh floor, and she told me where your office was. A perk of being blond is that no one ever thinks I'm a terrorist."

"Very privileged of you."

"I'm acknowledging it."

"So what did you bring?" Josh started clearing part of his desk so she could put the bags down.

"Well, we were going to get Italian, so I got some takeout from the restaurant. But I don't know what you like, so there's a variety here. Chicken piccata, spaghetti carbonara, ravioli marinara, and some tiramisu for dessert. Plus a couple of diet sodas."

"It all sounds delicious. You are my hero."

Paige started setting plastic takeout containers on the desk. "We could be classy and use the paper plates I got, but we could also just eat out of the containers."

"We've already exchanged bodily fluids. I'm not worried about cooties."

Paige laughed and pulled over a chair. "Seriously, is this okay? I don't want to get you in trouble or anything."

"Yeah, this is fine. My boss left about forty-five minutes ago. I still have a few hours of work to go, though, so I'm happy to take a break now."

"Don't you want to, I don't know. Go home? Sleep?"

"I'll sleep when I'm forty." He took the lid off one of the containers. "Oh, that smells divine."

"That looks like the chicken." She put a soda can next to his hand. "I know Diet Coke is not exactly a fine chianti like we probably would have had at the restaurant, but you do still have to work."

"Really, I'm grateful for all of this. Thank you."

"No problem. The atmosphere at this establishment leaves a little to be desired, but I still get to spend time with you. Although, seriously, has no one here heard of color? Everything is so gray."

"You'll have to help me pick out some art for the walls. I haven't gotten to it yet."

Josh dug into the chicken piccata and wondered how it was that he was sitting here with Paige, who had brought him dinner. He still couldn't believe it.

She moaned around her fork. "The carbonara is amazing. The place by my apartment does a pretty good carbonara, but this is much better."

"Don't make noises like that or I'll have to sweep everything off my desk and have you right here. And that would seriously set me back for the night."

Paige laughed. "Well, we wouldn't want that. And I gotta say, eating out of plastic containers in an office is maybe a little more boring a date than I would have asked for, and yet I'm not bored."

"Good food, good company. What else do you need?"

Though he was still getting over the surprise of Paige showing up in his office, he was completely, utterly charmed. And she *had* dressed up. She shrugged out of her coat to reveal a forties-style navy dress with white polka dots and buttons down the front. He believed the dress had what might be referred to as a sweetheart neckline, but whatever it was, it showed off her cleavage to maximum effect. She'd pinned her hair away from her face, too, giving him an unimpeded view of it.

"You look great," he said. "Cute dress."

"Yeah? Thrift store find, can you believe it? It has pockets!"

"Very cool."

"You look good, too."

He glanced at his arms, where he'd rolled up his shirtsleeves. "I'd intended to wear my suit jacket when I met you at the restaurant, so you could have the full effect."

"You did say you looked amazing in a suit. I'd hoped to judge that for myself."

"I'd get up and put my jacket on, but this ravioli is too delicious."

She smiled and rubbed his hand, then went back to eating. "How's Mr. Knightley?"

"Good, although his name is George now."

"George?"

"Mr. Knightley is kind of a lot to call a cat. So I looked it up, and in *Emma*, Mr. Knightley's first name is George. And that seems to fit the cat, too. It only took me a couple of days to get him to answer to it."

"Well, hey, that's something."

"I can't believe you guys talked me into getting a cat."

"We didn't have to try that hard."

Josh sighed. That was true. Deep down, Josh had known that cat had his number. George had pretty much moved right into his apartment. He liked to nap on the sofa or on Josh's bed or on Josh, sometimes. It was…nice. "He seems to be settling in well. I hired the teenage girl who lives down the hall to drop in and feed him on days when I have to work late so he doesn't get too lonely. Actually, I should text her that she should feed him now." He pulled out his phone and typed out the text with his thumbs.

"Aw, that's very sweet."

Josh put his phone down and eyed Paige, not sure if she was being patronizing or not. "Let me have some of that spaghetti."

———————

"So I put down my cards," Josh was saying. "Full house! Two kings, three eights. Because John was out of chips, he promised me something else, and I ended up with a ticket to an opera at the Kennedy Center, and I wasn't going to go, because opera, but then I thought, when will I ever get an opportunity to do something like this again? And you'll never guess who I ended up seated next to."

"Who?"

"Ruth Bader Ginsburg!"

"You're joking."

"No. Apparently she was a big opera fan."

Paige took the last bite of chicken and said, "Did you talk to her?"

"I introduced myself. Said I was a second-year law student. She wished me well."

"Oh, man, I would have asked so many questions."

"It took me the whole first act and most of the intermission to work up the courage to even say hello."

"Did you at least take a selfie? Please tell me you took a selfie."

"Of course. Here." He picked up his phone, touched the screen a few times, and passed it to Paige. There was indeed a photo of Josh and Ruth Bader Ginsburg. "That was my home screen for the rest of law school."

"So cool. We get celebrities in the Cat Café every now and then, but this is much more impressive than that." She handed his phone back.

"Who is the coolest person to come into the Cat Café?"

Paige had to think about it, but the first answer that came to mind was the shockingly handsome star of a popular TV show about an ex-con who led a dubiously straight and narrow life now. When she mentioned the actor's name, Josh scrunched up his face as if to say, *Really? That guy?*

"Look, I can't help it. He's even more gorgeous in real life. I also saw him in a play on Broadway last year. The play was very good and had something important to say about gay life in the twenty-first century, but, I'm not gonna lie, the most exciting part for me was that he was naked on stage for like five seconds, and while there was a screen that prevented the audience from seeing all the goods, what we could see was pretty impressive."

"Is this the kind of thing you should be telling to the man you're maybe pursuing romantically?"

She shrugged. "I'm a woman with a healthy sex drive, and if handsome actors get naked on stage, I'm allowed to appreciate them."

He smiled but shook his head. "I won't ask how I compare."

"Well, he's basically a Ken doll. I mean, he's hot, but he's also gay and doesn't know me from Eve. You are a heterosexual man who is right here in the same room with me, and you like me and know my name. So no contest."

"Well that's good to know."

"Don't be jealous."

"Perish the thought. Is there any of that carbonara left?"

Paige was so overfull that the presence of the big slice of tiramisu still in the takeout bag was making her feel a little nauseous, but she slid the carbonara container closer to Josh. He twirled some spaghetti around his fork and shoved it in his mouth.

As they continued to chat, Paige had to admit that there was definitely something between them. She also thought even that phrase was something of a sitcom cliché, but it seemed to fit here. It was a gut instinct, she supposed, a feeling like the person you were with was the person you were *supposed* to be with. She'd dated plenty and had even dated the same man most of the year she lived in London, but she had never really fallen in love. She'd definitely *liked* a lot of the men she'd been with, but she'd never had that feeling of rightness, of being able to see the future with someone. She didn't have that gut feeling that what she was doing was what she *should* be doing.

But she had an inkling of that with Josh.

Here they were pigging out on Italian food in his office and talking about nonsense, just casual getting to know each other without the romantic pretense that would have surrounded them in the actual restaurant. Josh had kept one eye on his computer monitor as they ate, occasionally stopping to answer an email, which made Paige aware that he was supposed to be working. But every time she volunteered to leave him alone to get back to his work, he said no, that he wanted her to stay.

And maybe that was the whole problem here. They liked each other a lot. Was that enough to override the risk?

"You ever date one of your sister's friends before?" she asked.

He paused with a fork halfway to his mouth. "Uh. Well, no. She's two years older than me, so when we were both still living at home, by the time I developed pants feelings for girls, her friends were all, you know, high school seniors, and I was an awkward acne-prone sophomore. And right now is the first time we've both lived in the same city since she graduated from high school."

"Let's stick a pin in that because I'm now for some reason very curious about how many of those high school seniors you had crushes on."

"Ah, no. Well, she had this one friend named Jasmine who was, like, eight feet tall. Probably actually a normal human height, but I was a short, scrawny teen, so she seemed impossibly tall to me. I couldn't even speak to her she made me so tongue-tied."

"Aw."

"I don't think Lauren and Jasmine are even really in touch anymore except on Facebook. Jasmine comments on Lauren's posts sometimes. My internet sleuthing reveals that she has a husband and two kids now and lives just outside Cincinnati."

"Sure."

"I mean, Lauren intended to introduce me to a lot of her friends when I moved here as a way to help me find a social circle. I think she had this vision of us being the Ross and Monica of our friend group. But I get to be the Monica, because Ross is the worst."

Paige laughed. "It's funny you should say that. Our friend Evan has been using *Friends* as his pop culture frame for everything lately. I, uh, mentioned to him that I'd met you. After he swore not to tell Lauren, he suggested that you and I might be Chandler and Monica, but I guess I worried we'd be Ross and Rachel."

"Ah, but Ross and Rachel ended up together."

"Yeah, eventually. After ten years of drama. And I don't know if I see Lauren as being as forgiving."

"But, see, that was kind of my point. Lauren had to know that if she integrated me into her friend group, I might end up dating someone in her circle."

That seemed so unlikely to Paige. But then, she was an only child and didn't have much firsthand experience of how sibling relationships worked. She thought she should probably talk to Lauren about this, but she didn't feel ready for that yet. At this point, if things didn't work out, then she and Josh could go back to being people who maybe might run into each other at a party.

"I somehow doubt Lauren wanted you to date her friends," she said.

"Well, maybe not. But…maybe we should try not to let Lauren get between us. Especially since I'm guessing she has no idea you're here right now."

"As far as she knows, you and I are two people who met while volunteering and are friendly and that's it. I told her I was going home after work tonight when she asked." She picked up her fork and poked at a stray ravioli. "I'd like to keep this quiet for now."

"Sure, all right. Also, let me just say, nothing kills the mood faster than talking about my sister."

Paige laughed despite feeling nervous about stepping forward into something with Josh. Then again, if it scared her, maybe it was exactly the right thing to do.

"I don't want to kill the mood," she said, leaning forward a little.

Josh lowered his eyelids. "No?"

"We came very close to kissing the other day when you picked up George from the Cat Café. Laur—er, no one is here now to stop us."

"I mean, my luck, some paralegal will—"

"Josh? Kiss me."

He grinned. "With pleasure."

The way they were seated, with the corner of the desk separating them, made kissing a little awkward, and Josh tasted like garlic, and still Paige wouldn't have changed anything. The kiss was sweet and romantic and held the promise of something greater in the future.

Paige supposed every relationship had risks. People overcame obstacles greater than meddling siblings all the time. Maybe it was time for Paige to take a risk.

So she said, as she pulled away from Josh, "I do still expect you to call me this weekend to set up another date."

"Now that, I can definitely do."

CHAPTER 11

PAIGE WAS SITTING IN THE cat room of the café, browsing children's books on her laptop to try to decide which she should try to buy from Stories, when Monique stuck her head in and said, "There's a guy here who asked for you."

"Who?"

"Dunno."

Paige wondered if it was Josh, which seemed impossible in the middle of the afternoon on a Monday, and besides Monique knew who Josh was. He had called her the day before, though, and they were scheduled to go out next Sunday, which she felt good about. Maybe nothing would come of it, but it was fun for now.

She got up and walked to the front of the café. The space was divided into three sections. There was a foyer in front where Lauren sometimes parked an employee to put potential customers on a wait list. There couldn't really be more than ten or twelve people in the cat room or the cats started freaking out and hiding under the furniture, which was sort of beside the point of a cat café. The foyer also acted as a second line of defense against any cats escaping. The middle section was the café. There was a counter that sold a wide array of pastries, all brought in from local bakeries and bagel shops until Lauren could persuade Diane to let a pastry chef make use of the full kitchen in the back. So the only place to get coffee within a few blocks was the Cat Café. And then the cat room, the largest part of the café, was in the rear. There were several rooms behind the cat room—Lauren's office, an employee break room, a room with litter boxes, and a storage closet full of cat food and litter. Lauren kept cat kennels in back, too, in case the cats had to be separated. And then there was that kitchen, because the space had been an Italian restaurant before Diane had come up with the idea for the Cat Café and hired Lauren to run it.

In the café section, Paige looked around. Monique walked back behind the counter and spoke to a man who faced away from Paige. He turned and looked at her. Paige recognized the mustache as belonging to Trevor, the guy she'd gone on a date with...god, when had that been? A month ago?

But ever the professional, she said, "Hi, Trevor."

"Paige! So good to see you. I had some time to kill this afternoon, so I decided to take you up on your offer to see the café."

She hadn't remembered offering that. "Oh. Well, after you get your coffee, come on back and I'll introduce you to some of the cats."

"I didn't order anything."

Of course.

Lauren and Caleb came in then, each carrying a huge bag of cat food. Once Lauren and Caleb were through the Café door and it closed with a click, Paige ran over to the cat room door and opened it for them. Once they were through, Paige said to Trevor, "Well, come on back then."

Paige was genuinely confused by Trevor's presence.

He walked into the cat room and looked around, his eyes wide with wonder. "Wow, what a cool space. Oh, hi there, kitty." He reached down to pet Mr. Willoughby, who was cautiously sniffing Trevor's shoes.

Sadie hopped up on a chair and tilted her head, as if to say, *This guy?*

"This is a cool mural. Did you paint it?"

Paige glanced at the mural that covered one wall of the cat room. It depicted cats drinking coffee. "No, I started working here after it was already up. The manager and one of her friends designed and painted it. It's based on the art of a painter in California who does these pieces that are very retro and colorful. Mid-century modern on acid."

Trevor laughed as if this were the most delightful thing he'd ever heard. "You were right, this is a really cool space. So, people come here and hang out and pet the cats?"

"Yeah, that's about the sum of it."

In Paige's peripheral vision, Lauren and Caleb came out from the backroom laughing about something. He gave her a quick peck and then left. Lauren then busied herself picking up cat toys from around the room.

"You ever think about having live music here?" Trevor asked.

Paige sighed. "No. Cats don't really like loud noise. The vacuum we use is pretty quiet, and that's too much noise for most of them. Besides, the point is to make people feel calm. Petting animals is supposed to help with stress. Loud music tends to stress people out more."

Trevor waved his hand dismissively. "Nah. I love loud music. I'm not really living unless I can feel the bass line in my chest."

It was a struggle for Paige not to roll her eyes. "Well, anyway, I have to get back to—"

"You never responded to any of my texts."

Oh, boy. "I've been busy."

"It takes like thirty seconds to respond to a text message."

"Look, Trevor, I—"

"I thought we got along great when we went out. I had fun. And then you blew me off. So I came down here today to see the cats, but I also wanted to talk to you because I think we'd be great together, and you should go on a second date with me."

Trevor was talking so loudly that everyone in the café, including Lauren, was staring at them now.

"Hey, Trevor, this is actually my place of business, so—"

"I won't wait. I won't let you brush me off again. I need you to tell me right here, right now that you'll go out with me again."

What was happening? How could Trevor think they had enough in common to be able to have a conversation through another date? "I appreciate your coming down here, but—"

"Come on, Paige. Why won't you go out with me again? Give me one reason."

Something in Paige snapped then. How dare this guy come to the place she worked to try to win her back. It was inappropriate, it backed her into a corner, and it was about to get her in trouble if she was reading Lauren's facial expression correctly. He must have known she wouldn't be rude in front of coworkers or customers. Except she couldn't deal with this anymore.

She'd been putting herself through this endless hunt for Mr. Right. Why had she thought she could find the love of her life by going on dates with twentysomething Brooklyn men who weren't really interested in anything more than sex and someone to hang out with? She was twenty-eight, and what would she have to show for it? Career success and financial security, sure, but also a lot of failed relationships, no husband or children, and this stupid, self-destructive pattern where she only went on dates with men she had nothing in common with.

So she said, "For one thing, I hate live music. It's too loud. I'd rather be in a quiet space where I can have a conversation. But live music is basically all you talk about. You only want me back because you find me physically attractive and you think my job is cool. It conforms to whatever hipster ethos you subscribe to because I work in a quirky café and not for 'the man.' I'm also an adult with my own apartment and a successful career, whereas you live with a bunch of guys over a pizza place. We're at different places in our lives, we have nothing in common, and you are currently making a scene in the place where I work. Is that enough reasons?"

Trevor had the grace to look chastened at least. "Well, geez. I had no idea."

"No, because you didn't listen to me when we talked the other night. You kept talking over me."

"How can anyone not like live music? That's like saying you don't like dogs."

"Get the hell out of here, Trevor. Don't contact me again, don't come to my place of business. I will be blocking your phone number."

He held up his hands. "Fine. Be that way." He stormed out of the café.

She hadn't even had to deploy the fact that she was, technically, seeing someone else. The live music thing seemed to have gotten the job done. At least he was gone. Paige turned to go back to work, and most of the customers had gone back to their computers or conversations once Trever had left the room, but Lauren was headed right for Paige and looked pissed.

Shit. Paige had been the one to make a scene, hadn't she?

Lauren said, "Come with me back to my office. Victor? Can you keep an eye on things in the cat room for a minute?"

Paige followed Lauren through the backrooms to her office, her heart in her throat. She was about to get a lecture. Lauren had pulled her back here so she could yell without doing so in front of customers. "Lauren, I'm so sorry."

"Are you okay?"

"What?"

Lauren frowned. "That guy was really rude. I've never seen you lose it like that. I just wanted to know if you're okay."

"I..." Paige took a moment to do a quick assessment. Her heart was pounding. "Yeah, I'm okay. Or I will be in a few minutes."

"Who was that guy?"

"Just some dude I went on a Tinder date with, like, a month ago. Did you hear everything?"

"Most of it. So he just showed up here? Wow, stalker much?"

Paige let out a breath. Her heart was starting to slow to its normal pace as she realized Lauren wasn't really mad. "Are you upset I made a scene?"

"Not your fault. You didn't invite that guy down here, did you?"

"No, of course not."

"I mean, Evan's here all the time. I suppose it would be hypocritical of me to tell you not to let your friends drop by during business hours."

"I didn't. I haven't seen that guy since the one date we went on." Paige sighed. "Why do I attract these losers?"

Lauren raised an eyebrow. "Dunno. I mean, I'm hardly one to talk, but I've wondered if true love could really be found in an app that treats dating like a game."

"I know." Paige rubbed her forehead. "I live in hope, I guess, but I think I'm, uh, looking for love in all the wrong places?"

Lauren cracked up at that. "I mean, stranger things have happened."

Paige was tired of all of it, though. She said, "I want to fall in love. I want to get married. It was all well and good for you to swear off romance and then meet your husband, but it doesn't work that way for all of us. I figured the best way to find a partner was to put myself out there, but all I meet are these guys I have nothing in common with. Why is it so hard?"

"I don't know. We live in a city of over eight million people and yet it seems impossible to meet any of them."

"Well, that's true."

It hit Paige then that guys like Trevor were not who she should be dating, but guys like Josh. Josh was mature and sexy and had a real job and his own apartment. Not that there was really anything wrong with guys like Trevor who were pursuing their dreams and trying to do something creative with their lives; they just weren't the sort of partner Paige wanted at this stage in her life. But she'd had more fun eating and talking over takeout Italian food in Josh's office last week than she'd had on all the dates she'd gone on this year, which mostly proved that she really had been looking for love in the wrong places.

Although, still, Lauren's brother.

Paige cleared her throat. "You're totally right. I'm sorry for bringing drama to the café."

"It's okay. Not your fault. I totally understand why you snapped." Lauren smiled. "What were you thinking about just then?"

Paige must have done something with her face while she'd been thinking about Josh. "I was just… I think this has really shown me I have to change something. I guess it all starts to feel like a habit after a while."

"Yeah. I worry about you sometimes. I mean, I can always be counted on for the bail-out phone call, but I would like for you to meet a nice guy and not make that phone call anymore."

"Me, too. You're right. I'm too old for this nonsense."

"It'll happen, Paige. You'll meet the right guy. And you deserve someone amazing. You're smart and you work hard and you're such a good person. *I* love you, just, you know, not in a pants way. But some guy out there will love you in a pants way and it will be awesome. I know patience is hard, but he's out there, you just gotta…wait for him to show up."

What if he had already arrived? Paige bit her lip to keep from blurting out anything and nodded.

"I bet he'll show up when you least expect it," Lauren added.

Ha. "Probably. Well. Thanks. I half expected you to snap my head off."

"Nah. I was mostly mad on your behalf. How dare that guy."

Paige smiled back at Lauren. See, *this* was why she had to respect her friendship. Lauren always had her back. Would she still if she found out Paige was seeing her brother? One could hope. "Thanks," said Paige.

"Anytime."

————————

It occurred to Josh as the subway train pulled above ground to go over the Manhattan Bridge that he was about to be home at dinner time, which meant he could see Paige. So he called her once he got a signal.

"What train are you on?" she asked.

"The Q."

"Get off at Atlantic. I'll text you my address. I'm cooking."

"Oh, yeah. What's for dinner?"

"It's Taco Tuesday, my friend."

He had to put Paige's address into the GPS app on his phone, but he found it without too much trouble. The doorman sent him up to the third floor of the super modern five-story building a couple of blocks from the Barclays Center. The building itself looked like a big concrete block with windows, but the lobby was sleek and well-designed, as were the elevator and the hallway to Paige's apartment.

Paige welcomed him in with a broad smile and a hug. "Welcome to Casa de Paige."

"Thanks," he said, walking into the apartment. It was small but very nice. Also quite feminine; it seemed very pink at first glance.

Off to the left of the front door was the kitchen, where Paige led Josh now. There was a small kitchen island with two stools next to it. Paige pointed at one of the stools, so Josh sat there.

"How are things?" he asked.

"It's been an interesting couple of days. This hipster guy I went on *one* date with, like, a month ago showed up at the Cat Café yesterday and begged me to take him back, so that was awkward."

That got Josh's back up. "Wait, he just waltzed right in and made a scene?"

"It was...not my finest moment. He was super annoying and I kind of snapped and told him off. Lauren saw the whole thing and I was worried she'd yell at me, but she was actually mad at the guy for causing a ruckus."

"I bet."

"I have to stop dating these guys I have zero in common with."

"Well, yeah. I could have told you that."

"You're biased because you want me to date you."

"True." Josh smiled at her. "We're going to have to tell Lauren that this is a thing at some point."

"Let's not do that just yet."

"I do usually wait until the fifth date to tell Lauren I'm seeing someone."

Paige laughed, although she looked a little uneasy. "Let's keep it in this little bubble for now."

"Fine by me. What's this I hear about tacos?"

Paige set a series of plates on the counter: a plate with crunchy taco shells, a plate of soft tortillas, a bowl with grilled peppers and onions, a bowl of lettuce, a bowl of shredded cheese, and then two skillets, one with chicken and one with ground beef.

"Wow, this is quite a feast."

"Taco meat reheats well, so it's a good solo meal, although I'll admit I only put the chicken on when you told me you were coming. It seemed better to have options."

He watched her get plates down from a cabinet and put two beside each other on the island. She handed Josh a fistful of silverware. Then she walked over to grab a few more things from the fridge.

"In case you didn't figure this out from our prior meals together," said Josh, "I'm basically an omnivore. If it's food, I'll probably eat it. Well, except I'm allergic to melon. Makes me break out in hives."

"Good to know. So the cantaloupe and honeydew salad I made for dessert is out."

"You didn't, did you?"

She laughed. "No. I don't have much for dessert. Maybe some ice cream."

"Or, uh, you."

She raised an eyebrow. "Oh, really? That's presumptuous."

"You're the one who invited me over."

"True. You want a beer?"

"Yes."

Paige handed him a bottle and an opener, then she got a beer for herself and a container of sour cream out of the fridge. She sat on the booth beside him and said, "Dig in."

Josh deliberately brushed her hand as much as he could as they assembled their tacos. He made a pretty big plate, as he was suddenly starving.

"Oh, I forgot the hot sauce," said Paige, hopping back up. "And do you want olives? I've got some black olives in the fridge."

"Sure?"

"My dad always puts olives on tacos. I didn't know that was weird until a guy I dated a few years ago pointed it out."

"I don't think it's weird. I love olives. Bring them on."

"Okay, cool."

As Josh bit into his first taco, Paige finally sat next to him and finished assembling her plate. He waited until she seemed satisfied with what she'd put together before he spoke.

"This is delicious, by the way. I like the spice blend on the beef."

"Yeah, I made it myself. From a recipe on the internet, but still. Well, I swapped out the chili powder for chipotle powder. It's smokier and has a little more of a punch."

"You cook a lot?"

"I like cooking, yeah." Paige looked at the feast arrayed on the counter. "My friend Lindsay is this big foodie. Went to culinary school and everything. *She* can cook. I'm self-taught and really just do this for myself."

"Hey, that's fine. I can't really cook. I mean, I can do basic things like boil water for pasta and heat things up in a microwave, but so much of my adult life has been grabbing food on the way to the next thing that I never took the time to cook a big meal."

"How old are you?"

Josh wondered if he should be offended by the question. "I'm twenty-eight."

"And law school only takes three years. What did you do between undergrad and law school?"

He smirked. He'd gotten this question a lot in law school, although he wasn't that much older than his classmates. A lot of people graduated, tried something, and then went back to school. "I decided to go into politics when I finished undergrad. I worked on Senator Green's election campaign, and he liked me so much he made me part of his staff. And after two years of that, I realized I couldn't do much as a low-level staffer, so I decided to go to law school."

"Interesting. I feel like I'm seeing a whole new side of you. Green is the senator from Ohio that is gung-ho about the environment, right?"

"Among other things, yeah."

"Do you see yourself running for office?"

"No. No way. I'm more of a behind-the-scenes guy."

"Ah, but you've got an altruistic streak, I bet. How much is the evil corporate law firm stomping on your heart?"

"A lot. But it's... I don't know. I got the internship at DCL at the right time, and I thought, sure, I can give this a try, get my feet wet. My boss when I was an intern was a great mentor, so I figured taking the job when I graduated would be a good way to get my law career off the ground. I've only been at it a couple of months, so it's too soon to say whether I made a bad choice, but I don't see myself staying with this firm until I make partner, if you get what I mean."

"I do."

Josh smiled. He supposed they had gone over this ground before. Big corporate job to pay off the student loans and get on his feet in his career, then he'd go off and pursue his passion. Just like Paige hadn't wanted to work for a huge international bank her whole life. So she understood. Maybe working in a cat café wasn't her passion, per se, but it seemed to make her happy.

He smiled at her. They ate in companionable silence for a few minutes. Then behind him, he heard a quiet *mew*.

He turned and saw a very fluffy white cat.

"That's Bianca," said Paige.

"Of course you have a cat. Lauren strikes again."

Paige laughed. "Yes. Bianca lived at the café when I started working there. I will admit, I loved her at first sight. I hope bad things happen to the family that abandoned her."

The cat stared at Josh intently, probably trying to work out the best way to kill him.

"She's kind of a diva," Paige said. "She already had her dinner, but she will now hover expectantly in case I decide this is the day I finally relent and let her have some people food."

"George is pretty low-key, but I worry about leaving him alone so much."

"Yeah. Cats are advertised as low maintenance, but they require more work than you think. This one lodges complaints about everything from the cleanliness of her litter box to the fact that her bowl is only half full. So I have to stay on top of things."

Josh chuckled. "Lauren and I had cats growing up. My mom never believed in letting house cats go out, so the ones we had were all pretty lazy. Lauren used to joke that one of our cats was really more ornamental than anything else. She didn't do much except drape herself over the furniture."

Paige laughed, which Josh appreciated. He wanted to make her laugh more because he loved the sound of it. He went back to his tacos as he tried to think of something to say that would get her to laugh like that again.

Josh insisted on helping Paige clean up after they finished eating, and he liked working alongside her in the kitchen, even with how small it was. The cramped space gave him an excuse to bump into or brush against her. She giggled every time he did it, which was endearing.

"So how'd you get sprung so early tonight?" Paige asked, leading him over to the sofa in the other half of the main room.

"Just...coincidence. I happened to get through everything I needed to before sundown. That almost never happens."

"I'm flattered you chose to spend your early night with me."

"Of course."

"You don't know a lot of people in the city, do you?"

"Aside from my sister and my coworkers? No, not really. But I would have chosen you anyway. I think you're awesome, if I haven't said so recently."

Paige's face went pink and she looked down for a moment. "Thanks."

"Hey, look at me," he said.

When her gaze met his, he leaned over and kissed her. She still kissed better than anyone he'd ever kissed.

"I was serious about having you for dessert," he said.

She blushed. "Oh, really?"

"Maybe you want to show me the bedroom?"

"Uh, sure. Right this way."

CHAPTER 12

A MAN COULD GET USED to waking up in a big soft bed with lots of covers and pillows that smelled like lavender. Even though Paige's apartment looked like a Vera Bradley catalog come to life, it was homey and comfortable.

He stretched and was about to get up when Paige stirred.

"What time is it?" she asked.

"Sorry, I set an alarm so I'd have time to go home and change before work. It's a little after five."

"Yikes." She yawned. "I guess I could get up. I'm opening the café today."

Josh gazed at her for a moment. He really liked this woman. She was gorgeous and sexy, of course, but he loved talking to her. He cursed his bad luck for meeting her at a time in his life when these too-short spontaneous nights were all he could squeeze in.

Her eyes met his. He felt some pull in his chest, some gut feeling that this might just be the real thing.

"Paige," he said, "I want you to know, this isn't just sex for me. I mean, don't get me wrong, the sex part is awesome, but I don't, like, want you only for your body."

She smiled brightly. "Well, thank you. And I agree. I keep thinking, you know, you're very different from the guys I usually date, but that's a really good thing. I like you, too."

"I want to see you again, but I also want to keep everyone's expectations reasonable. My coworkers tell me after the first year, the work is less crushing all around, but for right now, I'm putting in sixty or seventy hours at work every week."

She reached over and squeezed his hand. "I know. I understand. We'll figure it out."

"Okay, good."

Paige got out of bed. "You want some breakfast? I can make eggs."

Josh's stomach rumbled. "I think you might be my dream woman."

She shrugged into a robe and laughed as she left the room.

Josh wondered at his luck as he pulled some of his clothes back on. He heard eggs sizzling as he walked out of the bedroom. Bianca, who sat in one of the stools, eyed him warily as he sat at the kitchen island.

"You want your breakfast, too, Bianca?" Paige asked. She pulled a big bag of kibble from a cabinet under the counter and filled the half-full cat bowl on the floor. Bianca gave Josh one last skeptical look and then jumped down to eat.

"Any hot plans at the café today?" Josh asked as he watched Paige lay some breakfast sausages on a plate and put it in the microwave.

"I have a meeting with Diane around lunchtime. She's the owner."

"Yeah, Lauren has mentioned her."

"She wants a postmortem on the fundraiser. We raised enough money to cover everything I want to do, which is good. I'm going to present her with a more formal proposal for the youth programming I want to do at the café."

"Cool."

"Everything used to go through Lauren, did you know that? The first year or so I worked at the café, I pitched her all of my ideas and then she pitched them to Diane. But lately, she's backed off some. I think Caleb mellowed her out."

"Yeah, she was always kind of a control freak. The last time I had dinner with her and Caleb, they had a little spat about how much time she was spending at the café."

"Diane makes her take days off. But, basically, the result of Lauren backing off a little is that I'm meeting with Diane directly about financial matters, so I'm going to give her my plan for how to spend the fundraising money after we give half to the animal shelter."

"Are you nervous?"

"Nah. It's a good proposal, and I've already talked to Diane and Lauren about most of it. The meeting is kind of just a formality."

Josh smiled as she put a plate of eggs and sausage in front of him. He admired her confidence. She had no hesitation in her voice, and she knew what she was doing at work, which was more than he could say for himself most days.

Paige slid him a mug of coffee and then made a plate for herself and sat beside him.

"Bless you," he said, taking a sip.

"I'm fueled mostly by coffee, so I assumed you probably were, too. You want some creamer?"

"No, black is good. This is excellent coffee."

"It's the same stuff we get at the Cat Café. It's from a little place that does its own coffee roasting right here in Brooklyn."

Josh grinned. "You know, you spend a lot of time making fun of the hipster guys in Brooklyn, but isn't being pretentious about coffee on the first page of the hipster handbook?"

She had the presence of mind to look a little embarrassed. "Well, I guess we all have our eccentricities."

Josh left a little while later without showering, preferring to do that at home. But there had been a whole series of long, lingering kisses and, "No, really, I have to go…" but he had no regrets about that. He probably shouldn't make a habit of Paige delaying his leaving for work, but he could do it every now and then.

He was delighted to realize how close they lived to each other; once he got to the Barclays Center, he knew the rest of the way home. He caught himself humming as he walked home in the early morning, as the sun rose. Hardly anyone was out this early, which made the walk home fairly easy.

It reminded him of when he'd first arrived in Georgetown. He'd found a little apartment near the waterfront that was a shoebox but had a spectacular view. He'd get up in the morning sometimes and go out for coffee at a little cupcake shop near his building, then he'd walk around and explore the neighborhood.

And fine, he was a morning person. He loved the time just before rush hour when things were open but the masses weren't rushing to work yet. Such as right now.

He'd kept that Georgetown apartment for all of law school. Megan moved into it halfway through their second year. She rarely got up a second sooner than she absolutely had to, so even after she'd moved in, he'd had those mornings to himself. His heart still squeezed when he thought of Megan, not because he missed her but because the wound was still fresh. He couldn't say he had regrets about the way his life was going now, especially when everything with Paige was going so well, but it still hurt to think he'd once imagined Megan *here*, in his apartment, making it a real home and not just the barren place he slept.

When Evan sat across from Paige at Pop, he said, "I always kind of thought it was a sitcom cliché that people can tell when others have had sex, but...you totally banged Lauren's brother again, didn't you? You look like the cat who got the canary."

"Oh my god. Keep it down."

Evan grinned. "Lauren sends her regrets. It's safe to talk."

"Regrets? I thought she said she was coming tonight."

"She forgot she had a doctor's appointment or something. Although I suspect that was a lie and she's actually making sweet love to Caleb in a closet somewhere."

Paige screwed up her nose. "They are too much sometimes."

"Honey, I know. But I was right about them. I take credit for their sickening happiness. So I feel a little good about that."

Lindsay walked in then and sat across from Paige. "What a day," she said.

"What happened?" asked Evan.

"I got an assignment to write a story on farmers' markets, so I spent a good chunk of today researching and making phone calls about the food supply chain in New York, and it's *a lot*, you guys."

"Your job is weird," said Evan.

Lindsay rolled her eyes. "I'm patching together a career here. It turns out there is a finite number of restaurants in New York City that need to be reviewed, so I'm branching out into other food writing. Although I might write a story on pet food for my friend's website. There's a hot debate about raw food diets versus the canned stuff."

"Oh, boy," said Paige.

"There's something to it. I put my cat on a raw diet and—"

"You're not going to talk about cat poop in this fine establishment, are you?" asked Evan.

"Fine." Lindsay rolled her eyes. "What's up with you guys?"

Evan cleared his throat and raised his glass. "Darius and I have gone on a *second* date. It seems promising."

"Not the third date," said Lindsay, "so I'm guessing you haven't gotten into his pants yet."

"First of all, I never kiss and tell."

"Yes, you do," said Paige. "That's literally what we talk about every time we meet for drinks. We are here right now to tell about our kisses."

Evan sipped his water and sat up a little straighter. "Fine. Then

WHAT THE CAT DRAGGED IN   **133**

I will say that the whole 'sex on a third date' thing is a fiction of the television-industrial complex, and also Darius and I dated and bumped uglies repeatedly several years ago, so it doesn't count anyway."

"That means Evan totally slept with Darius," Lindsay stage-whispered to Paige.

"Yeah, I figured that out."

"Yes, fine. Darius and I consummated our relationship. And it was pretty great." He shrugged. "Now you go, Paige."

"I'm gonna need a martini or six first," Paige said, raising her hand to try to get the waitress's attention.

"That sounds promising," said Lindsay.

"Can I tell her?" Evan said excitedly. "No, you tell her. No, I want to tell her!"

"Knock yourself out, Ev. Here comes Jenny." Jenny was a regular waitress at Pop.

"Okay, Linds. Brace yourself. Also, cone of silence. What we are about to tell you does not leave this table."

Lindsay mimed crossing her heart. "I swear."

Evan let out a little gleeful noise just as the waitress appeared and they all ordered drinks. When the waitress was gone again, Evan said, "Paige is secretly banging Lauren's brother."

Lindsay's eyes went wide. "You… Are you kidding?"

"No." Paige sighed. "It's not just banging. Josh and I seem to be casually dating. And Lauren doesn't know. Don't say anything. We're working up to telling her."

Lindsay shook her head. "This news is amazing. Do I know Josh?"

"Probably not," said Paige. "He couldn't make it to Lauren's wedding, I met him for the first time a few weeks ago."

Evan nodded. "If I've said a dozen words to him in my whole life, I'd be surprised. But he moved to the city about two months ago and then Paige met him by chance, and now they're in *love*."

"We're not in love. We've been on a couple of dates. Yes, I like him, but it's very casual right now."

Lindsay narrowed her eyes at Paige like she was thinking this through. "How old is he?"

"Twenty-eight," said Paige.

Lindsay pursed her lips. "Okay. Relative maturity level?"

"I don't know how to evaluate that, but he's a lawyer and he has his own apartment in one of the big high-rises in downtown Brooklyn."

"Ah, but does he have a view?" Lindsay smirked. "My friend Rebecca lives in one of those buildings. You can see the Statue of Liberty from her window. It's amazing."

"I know you're joking and the view has no relation to maturity level, but no, he doesn't have much of a view. His windows face another building, but at an angle so you can't see into anyone's windows."

"Clever."

"Is Rebecca the one whose kid you babysit?" Evan asked.

"She is, yes. And for the record, I only babysit because that kid is sweet as pie and loves her Auntie Lindsay, so she's easy to deal with. Mostly, we read books, take naps, and eat Rebecca's officially sanctioned snacks. So don't get ideas if you guys decide to have kids."

Evan shook his head. "I would *never*."

"*Anyway*," said Paige. "Part of why I like Josh is that he seems to have his life together, and he doesn't spend all of his time obsessing over obscure indie bands or making cheese at home."

"People do that?" said Evan.

"Yeah." Paige sighed. "Tinder date I went on a couple of months ago was with a guy who was working out how to turn his spare bedroom into a cheese cave."

"So what you're saying," said Lindsay, "is that he has a job and a home and no whacky hobbies? Although honestly, I'm now mentally trying to work out if I can turn part of my apartment into a cheese cave."

"Well, he works a lot. That's the one potential negative as far as I can tell. He pretty much lives in his office, so he doesn't have time for hobbies. Or dating, really. All of our dates so far have occurred when he finagled time off." Paige sipped her cocktail as soon as Jenny deposited it in front of her. "And in defense of those Tinder dates, I do work at a cat café, and I like to do crafts in my spare time. Josh pointed out the other morning that I'm just as much of a Brooklyn hipster stereotype as the guys I make fun of."

"The whacky hobbies were never the issue," said Evan. "It was that you tend to attract men-children who are not at the same place in their lives as you are, honey."

"I have the opposite problem," said Lindsay. "Last time I tried online dating, I only matched with guys in New Jersey who were looking for wives. Where were all these Brooklyn guys then?"

"You probably had your age limit set too high," said Evan. "Not that I know anything about online dating." He whistled.

"Sure." Paige laughed. "I don't know. Are we at the point in our lives when everyone has baggage? I went on a date with a guy last year who was thirty-five and divorced. Not that this is a dealbreaker, it just seems like a lot of baggage to handle."

"Caleb was divorced when he met Lauren. That didn't seem to bother either of them much," said Evan.

"Okay, fine. And I'm really glad that worked out for them. Maybe the guy I dated was not in a good place mentally, I don't know. But then I met a guy a few months ago who had kids, and I couldn't deal with that either. So, see, I'm not even that mature."

"It's fine," said Evan. "And you are mature. You actually act like an adult most of the time. You have a job you love and a nice apartment and you pay your bills on time, right?"

"Right."

"So you've already got a leg up on a lot of people I know. And again, I don't think it was even the baggage per se that made those other relationships not work out. People get divorced. It happens. What was it Ross said on *Friends*? 'Divorced men are not *bad* men.'"

"That's what they put on the cocktail napkins at the divorced men's club," said Lindsay, laughing.

"My point, though, is that it's not the divorces or the kids or the cheese caves," said Evan. "It's that these men were not the right men for *you*."

"Yeah, okay," said Paige.

"But you're dating Lauren's brother and she doesn't know yet," Lindsay said with a "let me get this straight" tone in her voice. "And you really like him."

"I do."

"You're going out again soon, I assume."

"Yeah, this weekend, if all goes to plan."

"Are you going to tell Lauren or wait until you send wedding invitations?"

The thought of telling Lauren made Paige feel like she'd swallowed a rock. But the thought of *not* telling her didn't sit right either. Paige hated keeping secrets from her friends, especially something so big. "Eventually we'll tell her. But we don't want to cause any angst until we know if it's going really somewhere."

"They're already a *we* and not an *I*," Lindsay said.

"It's… No, I meant… Ugh."

Evan laughed. "Such a weird problem to have. But I get it. I honestly don't know how she'll react. She's pretty protective of Josh."

"Thanks," said Paige. "Like I wasn't already worried enough."

"What has you worried, exactly?" Lindsay asked.

"What *doesn't* have me worried? What if Lauren doesn't approve? What if Josh and I make some kind of commitment but then break up? Lauren's going to side with him over me, and then where will I be? What if she fires me? What if this whole thing changes our friendship?"

Lindsay nodded. "Yeah, that is a lot."

"But it also might *not* happen, you know. It could all work out. We could all live happily ever after."

Paige felt nauseous now. She loved her friends and didn't want to be responsible if she destroyed this little group that met for drinks a few nights a week. And she knew how this would go. Evan was Lauren's best friend and they'd known each other since college. Lindsay and Lauren had worked together at a café in Manhattan. Paige loved all of them like family, but she could very well lose all of them if Lauren disapproved of her relationship with Josh.

"If it helps at all," said Evan, "here's how I see it. Three things could happen. You and Josh will fall in love and tell Lauren and everything will be fine. You and Josh date for a bit, it fizzles, and Lauren is never the wiser. Or you get together, tell Lauren, and your relationship ends for whatever reason. And if that happens? We've got your back. Right, Linds?"

"Yes. Of course. We love you, Paige."

"So, yeah, things could get messy or uncomfortable for a bit, but if the end result is that we work through that and you end up happy with a really great guy, then that's awesome. So you have to decide if you want to risk some awkwardness for that possible future."

"He is really great," said Paige.

"I mean, it's a tough situation. Lauren might react badly. Or she'll think it's great. You don't really know. Do you really want to give up your potential future happiness because Lauren might flip out?"

When Evan put it like that, it seemed silly. What she wanted was to fall in love and get married and keep her friends and be happy. She could see the potential for that with Josh, although it wasn't a guarantee. But did she really want to give him up because Lauren *might* freak out? What she wanted was to see where things went with Josh.

"Fair point," said Paige.

"All right, good."

Lindsay's phone buzzed where it sat on the table. She picked it up and looked at it. "Oh, great."

"What?" asked Paige.

"Apparently the *Times* reviewed that new chocolate restaurant in Midtown."

"Chocolate restaurant?" asked Evan.

"Yeah. They serve both savory and sweet dishes, but everything has chocolate in it. Guess who the new head pastry chef is?"

"Oh no," said Paige.

"It's Brad, isn't it?" said Evan. "It's always Brad when you use that tone in your voice." Brad was Lindsay's ex, a man she was clearly still hung up on even though she denied it.

"Of course it's Brad," Lindsay said. She tapped her finger on her phone screen a few times and paused to read. "Lovely. Listen to this. 'After enjoying the novelty of chocolate in your savory dinner, be sure to save room for dessert, because the unique sweets offered by pastry chef Brad Marks are not to be missed. I particularly enjoyed the Mexican chocolate mousse.'... And it goes on in that vein for a while."

"Is it a crime to think Brad's food is good?" asked Evan. "Because I'm guilty. I still have dreams of that lemon chiffon cake he made for your birthday when you were dating. Best thing I've ever put in my mouth. And I've put a lot of good things in my mouth, if you know what I mean."

"Everyone knows what you mean, Ev." Lindsay crossed her arms and glared at Evan. "And you're not helping. We hate him, remember? We want him to fail."

"If you say so. Curse that man and his delicious baked goods."

"We have a lot of romantic problems collectively," said Paige. "You ever notice that?"

"What kind of New Yorkers would we be if our lives were completely fulfilled and happy?" said Evan.

CHAPTER 13

JOSH HAD ISSUED AN EDICT to Paige: show him what Brooklyn really had to offer.

Event planning was Paige's best skill, so she went about putting together a whole agenda for the day.

She met Josh in the lobby of his building late Sunday morning and said, "The first order of business is brunch."

"Is that... Did you make a spreadsheet and put it on your phone?"

"You asked me to plan an event, so I *planned* an event. You want to be with me, you need to accept my crazy."

"Fair enough. Lead on, General."

The first stop was a farm-to-table restaurant on Flatbush Avenue known for having a very good brunch. Paige had never been there before and only knew it by reputation, so this part of the plan was a bit of a gamble, but she was thankful she'd made a reservation, because the place was packed.

"I love brunch," Josh said as the hostess walked into the restaurant to make sure their table was ready.

"You seem to like food generally."

"That is true, and bless New York City for having lots of healthy takeout options so I'm not stuck eating hamburgers on the go all the time. But I also like sitting and really enjoying a meal in good company. And breakfast food. I'd eat eggs and bacon at every meal if I could."

"Not to be rude, but how is it you stay in such good shape?"

Josh grinned. "A lot of running on a treadmill in the gym in my building at odd hours of the night when I need to destress from the workday."

The hostess reappeared and brought them to a table in the back of the restaurant near a tall window that let in a lot of light. They had a view of the restaurant's backyard garden, which seemed to currently be hosting a baby shower.

"I'm buying, by the way," Josh said, opening the menu. "I'm starving and intend to order enough food for three men, so it's only fair."

"Thanks for the warning." Paige opened the menu and looked over the offerings. Fancy breakfast fare, mostly, a lot of creative plays on more traditional brunch dishes. Although the stuffed french toast sounded divine. "If I'd known eggs and bacon would get the job done, I would have taken you to Tom's."

"What's that?"

"It's this famous diner over by the Brooklyn Museum. It's famous for its breakfast. The space is tiny, and they really squeeze everyone in there, and there's usually a pretty long line to get in, but it's cheap and they make, like, six kinds of pancakes. They also make solid milkshakes and egg creams."

"That does sound good," said Josh. "We'll have to go there next time. But I mean, this is good, too. I like an avocado toast."

Paige laughed.

Josh smiled back at her. "For real, there are eight things on this menu I'd walk over my mother to try. It's going to be very difficult to pick."

Josh ordered only one entree but four side dishes and an appetizer, so he really would be getting enough food for three men.

"You eat like a teenage boy," Paige said.

"My mother says the same thing whenever I'm home."

They talked amiably about work, about cats, about things they'd read or seen on TV. After their food arrived, Josh told a funny story about a night in law school during which he and a friend had gone all over Washington looking for an all-night diner because Josh had been craving waffles. Paige told him about an event she'd run when she'd lived in London at which an attendee both kept kosher and had several food allergies, so she'd had to get creative with the menu, and then she'd gotten complaints that the special meal looked better than what everyone else was served.

As they wound down, Josh asked for the dessert menu. By then, Paige was feeling warm and floaty from the mimosa the waitress kept refilling, so she blurted out, "How do you have room for dessert?"

Josh grinned. "When I was a kid, my aunt Rita used to make the *best* pies at Thanksgiving. She made an apple pie with a cheddar cheese crust that was tart and perfect, but for my money, the best one was a chocolate cream pie. You may want to ask what chocolate pie has to do with Thanksgiving. I don't know and I don't care because it was my favorite part of the holiday. It never mattered how much turkey I'd gorged myself on, I was gonna get a slice of that pie. There was one year when, no joke, we ended up with six pies at the house because Lauren decided she wanted to try making one and some distant cousin came to dinner with one, too. So I only ate a modest amount of dinner food that year so I could eat as much pie as possible, and my mother was actually concerned I was coming down with something because I was eating so little."

Paige laughed, although the mention of Lauren made her nervous. "Was Lauren's pie any good?"

"I think it was passable. Lauren is not exactly known for her culinary skills."

"Yeah, I get the impression that Caleb does most of the cooking."

"If that's the case, they'll be just fine. I've had Caleb's cooking and…" Josh mimed a chef's kiss.

Josh opted out of dessert, citing Paige's stated intention to do a lot of walking to burn off the calories of that rich, delicious breakfast. But after he paid and they walked outside, she rethought her plan. She didn't want to tire Josh out too much; she had plans for when they got back to her place later. On the other hand, he did work out regularly.

"You up for walking a couple of miles?" she asked.

"Sure. I skipped the treadmill today."

"Cool. This way."

She headed west on Livingston Street and Josh explained again that he'd hardly seen any of Brooklyn. Paige said, "When I first moved to Brooklyn, I used to like to walk around here. I read a novel when I was overseas that took place in this part of Brooklyn in the 1870s, so I wanted to see it for myself. Obviously, most of this area looks completely different than it did a hundred and forty years ago, but pockets of it haven't changed much."

"Yeah, I would guess that big glass skyscraper in the distance wasn't here then."

Paige laughed. "Yeah, that's pretty new."

They talked amiably about the stores and restaurants they passed. When they got to Boerum Place, Paige led Josh to the right, up the street toward Borough Hall. "Your brother-in-law used to live near here," Paige said.

"Oh, really?"

"Yeah. He told me he liked to take his dog to the Promenade. That's a big cobblestone area right on the water that has a pretty good view of the Brooklyn Bridge and lower Manhattan. The view is great, but it's right above the highway, so it's loud. And I know a place with a better view of the bridge."

"Cool. Lead on."

As they walked, Paige pointed out various landmarks they passed: Borough Hall, the courthouses, a small farmers' market in the plaza in front of the courthouses, a hotel she'd used for a corporate meeting once.

And as they neared their destination, Josh looked around, amazement on his face. "Is your better place to view the bridge, the actual bridge?"

"Perhaps."

The entrance ramp to the Brooklyn Bridge looked like a tangled knot of roads, but Paige knew this route very well and led Josh to the walkway. "I don't want to go all the way to Manhattan, so I'll just lead you to the first tower. It's worth it, though. Come on."

The bridge's famous arches soared in the distance as they approached. Josh looked around him as they walked as though he'd never seen anything so amazing. It was a warm spring day and lots of people were out, so the walkway was crowded and they learned quickly that they had to be on guard for bicyclists who seemed disinclined to slow down or alter their routes so as not to hit pedestrians.

They paused at the tower and Paige pointed out that they could see the Manhattan Bridge on one side and the Statue of Liberty in the distance on the other. The skyscrapers of Lower Manhattan seemed to rise up from the base of the island like giant porcupine spikes. This view always awed and humbled Paige, and she'd wanted to share it.

Josh seemed happy to linger there for a few minutes to take it all in.

"I've seen photos," he said, "but I had no idea. The scale of this is so different in person."

Paige watched his face for a few minutes. She loved how impressed he seemed by the view. She loved that they'd already spent a few hours together and had not run out of things to talk about.

Did they have a future? Paige could see other Sunday afternoons spent together, when she showed him other parts of Brooklyn. They'd merely brushed against the surface today.

But really, making a mental list of places they could visit was like an elaborate excuse to keep seeing Josh, something she definitely wanted to do. Which meant they'd have to tell Lauren eventually, something Paige wasn't quite ready to think about. So she shoved it aside.

"If you walk the whole length of the bridge, it's about a mile. You end up near City Hall Park on the other side. I've done that walk when I've had business in Manhattan, just because I think the view is really cool. People always ask, 'Why don't you take the subway?' when I tell them that, but this is why."

"Yeah, this is really cool. Thank you for showing it to me." Josh took Paige's hand and wove their fingers together as they leaned against the tower so pedestrians could get around them. Paige squeezed his hand, but she focused on the view for a moment. Josh was right, this scale of the city seemed different from this view, more awe-inspiring, like a reminder that it wasn't just the dingy subway or their apartments or the shops and restaurants on the ground level.

"Shall we move on?" Paige asked.

"In a few minutes."

———————

Josh's calves and feet were starting to burn a little, but he didn't care.

After the Brooklyn Bridge, Paige had taken him on a mini walking tour of the historical parts of Brooklyn Heights, and Josh had enjoyed looking at all the old houses. She had been right; some little pockets of the neighborhood looked like they must have in the nineteenth century.

Paige explained as they walked south toward Whitman Street

that this was but one corner—an affluent, gentrified corner, to be sure—of Brooklyn. She rattled off the names of various Cat Café employees and which neighborhoods they lived in and what those neighborhoods were like.

"We're not going to the Cat Café, are we?" Josh asked.

"No. You've been there, you know what it's like. Also, Lauren still doesn't know about us."

"Right. I was gonna say."

Paige took an abrupt left turn, so Josh followed.

"Do you object to Lauren knowing?" he asked.

"Not...exactly. I'm worried about how she'll react."

"Why?"

Paige frowned. "My friends keep saying she's protective of you."

Josh paused and leaned against a brick facade. "Ah, all right. I bet Megan didn't help."

"Megan?"

"My ex." For some reason, he'd thought he could dive into a relationship with Paige without Megan coming up. "Our breakup was messy. The details aren't really important. I leaned on Lauren a lot when I was going through it. The short version is that I thought our relationship was more important than our careers, and she had a different set of priorities, so she took a job in Chicago knowing I had one in New York."

"I'm sorry."

Josh looked at Paige to try to gauge her reaction. He hated to bring this heaviness to their otherwise wonderful day. "It's... I'd rather not talk about it. I've been trying to move past it. But

Lauren knows how hard that was for me. And she's my big sister. So, yeah, she's a little overprotective." He rolled his eyes to show what he thought of *that*. "I am an adult capable of making my own decisions, and I've decided to spend time with you. Let's... leave it at that, for now."

"Yeah?"

"For now, we can live in the happy fantasy Brooklyn where sisters and exes are not allowed and continue our day. Okay?"

"Deal. So, this is Fulton Street," Paige explained, leading Josh around the corner. "This area is called the Fulton Mall because it's a big shopping district. I walk over here sometimes because there are a lot of outlet stores, so some good deals can be had."

"Not really a mall, though." So they were really going to blow past everything he'd just unloaded? Fine by Josh. He rolled his shoulders and tried to shake off memories of Megan. He didn't want her to intrude on this.

"There is a real mall close to Flatbush, if that makes you feel better."

Josh chuckled. "I never saw the point of malls in this city. In the suburbs if you want to buy a new jacket, you go to the mall, but here, it's easy enough to just go to the store you want."

"Real estate developers haven't figured that out yet. You know the Oculus in Lower Manhattan?"

"I've seen pictures."

"I had to go there last year to get my laptop repaired because it was the closest computer store. And even though, to me, it looks like a fish skeleton, it's this great work of modern sculpture, right? But actually, it's a big mall. So, when I brought my laptop to be repaired, I took a walk around the mall while they were fixing it, and I kept thinking, who would shop here? It's all high-end luxury stores. I mean, I love a cute handbag, but I don't want to spend four hundred dollars on one."

"It's also a transit hub, right? So most people probably breeze through it on their way to the subway or the commuter train."

"Exactly. It's so weird. I'm surprised they didn't put stores in that beehive thing they built in Hudson Yards."

"Are we going to become those New Yorkers who spend a lot of their downtime complaining about how the city is changing too much?"

Paige laughed. "No, sorry. I mean, I do find this part of Brooklyn really charming, and I think it's a shame that so many big chains have moved in because the little indie businesses are what give the neighborhood character, but I don't want to spend a lot of time complaining, especially with you."

Josh appreciated that. He smiled at her. He agreed; these times when they could talk and be in the same place were pretty valuable, given his work schedule. He wanted to keep things pleasant for now. He could envision a future in which, just like any other couple, they argued or faced challenges, but they weren't in that place right now. This was new and fun; he didn't need to make it complicated yet. No complaining, no exes, no complications.

His stomach rumbled. "After that feast we had for brunch, I can't believe I'm about to say this, but apparently all that walking built up an appetite."

Paige nodded. "I'm a little hungry, too. Where should we... Oh. Have you been to the DeKalb Market yet?"

"Isn't that the food court in the mall?"

"It is. The selection is pretty amazing, though. It's a good place for a quick meal. I go there for takeout sometimes."

It was a good thing Josh was hungry, because the number of choices overwhelmed him. There were tacos and burgers, but also sushi hand rolls, cheesy arepa sandwiches, a beer stand, and the thing that was making Josh's mouth water: an outpost of Katz's Deli serving up sandwiches as big as his head.

"It's dangerous that I know this is here," Josh said, "because I'm going to stop here on the way home from work every night now."

"Maybe we should split up and reconvene at the seating area at the foot of the escalator."

"Oh man. This is why I work out, I guess."

"Earth to Josh."

He laughed. "I heard you. Meet you back at the seating area by the escalator. I might be a while."

She shook her head but was smiling.

Ten minutes later, Josh walked over to the seating area with a pastrami sandwich and a beer. Paige was already seated, a bowl of ramen and a sushi roll spread out before her.

"So, do you feel like you've seen a sufficient amount of Brooklyn?" Paige asked.

"I'd say so. You're pretty good at this event organizing thing."

"That's what they tell me."

They ate silently for a moment, and Josh took the time to reflect on the day and his time with Paige. She really was remarkable. Smart, organized, but with an easy laugh and a sense of adventure. They'd gotten a little lost during the walking tour because Paige had taken a wrong turn, and even though Josh could tell the mistake had rattled her a little, she ultimately rolled with it, exploring a few blocks she'd never seen before with Josh. When she saw a familiar house, she'd gotten out her phone and confirmed that it had once belonged to Truman Capote.

He'd never once gotten bored. Even now, as the giant, delicious pastrami sandwich distracted him, he found everything Paige had to say interesting. They talked and joked, and he was enjoying himself immensely.

The food court was loud. Conversation from the crowded eating area bounced off the walls, mingling with the sounds of deep fryers and grills and squeaky wheels on carts from the adjacent grocery store.

But Josh hardly heard any of it. Paige was telling him a story about when she first moved to Brooklyn, and even though he only heard about every third word, he was riveted.

As they finished eating, she said, "I had fun today."

"Me, too, but you say that like it's over."

"Well, I didn't want to be presumptuous."

"Presume away, baby. My place is only a couple of blocks from here, just saying."

She smiled. "So, what you're saying is that we could have even *more* fun?"

"*Naked* fun."

"How fast can we get out of here?"

CHAPTER 14

A FEW DAYS LATER, JOSH was home when Paige texted to see if he was available. It was on the late side, and Josh had already eaten, so he wondered if this was a booty call. Not that he was opposed, but the level of effort it would take to change out of his gym clothes and walk to Paige's was more than his body felt equipped for. So he suggested she come to him. Why waste a night at home?

She arrived fifteen minutes later, which had only given Josh enough time to drink a big glass of water and pick up some of the general detritus from around his apartment. When he answered the door, he was still wearing his gym clothes. "Sorry," he said by way of greeting. "When you texted me, I had just gotten back from the gym."

Paige looked him over as she walked through the door. "You get in a good workout? You smell a little ripe."

"Yeah, I... Sorry. I had one of those work days that made me question every decision I've made in my adult life. Why did I take this job? Why did I think becoming a lawyer was a good idea?"

He sighed. "I don't want to talk about it, though. I did some lifting and then ran three angry miles on the treadmill."

"Is an angry mile longer or shorter than a regular mile?"

"Not sure. Shorter, I think. It seems to go faster. But I'm better now." He smiled to show that he really did feel all right. Provost had taken on a new client, some real estate tycoon, and had subsequently piled even more work on top of Josh. Running had long been his way of pushing everything from the day away, and he'd needed a good run tonight. He always put on some loud music, got the treadmill running at a challenging speed, and enjoyed the feel of his feet pounding on the surface. Usually by the second mile, most of the day had fallen off him, and by the third mile, his mind was mostly blank. "Sorry, though. I was going to change before you got here and ran out of time."

"I mean, why bother when you're just going to be naked very soon."

"So this *is* a booty call."

Paige shrugged. "Oh, I brought something for George." She reached into her bag and pulled out a bag of cat treats. "Caleb says these are basically cookies for cats. I thought George would like them."

"Shall we test that?"

George was lounging on the sofa. He stared at Paige as she walked over, probably wondering what this intruder was doing in his home. Paige opened the pouch of treats and shook out a couple onto the cushion beside were George sat. He must have smelled them, because he immediately jumped up and inhaled them.

"Well, you're going to be his best friend now," said Josh.

"Speaking of treats, did you eat?"

"Yeah. One of the partners is retiring, so there was a little party today. Well, someone hired a caterer to turn one of the conferences rooms into a buffet, and there was food there all afternoon. I may have made more than one trip. Did you eat?"

Paige took off the cardigan she'd been wearing and draped it over the arm of Josh's sofa. George immediately hopped up and smelled it, then leaned over to check out Paige. Paige pet his head; that and the treats seemed to persuade him that she was okay. "I did, a couple of hours ago. It's almost nine thirty."

Josh glanced at the clock on his microwave and saw she was right. "So did you come over to say hi to George or..."

Paige laughed. "Okay, honestly? I am so bad at this kind of thing. But I was just sitting at home watching TV and I missed you, so I figured I'd text and see if you were around. I'd been thinking we could chat on the phone, but when you said to come over, I was like, *Great! I'll spend the night with Josh!* And the whole way over here, I thought about how to best seduce you, or how to show you that I can be passionate and spontaneous. But honestly? I am not very spontaneous."

Josh laughed along with her. He appreciated that she'd been thinking about him and wanted to spend the night. He wanted her to spend the night, so that was enough. "It's all right. I smuggled a bottle of wine out of the retirement party. You want a glass?"

"Sure."

"Have a seat."

As Paige settled on the sofa, George sat beside her and rested his chin on her thigh, so Paige clearly met with George's approval.

George looked up at her with adoration in his eyes when she started to pet his back. Josh chuckled to himself and walked to the fridge, where he retrieved the bottle of wine. He didn't own proper wine glasses, but he had a couple of whisky tumblers, so he grabbed those and walked over to the sofa. The wine was a screw-top—"Only the classiest for office parties," Josh said—but it smelled crisp and fresh, which seemed like a good sign. After he poured, Paige held up her glass.

"A toast to…booty calls."

Josh laughed. "I'll drink to that." He clinked his glass against hers.

It was a pretty solid dry white wine. Josh took a couple of sips before he said, "I am really glad you walked all the way over here."

"I also have tomorrow off work."

"That's good news. Any hot plans?"

"No, not really. Sleeping. Catching up on my DVR."

Josh sighed wistfully. "That sounds nice. I miss lazy days off."

"I see you finished unpacking."

"I did. Mostly for George's sake. He loves you now, by the way."

George had fallen asleep with his head on Paige's thigh. He looked totally blissed out.

Paige laughed. "He's very sweet." She pet his head and his purring got louder.

"It's not all bad having a cat around the house."

"They do have a way of working their way into your heart."

Josh finished off his glass of wine and put it back on the coffee table. "Well, anyway…" He cupped his hand on Paige's cheek and kissed her.

Josh wasn't the most spontaneous person, either, but he knew when it was better to act than to talk. He licked into her mouth and felt her sigh against him. Her arms came around his shoulders and she pulled him close. Josh started to press forward, to try to get them more horizontal, but he was interrupted when George yelped and leapt off the sofa.

Paige burst into laughter, so Josh laughed along with her. "Whoops," said Josh. "Forgot he was there."

"I'm probably not his friend anymore," said Paige.

"Let's move this," said Josh, standing up. He held out a hand to Paige. She stood beside him and put her hands on his shoulder.

"You know," she said, "you are still a little sweaty, but it's sexy instead of gross."

"If that's the case, you're going to think I'm *really* sexy in a few minutes."

"Gonna get in another good workout, are you?"

Josh took her hands in his and then led her to the bedroom. "My old trainer used to stress the importance of cardio. Getting your heart rate up. So this is all to help us maintain our healthy lifestyle."

Paige giggled. "Sex for good health. I like it."

———————————

Paige writhed underneath Josh as he peeled off her clothing. He'd broken some kind of land-speed record getting out of his gym clothes, and now he was working on the buttons of Paige's shirt like he was worried about breaking one and Paige wanted him to hurry up. She reached between them and started at the bottom hem of her shirt, then lost patience, shooed Josh away, and pulled the shirt off over her head without finishing the rest of the buttons.

"Reasonable approach," Josh said, laughter in his voice.

He reached up and hooked a finger under her bra strap, then pulled her back down to lay next to him. She could feel him hard against her thigh. She wanted to get closer to him, to press their bare skin together. She reached behind her and undid her bra, which Josh pulled off and tossed over his shoulder. He put his arms around her and pulled her close, and it still wasn't quite enough. Arousal spread through her body and made her impatient.

She rolled their bodies so that she was straddling him. He held his hands up like he was surrendering, but he had a grin on his face. She stood up for a second, long enough to get her panties off, then she crawled back on the bed and straddled Josh's thighs.

"So," she said.

"You are the sexiest woman I have ever seen," said Josh.

Paige smiled, feeling powerful. Josh complimented her like that a lot, but something about the choked, breathless way he said it now made it sound primal. And maybe it was. Josh made her feel beautiful and sexy in a way few of her other partners ever had. He made her feel good, feel wanted, feel like she was someone he genuinely wanted to spend time with.

And it went both ways. Josh *was* sweaty and he still kind of smelled like the gym, but the scent was arousing instead of off-putting. He had strong arms and some muscle definition on his chest, and Paige loved when he put his arms around her, like he could take care of her, like he'd defend her if he needed to, like he had her back. He had beautiful eyes and disheveled hair, and the freckles on his face made him look a little boyish, but he was sexy and funny and they were good together. They were really good.

She reached for his nightstand drawer and pulled out a condom. As she rolled it on him, he said, "I could do that."

"It's more fun this way."

He raised an eyebrow. "Oh, really?"

Paige didn't answer. She loved touching him. His cock was hard and hot in her hand, his breath kept hitching as she touched him, and the look in his eyes was intense, aroused.

"You ready?" she asked.

"For you? Always."

She smiled and pressed a hand on his chest. Then she shifted so that she could slide him inside her.

She groaned, the feeling of him filling her satisfying. She sat on him for a moment, adjusting to him. He bucked his hips against her, likely trying to encourage her to move, but she liked that she could make him this impatient, too. She ran her hands down his chest and pinched his nipples, which made him hiss and bow his back.

Then she started to ride him.

Josh let out a strangled moan and put his hands on Paige's hips. At first he just rested his hands there, but then he started to apply pressure, likely trying to set the speed. But Paige loved the power she had now to drive him crazy, so she did what felt good for her and what made him grunt and moan.

Then she lowered herself to kiss him. He grasped her hard and thrust his tongue into her mouth, never breaking the connection between their bodies. He moved his legs so that he could better thrust into her, which felt amazing. Paige leaned up and met Josh's gaze and it seemed like everything he felt was right there at the surface.

It was too soon for love. That was Paige's first off-hand thought. But they sure liked each other in an intense way. Paige saw everything she felt reflected back at her in Josh's eyes.

Then she took control back.

She pushed back up and regulated the pace. Josh groaned. "You are going to kill me."

"Are you close?"

"Are you?"

"You could touch me more if you wanted."

"With pleasure."

Josh ran his hands all over Paige's skin, touching her shoulders, her breasts, her belly. He bucked against her, clearly trying to change her pace, so she accommodated him by riding him faster and harder. He groaned and his eyes rolled back.

"There it is," he said.

Thoughts fled out of Paige's head as she became honed on the places where their bodies connected. Her skin tingled and flushed, her face warmed, and the way Josh rubbed against her was just right. With a little more pressure, a little more, a little more...

Josh leaned up suddenly, grabbed Paige's face, and kissed her hard. The curve of his body gave her the friction she needed, and suddenly everything flew apart. Distantly, she heard Josh groan.

He threw his arms around her and held her close as they rode out their pleasure together.

As she floated back into her body and settled on Josh's chest, she thought, well, maybe she was awkward when it came to spontaneity, but they definitely had passion.

"So good," Josh panted.

Paige snuggled against him. "I'm really glad I came over."

"Me, too. But hold that thought."

Josh got out of bed and disappeared from the bedroom for a moment. There was something inefficient about the bathroom being on the other side of the apartment, but when Josh returned, still fully naked, Paige admired both that he had no apparent shame about his body and that he was still naked now.

He climbed back into bed and took her into his arms. "Okay, you were saying?"

She laughed. "Is this the part of the postcoital glow where we tell each other how awesome the other was?"

"If you like. I think you're awesome all the time, though."

Paige couldn't help but smile at that.

This *was* good, whatever was between them. Everything Paige had been looking for, in fact. They could talk, they could laugh, they could have amazing sex. And Josh liked and respected her, had never suggested she be anything other than what she was. She didn't want to change him, either. Well, she wanted him to work less, but she understood why he couldn't.

He stroked her hair now, and she closed her eyes, loving the sensation of that.

"So, ah, can I ask you something?" Josh said, a little sleepily.

"Anything."

"You're not seeing anyone else, are you?"

"No."

"So are we, like, a couple?"

Paige couldn't read his tone. "Is that what you want?"

"I mean, yeah. It is. It wasn't what I thought I would want at this point in my life, but I also didn't picture meeting someone as great as you are."

"I think you're great, too. I have such a good time when I'm with you. And not just in bed."

Josh kissed her temple. "I know about…well, everything else. And I'm not asking for a serious commitment. But maybe you could…not see other people some more."

Paige lifted herself up on her elbows so that she could look at Josh's face. He looked so earnest. She still wasn't at all confident that she could pull this off, and this still felt like an enormous risk given everything going on in their lives, but she also knew she hadn't felt this way about a guy…well, ever, really. She smiled. "I'm good with that."

He smiled back. "Cool. You know, I never did get that post-gym shower in. I still kinda want to do that before I fall asleep. You want to, her, give me a hand?"

She laughed. "Sure. I'll…give you a *hand*."

"Is that a sexy pun?"

"If you have to ask…"

He laughed and got out of bed. "You're the best. Come on."

CHAPTER 15

PAIGE DID NOT UNDERSTAND HOW something so small could make so much noise.

A six-year-old boy alternately laughed like a hyena and emitted high-pitched raptor squeals. He'd started encouraging the six other kids at Paige's Cats and Crafts event, and the volume in the cat room was deafening. Most of the cats had declined to participate and were instead hiding under the furniture.

Paige clapped her hands a few times to get everyone's attention. "Kids? Hi, kids! We're going to get started on the crafts in just a minute, but I need everyone to lower your voices. Hunter, you scare the cats when you make noises like that. If you guys want the cats to help with the crafts, you have to be a little quieter."

The boy looked chastened, but still talked through a lot of her presentation. She had set up supplies on the table for the kids to make cat masks with paper plates and tongue depressors. She'd gotten some cheap yarn from Stitches that the kids could glue to the masks to look like fur, and she had kid-friendly glue sticks, crayons, markers, and safety scissors she'd bought with the fundraising money.

Once the kids knew what to do, they calmed down and got to work. Even Hunter the Screamer mostly focused his attention on making his mask look like a lion. As the kids quieted down, the cats took tentative steps out from under the furniture. By the time the kids were almost done, a couple of cats were sitting on the table with them, sniffing at the kids' projects. Mr. Darcy got a hold of a ball of yarn and took off with it in his mouth, then rolled around on the floor with it, attacking it like it was his greatest enemy.

"And I thought cats playing with yarn was just something from cartoons," said one of the moms.

Evan showed up a half hour after the event began and looked startled as he walked into the room.

"Don't hate me," he whispered to Paige, "but I completely forgot this was happening."

"I don't suppose you want to make a cat mask."

"Are you kidding?"

Evan dove right in, sitting next to Hunter and drawing a beautiful cat face on a paper plate. Paige hadn't known Evan even liked kids, although she did know he'd never met a craft he didn't like. But Evan asked the kids questions and helped them draw and cut yarn. Considering he was working with crayons and yarn, the mask he made was surprisingly lifelike. Paige was grateful for the help, because the kids had started to overwhelm her.

Paige did not have a ton of experience working with children. A few of her friends and family members had kids, but she rarely saw them. Paige liked kids and had liked the idea of doing crafts with them in the abstract, but she had somehow not anticipated the kids would be this rowdy.

She had never thought much about having her own kids. She'd always assumed she'd have one or two, but in the same way she assumed she'd get married someday. It seemed like a logical part of her life plan.

She thought of Josh and how well their relationship was going, even though she hadn't seen him in a week. That was okay, though. Josh had been working, but so had Paige. Creating a schedule for today, managing sign-ups, and obtaining all the supplies had taken up most her time the last couple of days. But having Josh here would have been fun. It was likely that he didn't know any more about kids than Paige did, but she could imagine him throwing himself into this project with as much gusto as Evan had.

She smiled to herself. Yeah, Josh would have had fun here. Paige was surprised to find that she missed him a great deal. They hadn't spoken much in the last week, either, although Josh texted her whenever he had a little downtime.

She liked him. They had fun together. That sure seemed like a solid foundation for a relationship.

But she had to stop daydreaming, because one of the kids was waving a glue stick at a cat, who looked like she wanted to swat that glue stick out of the kid's hand.

A little girl in a purple gingham dress walked over to Paige with her mask over her face. She said, "Meow" a few times and then bent down to pet Sadie, who seemed very interested in these proceedings but not enough to get close to the table where the kids were working. But Sadie loved people and loved getting her head pet more, so she leaned into the girl's hand and started purring. Sadie had the loudest purr of any adult cat Paige had ever encountered, and this seemed to delight the little girl, who let out a little squeal of joy. Sadie tilted her head and shot her a questioning look.

Once the masks were done, the kids ran around the room meowing and growling at each other, which prompted the cats to dive under the furniture again, although an older tabby named Casey sat at the main table looking unfazed.

Still, the parents seemed happy, the kids were having a great time, and although their squeals and laughter made Paige think she'd go deaf if she did another one of these, the general feedback from people as they left was very positive.

"What do you think?" Lauren asked as the kids were packing up to go.

"I don't know if I'm cut out to run events for kids, but this worked out pretty well. Maybe we could get some guests to teach craft classes. One of the ladies from Stitches or art teachers or something like that."

Lauren laughed. "Not a bad idea. The kids had a good time, though. Three of the parents asked me when the next one is."

"Will there be a next one?"

"Yeah, I think so. The kids had fun, Paige. That's the most important thing."

Paige surveyed the cat room. Two cats were creeping out from under one of the sofas, as if to check if the coast was clear. The tables Paige had pushed together to make one big table were littered with marker caps and broken crayons and stray bits of yarn. "What a mess."

"I'll grab a trash bag," said Lauren.

———————

Josh's only day off this week was Sunday—thanks to Mr. Provost and his new client for making him come in to help him prepare briefs on a Saturday—but Paige was working at the Cat Café because it was the first day of her Cats and Crafts event.

The idea of going two weeks without seeing Paige seemed unbearable, so Josh reasoned he could casually drop by the Cat Café shortly after the crafts were over, maybe even on the pretense of seeing Lauren, who he knew was also working that day, and then he could get a dose of Paige before plunging into another crazy work week.

When he got to the Cat Café, he spotted Lauren near the counter. She looked happy but a little rattled.

"How's it going?" he asked.

"Hoo boy."

"That well?"

Lauren grinned. "It's crazy in the best way. Paige's craft event was a huge hit. We got a better turnout than expected and all the kids seemed to love it."

"That's awesome."

"The cats were a little afraid of the kids, but a few of them came out eventually. And we've got a lot of people who came to just check out what we've got going on here. Paige set up a newsletter and sent press releases to a bunch of local news websites, and now we've got bigger crowds than ever, which is awesome but overwhelming."

Josh didn't need Lauren to tell him Paige was good at her job, but he was still proud of Paige. They'd agreed they wouldn't tell Lauren about their relationship yet and Josh didn't want to give that away, so he said, "Who's a guy gotta bribe to get a cup of coffee around here?"

Lauren stepped to the side and gestured toward the register. "Be nice to Monique at the counter and she'll charge you $4.50 for a latte."

Josh glanced at the menu written out on a chalkboard above the counter and saw that lattes cost $4.50. "Wow, such a bargain."

"I aim to please."

He got in the short line at the register and considered asking Lauren where Paige was, but even that seemed like the sort of thing someone who was interested in Paige would ask and... How paranoid was he? He instead busied himself with staring at the menu. Lauren moved alongside him and said, "Paige and Evan are sitting in the back basking in their triumph. Evan helped out with the crafts. I thought he was just a digital artist, but it turns out he's pretty handy with crayons and a glue stick."

Well, that answered his question. He stepped up to the register and ordered that latte. As he waited for it to be made, Lauren got distracted answering a question from a customer. It was a little strange to see her in work mode. She looked so pleasant and serious.

When he had his latte in hand, Lauren stepped away from the customer and said, "Go join Paige and Evan in the back. I'll be there in a few minutes."

"Okay."

The cat room was pretty full. Paige and Evan were seated at a table in the corner, but there was an empty chair, so Josh headed for it. He sat without waiting for them to acknowledge him.

"Hi," said Paige, looking a little startled.

"Lauren told me to join you."

"You did just get the last chair," said Evan.

Josh put his cup on the table and looked around. There were no other free chairs in the whole cat room. Lauren hadn't been kidding about business being good. He turned back and glanced at Paige, who had schooled her face into something that looked placid and fake.

"Sorry to ambush you," said Josh. "I was a little bored at home, so I figured I'd walk over here and find out how the craft event went."

"Really well," said Paige. "I'm surprised you remembered."

Josh almost blurted out that she'd talked about it a lot the previous weekend, but he pressed his lips together instead.

"It's fine," said Evan.

"What is?" Josh asked.

Paige sighed and whispered, "Evan knows about us."

"Oh." Josh didn't know how to react to that.

"I had to tell someone. Sorry. I hope it's okay."

"It's...kind of a relief, actually," said Josh. He let out a breath. "But of course I remembered. You, in fact, told me you couldn't see me this weekend because of this event. So I thought I'd come to see you."

"Aw, thanks," she said with a smile.

"That's very cute," said Evan.

Josh couldn't tell if Evan was being sarcastic, so he said to Paige, "But it sounds like the event went very well."

"It did," said Paige.

"You've got yarn in your hair." Josh tentatively reached over and snagged a bit of brown yarn that had gotten twisted in one of Paige's curls.

"That seems about right," said Paige. "Cleanup ended up being kind of an ordeal."

"Hurricane Kid swept through here faster than we could stop it," said Evan. "The event was fun, but wow, kids can make a mess."

"And I don't even get much of a break." Paige sighed and rubbed her head. "We're starting the literacy program this week, too. A day care center up the street is bringing their first- and second-grade kids here after school Wednesday, and I've got a stack of books in the back that I was able to buy thanks to the fundraiser."

Evan frowned. "Pablo helped you pick those out, didn't he?"

Paige ducked her head sheepishly. "He did. But he's been working at the bookstore a long time, and he knows kids' books well. He gave me a bunch of recommendations."

"Who's Pablo?" asked Josh.

"He works at the bookstore a few doors down." Paige hooked her thumb to the east. "Evan's in love with him."

"I'm not *in love*. I just like him a lot." Evan turned to Josh. "I missed the window. Bided my time waiting for the right moment to ask him out, but now he's going out with someone else."

"That sucks."

Evan laughed. "It does, yeah."

One of the cats wandered over then and rubbed against Josh's leg. He reached down to pet the cat's head. The cat let out a little *brrup* and started purring.

"Don't get ideas, cat. I already brought one of you home. He's great, but I definitely don't need any more."

"That's Lizzy Bennett," said Paige.

"Cute. *Pride and Prejudice*, right?"

"Yup."

Josh looked at the cat. "Sorry, Lizzy. You and George aren't even from the same book."

Paige giggled. "Anyway, Evan had this whole elaborate courtship ritual plotted out. But since Pablo didn't know about it, he didn't follow the rules." She shot Evan a pointed look.

"On the other hand," said Evan, "I have another date with Darius next week. He got us reservations at Le Bernardin!"

"Fancy," said Paige.

"He better be buying, because that menu is a little bit out of my budget. Although, actually, I think he's throwing his money around to impress me and win me back."

"Are you impressed?" asked Paige.

"By the experiences, yes. By Darius? Remains to be seen."

"So, wait," said Josh. "You have a crush on Pablo, who is dating someone else. But you're dating a guy who seems to be going out of his way to impress you, and you feel meh about him."

"Ding, ding, ding," said Evan. "That's about the sum of it. I know I should get over Pablo. And Darius has been really great!

I'm just not sure if he's the One, you know? Or that I totally trust him."

"Fair enough." Josh wasn't sure that he even believed in the One. Megan hadn't been the One, that was for sure. He'd thought she was for a long time, but there was no way the woman he was supposed to be with would end things because she got a job that, rumor had it, she didn't even like. He'd loved Megan more than anything for two years of his life, and though he wasn't generally cynical, her leaving had made him rethink some of his ideas about romance and fate. Even setting that aside, he'd spent enough time around Lauren and Caleb since moving to Brooklyn to see that they were very much in love, but were they the One for each other? He doubted it.

He looked at Paige. She smiled back at him in a way that made his chest ache. Well, he wasn't sure if she was the One, but she was definitely someone he wanted to spend as much time with as possible.

A sound near the front of the café caught Josh's attention, and he looked to see what it was. He could see through the glass door that separated the cat room from the café that a dark-haired man walked in through the front door with a stack of what looked like picture books in his hands. Lauren greeted him with a smile on her face than gestured toward the back.

"I gotta go use the little boys' room," said Evan, standing up and quickly disappearing into the back.

Josh leaned over to Paige. "Is the guy with the books the infamous Pablo?"

Paige tapped her nose.

Lauren held the door to the cat room open for Pablo, who carried his books over to Paige. He smiled and said, "We got some donations! I put up a flyer in the bookstore, and a number of customers responded well and bought some more books for the program. So here you go."

"Wow!" said Paige. She stood to the side as Pablo put the books down on the table, and then she started looking at the covers. "This is amazing. Thank you so much, Pablo."

"My boss said I should come over here during the event Wednesday, so I'm at your service if you need any help."

"I can definitely put you to work. If today was anything to go by, the kids will need some wrangling."

"Cool. Is Evan here?"

Paige and Lauren exchanged a look. Paige said, "Uh, he had to step out for a moment."

"Oh, okay. Tell him I said hi. I gotta get back to work. See you Wednesday, Paige."

Evan stayed hidden until Pablo left, and Josh wondered a little about the dynamic of this group. Paige, Lauren, and Evan were the kinds of close friends who could clearly communicate with looks and gestures, almost telepathically. Evan snuck back out and made faces at Paige and Lauren, who giggled in response as if they understood what his expression meant. Josh felt a little like an interloper.

What would it be like to be Paige's boyfriend out in the open, someone who hung out with this group regularly and was in on the jokes? He liked the idea of it quite a bit. He looked at Paige, who shot him a quick smile before turning back to Lauren.

"I gotta get back up front," said Lauren. "There's actually a little bit of a line outside. If more of these people don't clear out soon, I'm going to make you guys leave."

"Hey, we're paying customers." Evan pointed to the paper cups on the table.

"That's the only reason I haven't kicked you out already."

Lauren walked back up to the front of the café and started talking to some of the customers milling around. Josh turned to Paige and said, "Well, this has been...interesting."

"Are you leaving?"

"Not if you don't want me to, but I don't want to get in the way if you're working. I just wanted to...well, the thought of not seeing you for another whole week was...unpleasant."

Paige laughed. "That was very carefully worded."

"*I* have to go," said Evan as he began to pack up his stuff. "I have to make an appearance at a dinner party this evening and need a little time to pretty myself up."

"Are you an Upper East Side aristocrat now?" asked Paige. "Make an appearance?"

Evan sighed. "One of my exes is newly married, and I skipped the wedding, because awkward, but now I feel a little guilty, so I'm going to this dinner party. My guess is it will mostly be the happy couple flaunting their new love and showing off their new china, but I promised I'd go. I'm giving myself permission to leave before dessert if it sucks, though."

"Your life is weird," said Josh.

"I seem to be in that awkward part of my life when all of my friends are getting married, but I am still mostly single, unless you count Darius, and that's not even a real thing yet." Evan slung his bag over his shoulder. "See you later, kids."

When Evan left, Paige sat back down, so Josh took Evan's seat to be closer to Paige. He looked over her shoulder and saw she was making up some kind of schedule. "You're sure I'm not in your way?"

She nudged him with her shoulder. "I like your company."

On their previous big date, as they'd walked around Brooklyn, Josh hadn't felt inhibited in any way about touching Paige or holding her hand. They'd been a couple then. Now, he felt like he had to be careful so that Lauren didn't see something that made her suspicious, and it made his fingers itch. He wanted to run his hand through her hair, put his arm around her, kiss her cheek. Instead, he wrapped both hands around his cooling coffee cup and contented himself to sit silently while Paige finished whatever she was working on.

"This week busy for you?" Paige asked.

"Yeah. My boss's very guilty client is going to court. My boss is going to argue before the jury that the plaintiff has some kind of personal vendetta, not that she was sold a shoddy product."

"That's some justice for you."

Josh shrugged. "I think any jury with a few brain cells and a pulse will heap some hefty financial penalty on this guy. My boss, meanwhile, just took on a new client who is equally sketchy and I have to rush to get up to speed on this new case." Josh didn't specify that the client was a shady real estate magnate who had been snatching up old buildings in Brooklyn and replacing them with shiny new high-rises. This guy was apparently not happy with the lack of aggressiveness of his previous law firm, and had hired Provost to—well, Josh wasn't entirely sure, but it sure looked like he wanted Provost to help him kick little old ladies out of their apartments. Not exactly something Paige would look highly upon.

"What's your role in all this?"

"My boss is letting me sit second chair at the trial, as a way to give me trial experience. So I gotta put on the good suit tomorrow to go to court."

"There's only one good suit?"

"Your question assumes I've had time to shop. It's hard to buy a suit online. You have to get it tailored, and I have short legs for my height, so…"

Paige laughed. "I'm just teasing. Although you don't have to work today, do you? You could go buy a suit now."

"But then I wouldn't be spending time with you."

When Josh hadn't been paying attention, he and Paige had gradually moved closer together, and now she was close enough that if he tilted his chin, they'd be kissing. His desire to kiss her was like a magnet pulling him forward, but he recognized where they were and who was around, so he sat back.

"You, uh, need anything?"

Paige grinned. "Could you get me a refill on my tea?" She handed Josh an empty cup. "Ask Monique for the jasmine green tea."

"Sure, okay."

Josh took the cup and walked up to the counter. As he handed the cup to Monique, Lauren walked over.

"So, hey, stupid question," said Lauren. "But is something going on with you and Paige?"

"Why do you ask?" But Josh knew they were busted. Lauren must have seen how closely they were sitting. His stomach flopped.

"Oh, no you don't," she said. "I don't believe you would do anything so stupid as to have something going on with one of my friends."

So here they were. Josh had been dreading this moment. Part of him had always known Lauren wouldn't really approve, no matter how hard he tried to rationalize it. He'd been hopeful that she'd get over that quickly, especially now that he'd really fallen for Paige. "So if, hypothetically, I went out with Paige, you would not approve?"

"First of all, when do you even have time to date? Don't you work all the time? And second of all, Paige is... And you are... No. I don't like it."

"Why? Hypothetically, of course."

"Well, for one thing, it puts me in an awkward position."

"So, this is about you?"

"Are we having an argument?"

Josh grunted and pulled out his wallet. He handed Monique a five and told her to keep the change. Then he picked up Paige's refilled tea. "I don't want to have an argument. But I do like Paige. If you have a problem with that, I think I have the right to know why. It's kind of bullshit if your only reason is that it makes you feel awkward."

Lauren rolled her eyes. "Why do the people I love insist on making drama during business hours." She pointed at him. "I'm not going to argue with you here, but this is not over."

"Fine. I'm going to bring Paige her tea."

Josh headed back to the cat room. Paige looked up with a smile as he sat back down beside her.

"I don't know how to tell you this," said Josh, "but the jig is up."

"What do you mean?"

"Lauren is onto us."

Paige clasped a hand over her mouth. "Oh, shit."

"She's not happy about it either."

"What does that mean?"

"She didn't want to argue with me here. I was all set to defend us, but she's busy and said she'll fight with me later."

"Oh, no."

Paige looked terrified. Josh wanted to find some way to make this better, but he had no idea how right now. "I'm sorry if I've made this bad. I didn't say anything. Lauren figured it out. But I guess now that the cat is out of the bag, we don't have to sneak around."

"This is so bad," Paige said, pressing a hand to his forehead.

"I'm sorry. I should probably go."

"I'm tempted to sneak out of here with you, so I don't have to talk to Lauren. I can't deal with this right now."

"You're welcome to do that, too. But, like, I don't think this is that big a deal. She'll come around when this news sinks in for her."

Paige shook her head. "You sure about that?"

"I've known Lauren for all of my twenty-eight years. I think I know her pretty well. Besides, it's not like we need her permission."

Paige frowned deeply, which made Josh remember that Paige

was worried this relationship could harm her friendship with Lauren and her employment status at the café.

"Sorry," he said softly. "I just really like you. We'll have a rational conversation with Lauren once things settle. Deal?"

"Yeah, I...I guess."

"Come on, let's get out of here."

CHAPTER 16

IT TURNED OUT THAT IT was easy to avoid a pending fight with one's sister if one had a demanding job.

He hadn't wanted to hear anything about it, if he was honest. First of all, Lauren didn't know the whole truth yet, and he was loath to tell her that, not only was he interested in Paige, but they'd been secretly dating for almost a month. Still, he couldn't believe Lauren would be so selfish as to try to keep him and Paige apart. And so what if she didn't approve? She was not *his* boss.

Although she was Paige's, and that had the potential to be awkward.

So maybe Josh was being selfish now.

He and Paige spent Sunday night together at Josh's place, and Josh's alarm woke him up Monday morning just as the sun was rising. Paige grunted, rolled over, and fell back to sleep.

She'd been in a full-on panic as they'd walked to his place from the café. One would have thought she'd been caught stealing money from the cash register. Josh had tried to talk her down, explaining that they hadn't done anything wrong, and besides,

Lauren only thought she knew something. Josh hadn't actually confessed that he and Paige had been dating, although he supposed the fact that they'd left together probably convinced her they were.

They liked each other. What Lauren thought was immaterial.

He understood that was not true. He knew this made Paige worry about her job and her friendship with Lauren. He still thought her freak-out was disproportional to the situation, but he hadn't said anything, just listened to her talk through her panic.

Still, they'd gotten to his place last night and Josh had done everything he could to distract Paige. They'd talked some, and Paige had said she wanted to be with Josh and would have no hesitation about it if not for Lauren. Maybe it was the wrong thing to do, but Josh had pounced on that idea and went about romancing her. He got dinner delivered from the same restaurant where they'd had their brunch date a week ago, and they fed each other delicious food and talked about nothing stressful and watched a stupid movie on TV. George had been charming and cute, rolling around on the sofa and trying to convince Paige to pet him, which she did. Then Josh had seduced Paige and distracted her with sex. He hoped she wasn't panicking anymore.

Somewhere in there, he'd had an unwelcome thought about what this could all mean. The last time he'd put this much energy into convincing someone to be with him had been with Megan, and look how that had turned out. It was the first time since he'd started pursuing Paige that he'd been struck by real doubt. He thought Paige was amazing, but he'd thought Megan was amazing, too, and she'd still bailed on him nearly the instant they were faced with a challenge to their relationship. He and Paige were having fun together, but her freak-out had shown him that she was likely to do the same.

Megan and Paige were very different women, but it was hard not to remember that sinking feeling from watching Megan wheel her last suitcase out their apartment door. It had been like something in his body had soured, had spoiled to the point that it was no longer good or useful, and his life had changed irrevocably because his vision of the future would never come to pass. It had physically hurt him, Megan's leaving. He'd never wanted to feel that again.

He didn't want the ghost of girlfriends past to haunt his future relationships, and he'd worked hard to put all that behind him, but Paige was making him feel an inkling of that again.

On the other hand, he and Paige were just having fun, right? They weren't planning a future. A tiny voice in the back of his mind objected to this, but he pushed it aside.

He got out of bed and hopped in the shower, seething about Lauren. He couldn't see any viable reason for Lauren to disapprove.

He didn't have enough food in his apartment to make Paige a fancy breakfast, but they ate cereal together before leaving the building. Paige had the day off, and Josh started to offer to let her stay, but she insisted she needed to get home. She didn't seem panicked, but Josh couldn't help but worry that her wanting to go home was maybe her way of saying she wouldn't be coming back. He did not want to let that happen.

Maybe he was kidding himself. Maybe he worked too much. Maybe Lauren had spooked Paige. Maybe this was a fun thing for now that ultimately had no future.

He sat all day with the idea that this could end.

It weighed on him all through the morning court appearance. He went back to the office afterward feeling completely out of sorts, so of course Provost pulled him into a meeting with the new client, a Mr. Randolph, who was trying to turf out the last holdout in a crumbling brick apartment building in Fort Greene, a feisty old woman who had been living in that apartment since 1973.

"And you want to do what with this apartment?" Josh asked, realizing after he spoke how rude he sounded. "Apologies. I was just curious."

Randolph smiled. "Modern apartments. I've already got an architect at work. Here's the preliminary mock-up."

Josh looked at an image of a frankly hideous apartment building. It was brutalist in style with a dark gray concrete exterior and stark white horizontal slashes that Josh assumed were balconies. He schooled his face not to react to it.

"And," said Randolph, "I finally found investors for the restaurant I want to open on Whitman Street. That's near Downtown Brooklyn."

"Yeah, I know it," said Josh.

"I bought a building there almost two years ago. There's this gorgeous space on the first floor that used to be a coffee shop that I want to convert into a sit-down restaurant, and I'm close to a deal on that with a celebrity-turned-restauranteur." Randolph grinned. "I *tried* to buy the building across the street, but this aging hippie owns it and wouldn't sell, not even after we tried to get the health department to shut down the Cat Café on the first floor."

It hit Josh suddenly that he was sitting across a conference table from the very real estate developer Lauren had complained about, the one who wanted to buy Diane's building.

As if Josh needed another reason to quit this job.

He schooled his face again and got through the rest of the meeting, but he felt deeply ambivalent about everything by the time he left the office.

He got home after eight that night, fed George, and collapsed on the sofa before picking up his phone and calling his mother.

"Joshua! We haven't heard from you in so long! How is your job?"

"It's good, Mom. Well, I'm working insane hours. There's a lot going on right now. I actually only just got home."

"That's terrible. Did you eat?"

"I got food delivered at the office. And the firm has a car service on call, so I got a ride home. I'm fine, just tired. Actually, I was in court today. I'm helping my boss with a trial, so that was great. But then I had to go back to the office afterward, so I worked a pretty long day."

The morning's court appearance had been a preliminary hearing to resolve a couple of issues; the trial proper would start the next day. But Josh had still been excited to be in the court-room, and it was a reminder, sort of, of why he'd gone to law school. Too bad his boss's clients were all such terrible people.

"That's exciting. I'm glad you're getting court experience. Those must be a lot of hours you're working. Your sister said she's hardly seen you since you moved to Brooklyn."

"That's true. I did see her yesterday, though."

"Oh?"

"I went by the Cat Café, just to say hi. The place was mobbed."

As if he'd heard the word "cat" and interpreted it as a summons, George hopped up on the sofa and put his front paws on Josh's thighs. Josh pet him and he started to purr and knead Josh's leg.

His mother chuckled. "I'm glad that place is so successful. I did wonder when she told me she'd taken that job."

"Mom, let me ask you a question. Do you think it's totally inappropriate for me to date one of Lauren's friends?"

"What?"

"See, Lauren has this friend Paige, and I really like her. I think you would, too. She's friendly and sweet and very successful at her job."

"Oh, sure, I met Paige at the wedding. She was one of Lauren's bridesmaids."

"Right, of course. Well, see, I met Paige here in New York and we hit it off and I really like her. But Lauren doesn't approve of us dating."

"Why should that matter?"

Josh laughed. "I mean, exactly."

"Did you and Lauren fight about it?"

"Not yet. She's mad about it, though. She said she wants to have a talk with me. But you know how Lauren is. I'm reading that as she wants to sit me down so she can yell at me for a while."

"I suppose I can see why that would make Lauren feel strange. But she's got her own life now, honey. I don't see why she would need to worry about yours. On the other hand, I want to know more about this Paige. You like her, you said?"

Josh sang Paige's praises for the next few minutes, and he recognized that he was manipulating his mother a little to make her see his side of things.

Still, shouldn't this have made Lauren happy? She liked both Paige and Josh. Surely she could see how good they were for each other. Josh was certainly better than the losers Paige had been dating before.

"Lauren will come around," said his mother.

"Are you sure? What if she doesn't?"

"Well, deal with that when you have to. Lauren can be stubborn, I know, but really, I don't see why it should matter. If this girl is as great as you say, and if you and Paige are happy, then Lauren will see that and get on board soon enough."

"Thanks, Mom. I'd been hoping that was the case. Lauren doesn't know this yet, but Paige and I have been dating for a month, and it's going really well."

"Well, I'm happy to hear that, then. I was worried that when things ended with Megan, you wouldn't want to date for a while."

"I didn't." Ugh. Leave it to Mom to bring up the thing he'd been trying to forget. "I mean, I was hurt after Megan left. I had planned to focus on work when I got to New York. But, you know. Things happen." What he thought, but did not say to his mother, was that he didn't want to live his life like a monk. He'd intended this thing with Paige to be sexy and fun, but if he was talking to his mother about it, their relationship was more than that, wasn't it?

His mother clucked her tongue in an affectionate way. "I miss you kids all the way over there in New York City. As soon as you get some time off, you'll come visit us, won't you?"

"Of course."

"The two of you may be adults, but you'll always be my babies."

"Yeah, yeah."

"Don't sass me. I love you, Josh. Call more often."

"I will. Love you, too."

Once he got off the phone, he lay down on his sofa, with George settling on his chest. Josh was pretty glad now he'd gotten this cat, because at least he wasn't totally alone with his thoughts. But he couldn't help thinking about Paige, because he always thought about Paige when he was idle. In a way, Lauren's finding out was like popping a bubble. He and Paige had been in a little private space where they could enjoy each other's company without anyone else getting in the way, but that was over now. More than that, though, it was like a fantasy world of flirty banter and getting to know each other and amazing sex, but now they'd have to face the real world. Hopefully, they would do that together.

———————

Paige took a deep breath before walking into Pop. She'd felt bad about ducking out of the café with Josh yesterday, so she'd walked to the café that morning to apologize, but it was Lauren's day off, too. When Evan sent a group text inviting them to Pop that evening and Lauren said she'd be there, Paige had held out some hope that Lauren would be willing to talk to her.

Lindsay and Lauren were sitting at their usual table near the front, so Paige joined them. Lindsay greeted her enthusiastically. Paige was about to broach the subject of Josh when Evan breezed in and sat at the table.

"Guys," he said, "did you see the sign on that empty store-front near Henry Street?"

"No," said Lindsay, "but I'm sure you'll tell us all about it."

"I walk by that store on the way here all the time, and I keep assuming it'll be a bank or a cell phone store, because we need more of those in this neighborhood." Evan rolled his eyes. "But now there's a sign out front saying it's going to be Whitman Street's own vegan bakery. It's owned by the same restauranteur that owns that place in the Village we used to eat at all the time in college."

"Vegan bakery?" said Paige, playing along. "So, like, baked goods without milk and eggs and butter and everything that makes desserts delicious."

"Hey, don't mock it," said Lindsay. "That place in the Village makes the best lemon bars in the city. They serve them with a little dollop of heaven on top. I don't know what they make their vegan whipped cream out of, and I don't really want to know, but it's like eating a cloud of magic."

Evan laughed. "I understand why you're a food writer now."

"It's cool that it's a bakery and not a bank," said Lauren. She glanced at Paige.

Paige frowned. Lauren was still mad.

Evan signaled to the waitress and said, "When our drinks get here, we should probably acknowledge the elephant at this table."

"What elephant?" asked Lindsay.

"Do we have to?" asked Paige, reluctant to talk about it now. She'd been grateful Josh had tried so hard to distract her Sunday night, and she totally knew that was what he was doing. She suspected that had been their last relatively low-stress night together. The honeymoon was over. Their relationship might be, too. Paige couldn't help but feel sad about that.

They all ordered martinis, then Evan said, "This is going to be a ball of tension until we talk about Paige and Josh."

"Way to cut to the chase," said Paige, although her stomach churned. She didn't want to have this conversation at all, but she supposed it was better to get it over with.

"Do you not think we should talk about how you and Lauren's brother are in a secret, lurid tryst?"

"Geez, Evan," said Paige. "It's not like that at all."

"Then what's it like?" asked Lauren.

Paige's heart pounded and blood rushed in her ears. Lauren's face was flat and unreadable, so Paige couldn't guess how she would receive this. She said, "All right. Fine. Josh and I have been dating for the last month. We met at Mitch's cat rescue event and have seen each other a few times since then. It's not very serious yet, because he works all the time."

"But you like him," Evan prodded.

Paige wanted to punch him. "Stop helping, Ev. But yes, I like him."

Lauren stared at the middle of the table for a long moment before she said, "Why didn't you say anything?"

"We wanted to wait until we knew it was something real before we told you. If we went on, like, two dates, but then things didn't really go anywhere, we could go our separate ways and not make you freak out the way you're freaking out now. But since we're still seeing each other, we were warming up to telling you soon. I promise."

"Okay."

"How angry are you? Really?" asked Paige.

"I'm not angry," said Lauren. "I'm...surprised. Shocked. Still wrapping my head around it."

"Thrown for a loop," said Lindsay.

"Bowled over," said Evan.

"Flabbergasted," said Lindsay.

"Leave it to the writer to pull out the ten-dollar words," said Evan. "Er...dumbfounded."

"Thunderstruck!" said Lindsay.

"That's quite enough," said Lauren. "I'm just saying, the news was definitely not something I ever expected. You're...dating."

"Yeah. I mean, we've gone on a few dates."

"Have you slept together? No, don't answer that."

Paige bit her lip.

"Ugh, gross," said Lauren.

"I'll end it if you want me to," said Paige. Although, she hated how that sounded as soon as she said it. She felt disloyal to Josh, and it wasn't what she wanted. She wanted to keep seeing Josh. She wanted to be with him, could see a future with him. But she loved her friends, and she couldn't lose this group of people. So she said, "Josh and I have barely started seeing each other. Your friendship means a lot to me. If this makes you uncomfortable—"

"No, it's...it's okay. It's weird, but okay."

"Are you sure?" said Paige. "Because I really don't want to do anything to upset you. I didn't know he was your brother when I met him at Mitch's event. And then we hit it off, and by the time we figured it out, we'd both grown to really like each other. And I'm so sorry, but I—"

"Give me some time, okay?" said Lauren. "I mean, Josh said he was interested in you, but I didn't know you were actually dating. I need some time with this."

"Okay," said Paige. "But I swear, I never meant—"

"It's okay. I mean, don't get me wrong, it's *weird*. But it's okay."

Paige tried to take that to heart. Maybe with time, Lauren would get used to the idea and everything would work out. Because the difficult part of this situation was that Paige could feel herself falling in love with Josh. She'd never been in love before, but she figured the way she felt about Josh, the warmth in her chest she felt when she saw him, the way she thought about him at random times of the day, the sweet way he'd tried to distract her from this uncomfortable situation the night before... Well, Josh was amazing and Paige would be a fool to walk away from that. But if Lauren didn't come around, what would she do?

"Is this going to be like that episode of *Friends* when Joey dates Phoebe's twin?" asked Evan. "At first you're all like, 'Why not?' But then it gets ooky."

"Time will tell," said Lauren, which wasn't encouraging.

But Paige supposed that was that. They all drank silently for a few minutes. It seemed like permission, but Paige was still worried about how this might damage her relationship with Lauren, if this would drive a wedge through her whole friend group. She liked Josh, but she wasn't in love with him, at least not yet. But Lauren was like a sister. These people at this table, they'd become her family. Having to choose between them sucked, but she knew she'd choose Lauren.

"Well, now that that's out of the way, can we talk about me now?" Evan asked.

Lauren laughed, which made Paige feel a little better.

"Sure, Ev," said Lauren.

"Okay, so, Darius was also at the dinner party I went to last night, so I took him home. And instead of sexing him up like I should have, I asked him why he dumped me the last time, since he never really gave me a reason, and I decided that if I'm going to keep seeing him, I need to know. And do you know what he told me?"

Well, this would probably be dramatic. Hoping it would deflect attention from the tension she still felt between herself and Lauren, Paige said, "Is he still the worst?"

"The very worst. So here's what happened." Evan mimed rolling up his sleeves. "You may recall that the last time I went out with Darius was around the time I quit my job to go freelance. There was one night when he and I were out at dinner before I quit my job but after I'd made the decision to leave the company. And I was telling Darius all about my plans. And he was like, 'Gee, it seems like a bad idea, the freelance market is unreliable income, wouldn't it make more sense to stick with what you know and the reliable paycheck?' And blah blah blah."

"I remember that," said Lauren.

"Right. And I explained to Darius like I was talking to my parents that I already had some jobs lined up and I had a good savings cushion and I was being very responsible and so on. And

Darius let it drop, but he dumped me a few days later. I had always kind of assumed he met someone else, but no. He dumped me the day after I quit my job because he's such a flipping control freak he was bothered by the fact that I didn't listen to his career advice."

"Are you kidding?" said Lindsay.

"Nope. And I think his pride was tied up in it, too. Like, he couldn't date a *creative person*."

"That must have narrowed his dating pool quite a bit," said Lauren.

Evan smiled. "I know. At least when I had a job at a big ad agency, I was part of the corporate world. I wasn't an *artist*, perish the thought. He wanted to be with someone who had career stability and some boring, traditional job. Not that there's anything wrong with traditional jobs, and I like stability, too, but he had no faith in me. I'm very good at what I do and always have a decent stable of clients. But Darius never had faith that I could pull it off."

"So he dumped you rather than supported you, in other words," said Paige.

"It's making me rethink some things now. Do I really want to be with someone like that? Even if he's gotten over that train of thought, he may only be interested in me now because I have a successful business. He's so petty and untrusting that he needed me to do exactly what he wanted me to do or he couldn't be with me."

"That's stupid," said Lindsay.

"I *know*," said Evan.

"You've had reservations about this guy all along," said Lauren. "At least you know the whole truth now."

"Did you dump him?" asked Lindsay.

"I did," said Evan. "Nice try, Darius, but I can't be with someone that manipulative. I mean, he started lecturing me on accounting software and then tried to refer me to some friend of his who handles insurance, and I was like, nope. Not doing this. So that's the end of that."

Paige sat back in her chair and contemplated her own situation. She'd dated a Darius or two over the years. They couldn't believe she would quit a well-paying corporate job to work at a cat café. One of the things she really liked about Josh is that he respected her career choices. She couldn't picture him ever telling her what to do or getting mad if he didn't follow her advice.

And yet she still had misgivings and doubts. Sitting here listening to Evan was a sobering reminder that not every relationship was meant to be. Should she listen to her heart, which told her to go for it with Josh, or her head, which told her there were a lot of ways it could go wrong?

Lauren was one of her best friends. And she still kept shooting Paige disapproving looks. Josh had said last night that Lauren had protested primarily because their relationship put Lauren in an awkward position. And Paige didn't think the tension at the table now was just in her imagination.

So where did that leave things?

"Earth to Paige," said Evan.

"Sorry, my mind wandered off. What?"

"You want some appetizers or no?"

"Sure, I'll eat whatever you guys order."

Evan nodded and said something to the waitress, whom Paige hadn't even seen standing there. Paige sighed.

"Only a few dates," said Lauren. "You and Josh, I mean. I can't believe I didn't know about it."

"I'm serious. If you say the word, it's over."

"And I said it's fine. Weird, but... I'll adjust, I guess. If you think it's really going somewhere."

"You don't like it."

Lauren shrugged. "It's not that, exactly. I'm trying to picture it."

Paige wasn't eager to mount a defense of her relationship with Josh. "We have fun. I don't know what you want me to say. You must agree he's a good guy."

"I do, but he's never dated one of my friends before."

"Right."

"Josh is great, and I love him, obviously. But he *just* got out of a relationship that really messed him up, and on top of that, his firm works him pretty hard. I've hardly seen him at all since he moved here, and aside from you apparently, I'm the only person he knows in the city who doesn't also work for DCL. I guess I'm worried. For both of you."

"So you don't want me to date him?"

Lauren frowned. "I need some time to get used to the idea."

Caleb walked into the bar then, which at least distracted Lauren for a few minutes. Lindsay changed the subject to the restaurant she'd reviewed a few nights before, but Paige felt her heart sink.

CHAPTER 17

IT HAD BEEN A FEW days since Lauren had found out about Paige and Josh. It didn't feel like anything had changed much. Lauren had been cold and aloof at work. Paige had asked her if things were okay between them a few times, and Lauren always said they were, but it didn't feel that way.

Josh was Lauren's family. He was forever. If this tension couldn't be resolved in some way, then Paige would be the one pushed out. She could already feel her friendship with Lauren unraveling, which was frustrating because she couldn't work out why. Lauren didn't like that Paige and Josh were dating, but they weren't doing anything to hurt Lauren. But Lauren was treating it that way.

Lauren wasn't even there on Wednesday afternoon when Paige and Pablo ran the literacy program. They had a very enthusiastic group of six- and seven-year-olds who were very cute and surprisingly patient.

"I'll tell you a secret," said the teacher, a woman named Annette. They were helping kids pick books. "A lot of my students have working parents and have been in day care since they were two. They've had routines drilled into them since they were toddlers. They know what to do. I mean, every now and then you get an excitable kid or one whose parents did preschool at home. Take Owen, for example." Annette gestured at a dark-haired boy who was chasing one of the cats across the room. "But these are well-behaved kids, for the most part."

Paige found that a little cynical, but she nodded to make the teacher go away.

Between donations and the books Paige had bought with fundraising money, they had enough books on-hand for each kid to take three with some left over, so the kids had plenty to do. In most cases, once each kid picked a comfortable spot, at least one of the cats came over to sniff him or her and see what the kid was about. A few kids got two cats to sit near them, or sat together and had a rapt audience of cats.

A little boy had snuggled up to Mr. Darcy and read *The Cat in the Hat* to him, and it was so cute that Paige worried her heart might burst.

By the end of the hour, some of the kids were ready to beg their moms to get them a cat. Paige told them they could come back to the café to visit the cats at any time. Annette and the other teacher who had come were impressed that the kids had been so excited to read to the cats. The articles Paige had read were right; the kids seemed less inhibited when they didn't think adults were listening.

As the kids filed out, Pablo agreed that it was a great success and they should do it again.

Sometimes it hit her how odd it was that she'd gone from arranging annual meetings for a big corporate bank to, well, this. She had no regrets, though. She loved this work and coming to the café was fun. She felt good about helping the cats. Paige had done so much outreach to shelters, volunteer organizations, and pet websites in Brooklyn, the Cat Café felt like a community space, and Paige was an integral part of that community.

Which was why she couldn't lose this. It was *hers*.

So Paige felt good about that. *This* she could do. Romance, though?

She'd tried in vain to catch Josh on the phone all week, hoping for some kind of reassurance, and kept getting his voicemail message. He'd texted to apologize, but he was busy with his boss and the court case, which was apparently going as poorly as predicted. She wasn't sure why that thought had popped into her head as she and Pablo picked up the books from where the kids had left them.

As they were adding the last of the wayward books to the stack on one of the tables, Diane appeared in the cat room. "Well, this must have been a success."

"It went very well, Diane," said Paige. "We had seven kids here, they each read at least two books, and even the most, uh, undisciplined kid sat and read a book aloud. The teachers were thrilled."

"We should do this again," said Pablo. "Maybe invite different schools or after school programs."

"Weekday afternoons are usually our quietest time," said Paige. "I think it could work. I'll draw up a schedule and we can create a sign-up form for groups on our website."

Diane laughed and said, "That is delightful. I am so glad this worked out."

Pablo looked at his watch. "I gotta get back to the store. Thanks for letting me help out, Paige. This was fun. I'll let my boss know it went well. If you need anything, let me know."

"Sure. I'll let you know about scheduling the next one, too."

Pablo nodded and left.

"He's cute," said Diane.

"That's the infamous Pablo that Evan is in love with. He works at Stories and has a boyfriend."

Diane frowned. "Oh, pooh. Well, let's get tea and you can tell me more about this event."

After Paige gave Diane a recap over cups of Diane's favorite rooibos tea, Diane asked, "Anything else going on?"

Paige was normally reluctant to disclose details about her personal life to Diane, who was a busybody of the first order and would likely give inappropriate and unworkable advice, as was her wont. But Paige remembered suddenly that Diane was a retired lawyer. "Actually, I have a weird question for you."

"Shoot."

"You used to work at a big corporate law firm, didn't you?"

"I did. Why? Are you thinking about a career change?"

"No, no, nothing like that. I'm dating a lawyer. He's a first-year associate at a big firm in midtown."

"I assume you're using the word *dating* loosely. If he's a first-year associate, you must never see him."

Paige laughed. "Yeah, that's true. I saw him on Sunday, but we haven't been able to connect since." He had, in fact, canceled on their tentative plans, something he'd had to do more than once since they'd started seeing each other, and Paige wasn't a fan, but she tried to be sympathetic. "And I guess maybe I was wondering if it would be worth it to wait out this first year or if it would get easier or what."

Diane nodded. "It does ease off a little, but we worked our associates pretty hard at the firm where I worked. I mean, even back in my associate days, I was only able to see Winnie because she was a paralegal at the same firm. We tried to meet for lunch in the company cafeteria every day, and even then, I still had to miss it quite a bit." Winnie was Diane's late wife.

"I don't think he likes the kind of law he's doing. His boss is representing a shady businessman in a civil suit, and Josh, the lawyer I'm seeing, thinks the client is guilty, which I think is making him have second thoughts about taking this job."

"Well, that's something." Diane smiled. "Although I guess it's all relative. When I was still practicing law, I had a colleague who'd had enough of seventy-hour weeks and quit to take the lead council job at a start-up company so that she could, in her words, get her life back. And then the startup's IPO ended up being a major disaster, and the job ate up all her time again. It's sort of the curse of ambitious people. We want success, we want to work hard, but then what does that do to our personal lives?"

Paige sighed. She was conscious it was Diane she was talking to, and still she confided, "I really like this guy. More than anyone I've liked in a really long time. But the universe keeps throwing all these obstacles in our way. And I guess I'm wondering if it's worth it to try to overcome those obstacles or if this is more trouble than I want to take on." And that was really the crux of Paige's problem now. She liked Josh, but did she like him enough to sacrifice her job and an important friendship, and did she like him enough to accept the scraps he could give her while he was getting established as a lawyer?

"Only you can answer that," said Diane. "In my experience, love is always worth it, but if you don't know if that's what's waiting for you on the other side, it can be hard to know."

"How could anyone know that?"

"Well, exactly. That's why love is always a risk. Love is putting yourself out there, making yourself vulnerable, and maybe you get hurt along the way, but maybe what you get is beyond your wildest dreams." Diane smiled wistfully. "I can't speak for Winnie or what was in her head all those years ago, but I like to think she waited me out because she knew we'd be great together."

Paige nodded, but that didn't get her any closer to a decision. "I don't think I feel that way now. I mean, we've only been on a few dates. I can see where we have some potential, but I don't know if it's, like, forever, you know?"

"Maybe that's your answer."

That seemed cryptic to Paige and didn't get her any closer to a decision.

"Well," said Diane, "I'm having dinner in the city tonight, so I should get ready for that. It was wonderful speaking with you, and I am thrilled the event went well. I hope I was able to give you some useful advice, too." She winked.

"Yeah," said Paige, feeling more confused than ever. "Thanks, Diane."

Josh's case wasn't being heard in the famous courthouse with the columns and the stairs, scene of many a tight-lipped argument or shoot-out on *Law & Order*, but rather at a different and far more nondescript courthouse up Centre Street. Josh couldn't even get a good look at the architecture because the whole facade was covered in scaffolding while the building was being cleaned. He didn't want to say he was disappointed—he was still getting to sit second chair on a trial—but everything from the building facade to the organized chaos at the security checkpoint to the inside of the courtroom which, frankly, looked more like a hospital room with benches than a courtroom, were not what he expected. And, really, how did people not get headaches sitting all day in a room with such bright lighting?

Mr. Provost didn't do much more than let Josh observe, but Josh sat in a very uncomfortable wooden chair and jotted down notes as the plaintiff presented her case. The case itself was convincing and the jury looked bored. Josh had never been on a jury—the one time he'd been called for jury duty, he'd explained that he was in law school, and the attorneys had fallen over themselves to dismiss him—but he imagined sitting there listening with no phone or other distractions must have been dull as hell. The only time the jury perked up was when a court officer wheeled in a TV and they were shown the original commercial and a demonstration of a rubber mallet destroying a window from the defendant's store.

Josh was allowed to keep his phone, and it buzzed eight or ten times in his pocket during the morning session. He was afraid to look at it, worried the judge would say something if the proceedings were not commanding his full attention. Provost focused on the testimony and asked some excellent questions on cross-examination, setting up his counter-theory of the case that the plaintiff was motivated to sue out of some nefarious agenda against the defendant and not because her window had shattered.

Around one, they recessed for lunch, at which point Josh thought it was safe to check his phone. As he pulled it out of his pocket, Mr. Provost said, "Good job today, kid. Let me take you to lunch."

"Sure," said Josh, although he wasn't sure what job he'd performed aside from sitting there quietly.

Most of his messages were work related, but there was a text from Paige in there asking if he had time to talk. As he followed Mr. Provost to the restaurant, he texted back that he did not have time because he'd be in court all day, and he hoped that was okay.

"Responding to stuff from the office?" asked Provost as they walked to the restaurant.

"Oh, no, sorry, my girlfriend," Josh said without thinking. Probably he should have said work, but too late now. He sighed and pocketed his phone.

"I dated a girl my first year as an associate," said Provost, sounding a little nostalgic. "Great girl, but I hardly had time to see her."

"I suppose that didn't work out, did it?" Josh asked, pocketing his phone.

"She's not my wife."

Of course.

"I realize it's tough the first year or two. We do put you new lawyers through your paces. But it's in the interest of helping you learn. And certainly, the more hours you bill, the more money the firm makes, so it's in our interest to keep you busy. But I remember how difficult it was."

Josh supposed this was Provost's way of being supportive and sympathetic. Josh nodded and thanked him. This didn't stop Josh from fretting about Paige being mad at him all through what turned out to be a very good lunch at a little bistro two blocks from the courthouse. Once they were seated, Provost only wanted to talk about work, which was probably for the best because Josh wasn't that interested in sharing his personal life with his boss.

When they returned to the courthouse, Provost said, "Your job this afternoon is to keep your eye on the jury and let me know if you have any impressions about how they react to testimony."

"This morning, they looked bored, for the most part," said Josh.

Provost nodded. "I worried about that. Extracting from the plaintiff witness list, this afternoon is going to be a lot of technical speak about the chemical properties of various kinds of window material, which will bore them more. My hope is that a good scandal will wake them back up when we present our defense."

Josh was skeptical of this, but he nodded.

Provost's prediction was correct, and Josh spent all afternoon sitting through testimony from a chemist who specialized in developing new kinds of clear, unbreakable materials. He was there to argue that, if the windows Giardino sold the plaintiff were indeed made out of the material he said they were, they wouldn't have shattered in the way they did. Provost got him to admit that

the storm that did break the plaintiff's windows was a rema.
able occurrence. A tornado had touched down in Brooklyn that
night, and though it was a small one, the wind had been significantly faster than New York City typically saw, and there'd been
more flying detritus in the air. Although there was no evidence
that anything more harmful than a tree branch had gone through
the plaintiff's window, Provost got the expert to admit something
larger could have. Josh knew there was a weather expert witness
on the defense list who would testify about how rare tornadoes
were in New York City.

When court adjourned for the day, Josh saw he had another
text from Paige, but then he found himself in the DCL company
limo headed back uptown as Provost peppered him with questions
about juror facial expressions and whether the glass guy seemed
reputable.

So when Josh returned to the office, he was so distracted he
forgot to respond to Paige and wasn't reminded again until about
9:00 p.m. as he took a car service to his apartment for a few hours'
sleep before he head to do this all over again. Being in court was
no excuse for not getting through his regular workload, according
to Provost.

He glanced at his phone and his heart sank. He texted Paige that
he was sorry, but he wondered if he wasn't adding fuel to the fire of
the idea that now was not the right time for them. He thought about
calling her, but he didn't want to be overheard by the driver, and by
the time he got home, he was so tired that he went straight to bed,
Paige on his mind.

CHAPTER 18

BY THE TIME FRIDAY MORNING arrived, nothing with Lauren had been resolved and Paige hadn't been able to talk to Josh much either. Josh had been too busy all week to talk, and maybe that was the answer Paige needed. She would be willing to wait him out if she thought they had a future together, but as the week went on, she was less sure they did. Worse, whether it was in her head or not, Paige couldn't tell, but it sure seemed like Lauren was keeping her distance. It was starting to feel like she was holding out hope that something would work out with Josh but sacrificing Lauren in the process, and she just wasn't sure that any of it was worth it or that any of this would work out.

As a result, she'd felt nauseous all week. The harder it was to get in touch with Josh, the more she worried about their future. And with Lauren basically avoiding her, it was hard not to feel like she was about to lose everything. And something had to give.

Midafternoon, when the café was empty, Paige finally said, "I'll break up with him if that's what you want."

"What?"

"Josh. I'll break up with Josh if that's what you want."

Lauren furrowed her brow. "Is that what you want? Because you've offered a few times."

"No. It's not what I want. I thought it was what you wanted. I get that this is weird for you, but you've been holding me at arm's length all week, and I want things to go back to how they used to be. If you don't approve of me going out with Josh, I'll end it. I just... I just want things to go back to how they were." And that was really it—she wanted her friends and her support network, and she wanted Josh, and she didn't see how both were possible.

Lauren sighed. "You want my honest opinion?"

"Yes. Please tell me."

But Paige wasn't sure she wanted to hear this. And she wondered if she'd been too defensive. Perhaps she should have stood up for her relationship with Josh more instead of offering to break up, but she'd hated the tension between herself and Lauren and couldn't help but wonder if all of this could have been avoided if she hadn't gone out with Josh to begin with.

Lauren stared at her for a long moment with her lips pursed. "It really doesn't have much to do with you. I mean, it does, because I love you and you're one of my best friends and I want you to be happy. But Josh is...he's barely over Megan. Has he talked to you about what happened?"

"He's mentioned her but hasn't said a lot."

Lauren nodded. "I don't want to betray his confidence, but the short version is that they met in law school, fell in love, and were planning a future together, but once they were facing the real world, it all fell apart, or this is how Josh tells the story. Secretly, I think she wasn't as serious about the relationship as he was. I mean, I'm sure she cared about him, but he was law school companionship, not a long-term relationship. But Josh didn't know that, and he was crushed when she ended it. I think she actually got the job in Chicago to put some permanent distance between them."

"He missed your wedding because he had a job interview in Chicago. I remember you being upset about that."

"Yup. And he still beats himself up about not being there for me. He didn't get the job, and he didn't get the girl, and he was really unhappy for a little while. He's been better since he started the new job, but I assumed that was because the job was distracting him from what happened."

"Probably it was."

"You probably were, too. Which I don't say because I think it's a bad thing, but I...I couldn't stand to see him get crushed again. Megan broke his heart. And you, well, I started picturing him falling in love with you, which of course he'd do, because you're wonderful. And if things didn't work out and he got crushed again... Not that I think you'd string him along or anything... Ugh, I'm not explaining this well."

"You're being protective." Paige felt her heart squeeze. "I wouldn't intentionally hurt him."

"You say that, but you just started dating. What happens if you break up?"

What indeed? "Believe me, I've spent a lot of time wondering about that question."

"And?"

"And I worried that, if we broke up, you'd choose him over me."

"Really? You thought that?"

"Yeah, of course. He's your *brother*. He's family. So being with him is a pretty big risk. Because if things don't work out, I lose you and I lose this job that I love. But then some days I think it's worth the risk." Paige took a deep breath. "But you've been kind of avoiding me all week, so maybe I'm wrong about that."

"I needed time to process this. And like I said, I worry. About both of you."

"I know. And maybe you're right. But I... Well." Paige ran out of things to say. "I guess I know what I have to do."

"No, wait." Lauren's brow furrowed. "You know what sucks about this? I don't want to lose you, either. Josh is family, but you are, too. You, Evan, Lindsay, you guys are my family here in New York. I know I didn't react very well to the news that you and Josh were seeing each other, but it's only because I want you both to be happy, and this situation could get complicated. I know your luck with romance hasn't been the best recently, and I hate watching you go through that because I want you to find a great guy. I'm not telling you not to date him, or even how I feel about the two of you together should even matter. But just, you know."

And Paige did know, or she thought she understood what Lauren was telling her. When Lauren offered a hug, Paige hugged her back.

Customers came in then and ended the conversation, but as Paige got the cat room ready for that evening's book club meeting, she made some decisions. She wasn't happy with any of it, but it was the only way she could see to keep her life together.

"The jury is going to find Bobby guilty," Josh said as he stood with his boss in a little anteroom near the courtroom. "Jurors number five and seven, the older women? They recognize the bill of goods Bobby's selling."

Provost frowned. "I know. Mrs. Rossi's counsel knows it, too, because he's still refusing to settle."

"What if you upped the financial ante? She's suing for damages to her house, but if Bobby will agree to double that, she might back off."

Provost chuckled. "Well, Joshua, you are about to get a lesson in where the line is between greed and the principle of the thing."

That line was apparently somewhere around five million dollars.

Josh walked out of the courthouse an hour later, after Bobby Giardino had agreed to fork over a substantial percentage of his assets in exchange for being spared the humiliation of a guilty verdict. The judge had even given Bobby a lecture on not lying to customers.

So now that he and Provost were actually leaving and the case was over, Provost said, "Go home, Josh."

"Are you sure? What about the Randolph case?"

"Yes, I'm sure. It's Friday. This week has been long enough. Go home and we'll resume with Randolph on Monday."

Josh glanced at his phone as he walked to the subway. It was just barely past four o'clock. So before he went underground, he called Paige to share the good news.

"That's timing for you," she said.

"What does that mean?"

"I need to talk to you. I'm wrapping up at the café, but I'll be home by the time you get there."

Josh's stomach churned as he sat on a surprisingly empty subway train into Brooklyn. Something in Paige's tone told him Paige had bad news. He felt a little bad for blowing her off the last couple of days, but he really hadn't been available. He'd been putting in fifteen-hour days on this case all week. Even now, as he sat, fatigue was seeping into his muscles. It was like his whole body was finally exhaling. That infernal case was finally over.

And Paige was, in all likelihood, about to dump him.

But he was a lawyer, wasn't he? He knew how to put forth an argument.

Paige's doorman told him to head on up when he arrived, and he had most of his argument formed by the time he knocked on her door.

Paige let him in. Her cat was curled up on one of the stools at the kitchen island, and she gave him an intimidating sideways glance before going back to sleep.

Paige stood near the island and looked at her feet. "I could order some food, or...?"

"Am I staying?"

"Are you?"

Josh sighed and walked over to the kitchen island. He parked on one of the stools and rubbed his head.

"Rough day at work?" Paige asked.

"Rough...year. My boss's clients are terrible people. I just spent a week in court sitting second chair to defend a man I know is guilty, and now my boss is representing an evil real estate developer who wants to kick little old ladies out of the apartments they've lived in for decades so that he can put up ugly modern buildings and charge premium rent. So, you know, eighty-hour weeks, uncomfortable moral crises, just another day at the office."

"I'm sorry. You know that an evil real estate developer almost shut down the Cat Café last year."

Josh didn't want to add more fuel to the fight he sensed was coming, so he did not confess that it was the same developer, but he nodded. "I don't feel great about working for him." He rubbed his forehead. "And you? How was your week?"

"Better than yours, it sounds like. The event we did this week with the kids reading to cats went well."

Josh felt like they were stalling. "I'm glad." He tried to smile but found his heart wasn't into it. He was too tired for small talk. "Not to be a dick, but we should probably cut to the chase. What did you want to talk about?"

"Well, I talked to Lauren."

"Ah. So is she mad, or..."

"No, not exactly. She mentioned Megan."

Of course she did. Josh shook his head. "I've put all that behind me."

"I don't want to be a rebound."

"You aren't! The thing with Megan ended months ago. It sucked, but I've moved on, and I was looking forward to a future with you." He caught his use of the past tense too late and noted the expression on her face, one of resignation. But here came those doubts again.

If she was gonna leave him, better to have it be now rather than later when his heart was more fully engaged, right?

He groaned. "What did Lauren say?"

Paige shook her head. "It's not important. The gist was that she's worried we're both making a mistake."

"A mistake? She said that?"

"Well, not in so many words, but just...if this ends, then what?"

"What if it doesn't end?"

"Everything ends!"

Josh sighed. He glanced at Bianca lounging on the stool beside him. "Until it doesn't," he muttered. He still hadn't had his big fight with Lauren, and he cursed the timing of the trial. If he'd had time this week, he could have answered Paige's texts or spoken to her on the phone or in person and helped quell some of her panic, and he could have talked to Lauren and gotten all this square so that Paige hadn't come away from that conversation convinced this story had some tragic ending. But he'd been so caught up in the case and his work and so tired when he got home at night that he hadn't talked with anyone about anything.

Paige stood near the kitchen island and wrung her hands. "What I said the first time we slept together hasn't changed. If we keep dating and get more involved and we have a fight or we break up or something else goes wrong with us? I still think Lauren would take your side, but even if she didn't, it would be a huge mess. And I'm sorry, but my friendship with Lauren and my job at the Cat Café are too important to me. So I think it's better that we end things now before we get too involved emotionally."

Josh nodded, because it was what he'd been expecting her to say. His stomach flopped as he realized that her ending things was not just theoretical. But he had a multipronged argument prepared, so he dove into it. "I hear you," he said, "but first of all, I don't know about you, but I'm already involved emotionally. So it's too late for that. If I walk away from you today, I will regret it for a long time."

Paige's face fell. "Don't say things like that. Don't make this harder."

"Breaking up is not what either of us wants, is it?"

"No, but..." Paige started to pace across her kitchen. Bianca hopped up on the counter and curled into a ball but kept an eye on Paige. Paige pet her head absently, but said, "You ever feel like, no matter what we want, the universe is trying to tell us this was not meant to be?"

"What are you talking about?" But Josh knew. He knew because he'd been through this very thing once before. It was the feeling he'd had once he'd finally gotten a plane home from Chicago and knew that everything was over.

Paige continued to pace. "I mean, you still have a demanding job. In the time that we've been dating, you've had to cancel on me several times because of work. And not only that, but you're working all those hours at a job you don't even seem to like very much, for the very sorts of clients who would have businesses like the one your sister and I run shut down!"

"And you worked for a bank. What's your point?"

"I like you, I really do, but you're too busy, and if my job and other personal relationships are also at stake, I can't help but think that this is the universe telling us we should not be together."

"Paige." Josh did completely understand what Paige was

saying, but he disagreed. They could find a way to make this work. Although if Paige was already looking for a way out, maybe it wasn't worth it. If she was just going to leave the way Megan did, maybe he shouldn't bother.

No, that didn't feel quite right. They wouldn't be feeling this much turmoil about this if they didn't care about each other. They'd be able to just walk away. Something in Josh was very stubbornly refusing to walk away.

"Let me talk to Lauren," Josh said. "She wanted to have it out with me, and I haven't had time to let her. But I think I can bring her around."

"She's avoiding me. I called her on it today, and she didn't deny it. See? It's already starting."

"But I think I can—"

"Josh." Paige pinched the bridge of her nose and furrowed her brow. She looked like she was in physical pain. "I don't know what to tell you. I hate how I feel right now. I don't want to say goodbye to you, but I don't see a way for this relationship to work."

"We could also just…not break up and see where it goes."

"I don't think that's an option," said Paige.

"We give Lauren some time to come around to the idea of us together and I keep working until my schedule becomes a little easier. Or I could take the time off my boss keeps telling me I have coming, and we could spend a whole week together. Or, hell, maybe I'll quit my job. And maybe it turns out that, when we spend more time together, we don't like each other so much after all, but maybe we do have something really special that is worth fighting for. I don't know. But I hate not trying."

"No, don't quit your job. I don't know if I can... I mean, it's such a big risk, and..."

Josh probably should have taken Paige at her word, but he wanted to fight for this. He wasn't sure if this was love, but it was something, and he refused to give it up. "Let's not make any decisions we can't take back right now. Maybe we have dinner together tonight, and then I go home, and then we just see where things go."

Paige shook her head. "I need some time to think."

"All right. I can give you that. But don't give up on us, Paige. I know this puts you in a terrible position, and I do feel bad about that, but I care about you and I want to keep caring about you, all right? And I think that you want to keep caring about me, too, but you're afraid of the fallout. And I get that, I do."

Then everything became quite clear to Josh. If what Lauren had told him was true, and based on things Paige herself had said, Paige had been dating a series of guys she met on apps who were all wrong for her. And this was a woman who had the rest of her life together—a job she loved, financial security, a lovely home. Why was she pushing away the one man who had come along whom she did connect with? Because she was terrified. What she was terrified of was not completely clear. Commitment? Love? There were a lot of possibilities here. But Josh felt like he finally had her pegged.

"Take some time to think," Josh said. He moved toward the door. "I think we both know where we stand and how we feel. I don't want to lose you. If you're breaking up with me now, well, I refuse to accept that."

"You refuse?"

"If I thought that you didn't want to be with me, I'd walk away right now. But you do want to be with me. These obstacles between us? I think these are things we can overcome. But if you're not willing to fight for it with me, then maybe this is a lost cause. Because I've been through that once before and I won't put myself through it again if I can help it. So you think about what you really want. And I'll go for now. Okay?"

"I…" Paige bit her lip and nodded. "Okay."

"Good." Josh walked to the door. Then he changed his mind and walked over to Paige. He leaned over and kissed her, and it quickly became something bigger, hotter, the sort of kiss that stirred something in his chest. He ran his fingers through her soft, silky hair just in case this was the last time he'd be able to do that. And he made it clear where he stood.

But he knew, too, that he could not be the only one fighting for them. If she wasn't with him all the way, this really was over.

He pulled away, leaving her looking dazed. She gaped at him as he walked to the door.

"Something to think about. Good night," he said. Then he made himself leave.

CHAPTER 19

JOSH WALKED INTO THE CAT Café and was relieved to see Paige was not working that day.

It was close to closing. The sun had started going down outside. Most of the staff was busily cleaning the café. Monique walked over, probably to tell him to leave, but then she recognized him.

"I just need to talk to Lauren," said Josh. He'd come here to finally have that talk. It was Monday evening, three days after Paige had tried to break up with him, and although he figured convincing Paige to take a risk on him was going to be a challenge, he thought he might be able to convince Lauren to back off.

"She's in the cat room."

Josh nodded and found Lauren there wiping down tables.

Rather than preface his comments with anything charming, he asked, "Did you tell Paige to break up with me?"

She looked startled. She tossed the rag she'd been using on one of the tables. "No, of course not."

"Are you just saying that to appease me?"

"No. I promise. I told her I was okay with you guys dating."

"Okay. She broke up with me. Or she tried."

"She...what? Why?"

Josh squinted and tried to measure whether Lauren was genuinely surprised or not. While it was true that he and Paige had left things ambiguous, the fact that Paige had not returned any of his calls or texts over the weekend told him a lot of what he needed to know. And now he was mad, but he didn't know where to put his anger, so he started with Lauren. "Well, she got the impression that you did not approve of our relationship."

Lauren looked chastened for a second, but then her brow furrowed. "That's not what I said."

"She also thinks that, if something goes wrong between her and me, you will choose me over her, and she doesn't want to lose you as a friend. Although honestly, if you did try to talk her out of what could have been a really great relationship, you're not a very good friend."

Lauren frowned. "Are you kidding me right now?"

"I like this girl! We get along great! I think we could really have something. But she dumped me because your approval is more important to her."

"Okay, first of all, stop yelling. Second, that's not what I told Paige. I mean yes, if you guys got together and broke up, this would all get very complicated, but Paige is one of my best friends and I wouldn't dump her just because she and my brother dated. I *did* warn her that Megan had done a number on you."

That Josh brought up short. "What did you say, exactly?"

"Just that you took your breakup with Megan hard, so I was worried about you because I didn't want you to get your heart broken again. Maybe I didn't say it well, but what I was trying to say was that Paige should only keep dating you if it was for real."

"Well, it is for real," said Josh, although now he was less sure. What had Paige been trying to tell him the other night?

"And, no offense, but it's not like you have an abundance of free time."

"I have some time. And I will have more soon enough. I'm not going to be a first-year associate forever. Besides, it's actually not any of your business."

He shouted that last part. He and Lauren were close, but sometimes fighting with her brought out a side of him he didn't love. They'd had some drag down fights when they'd been kids, although they hadn't fought like that in a very long time. Josh loved his sister, but there were few people on Earth who knew him so well and so knew exactly how to piss him off.

She put her hands on her hips now and glared at him. "Right. You guys have known each other for five minutes, but you're already thinking long-term? Or are you thinking with your dick?"

"That's low. It's not like that at all."

Lauren shook her head. "I don't know what you want me to say. Did finding out that you guys were dating freak me out? Yeah. Did I handle it well? Probably not. But if she broke up with you, it is not my fault."

"It's a little your fault."

"Again, I told Paige I was okay with it. I did *not* tell her to break up with you."

Josh let out a breath and felt his argument deflate. "Well,

it doesn't matter now because on Friday she said she wanted to break up."

"She really said that?"

"Well, yeah. Sort of. I think. I'm not really sure, actually."

"What does that mean?"

"The idea of breaking up with me seemed to upset her." He glanced at Lauren. "Again, to be clear, my love life and your friend's love life are actually none of your business."

"Uh, you came here to talk to me about it. You made it my business. And if you guys are so close, why did she offer—repeatedly—to break up with you?"

"She said that?" Well, that was discouraging. Had Paige really been willing to give up on them so easily.

"She said she didn't want to break up with you, but she would if I had a problem with your relationship. I told her I didn't. She broke up with you anyway?"

"Well, we left things kind of ambiguous, but she stopped returning my texts, so…"

"I guess that explains why you're so mad." Lauren sighed. "Look, I'm sorry. It was not my intention to meddle, and again, I told Paige I was okay with it. Yeah, I freaked out. But you're right, it's *not* my business. I still feel weird about it, but I don't want to be in the middle of this, and frankly, I resent that you guys put me there. But, I mean, if you guys want to date…I'll have to learn to live with it. But she tried to break up with you. So maybe she's not as committed as you thought."

Josh's head swam with that. He could so easily picture some future where they all hung out together. He dropped in on drink nights at the bar up the street on nights he didn't work late. He'd come by the Cat Café and tease Lauren and hang out with Paige while she did the schedules for the week. Maybe they'd live in the same apartment and explore the city on weekends. He could see all of it before him like it was a movie. If Paige was using Lauren as an excuse to break up, and it seemed like that was the case, maybe she wasn't as committed to making it work as Josh was. Maybe she had really meant to break up with him.

Josh grunted and dropped into an empty chair. "Well, now what do I do?"

Lauren picked up the rag and started wiping the table again. "You are my brother and Paige is my friend, and I want both of you to be happy. If you're happy with each other, that's wonderful. If not, that's okay, too. What do you want?"

Well, he wanted Paige, but not unless she really wanted to be with him. "Maybe it's time to move on. Probably I should be focused on work anyway. But I just want to register the complaint that I do not appreciate your interference in my love life, and I do really like Paige. For the record."

"So noted. But also I did tell her I was okay with you guys, so I don't deserve all the blame. I just... I know how bad Megan hurt you and I didn't want someone I loved to do that to you again. Not that she would on purpose. Well, anyway. I'm done. No more meddling. You kids have to work this out on your own."

"Right. Thanks, Mom."

"Oh, come on, now. That's not how this is."

"Mom didn't like me dating Jennifer O'Malley in tenth grade

and gave me a very similar speech. Is this what happens to all married people? You become your parents?"

Lauren mock gagged. "How dare you. Why didn't Mom want you to date Jennifer O'Malley?"

"I forget. I think Mom and Mrs. O'Malley had clashed at a PTA meeting or something. When Jen dumped me, Mom gave me that speech. 'You kids have to work this out on your own.' Like, verbatim. But she added a chorus of, 'It's for the best.'"

Lauren reached over and pulled Josh into a hug. "I swear, that's not what I'm doing. I'm…bowing out. I have no role in what happens between you and Paige."

Josh sighed and hugged her back. "Well, thanks for that, I guess."

"You gonna talk to her?"

"Yeah." Josh stepped back. "Not sure what I'm going to say yet. But if she doesn't want me, there's no sense in prolonging the inevitable."

"I'm sorry, for what it's worth. I hate seeing either of you upset. But you'll have to do what you think is right." Lauren picked up the rag she'd left on the table. "But if it is over, don't date anyone else on my staff."

Josh chuckled. He did forgive Lauren and believed her. So the question now was whether Paige was using Lauren as an excuse, and why.

Maybe it really was time to move on.

To prove he could joke about it, he said, "Does Caleb have a sister I could date?"

"You *think* you're funny," said Lauren.

One of the cats—Josh still hadn't learned any of their names—jumped up on the table and meowed at him, so he reached over to pet the cat.

"You done with work for the day?" Lauren asked.

"For now, yeah. I have some briefs to read before I can sleep."

"You want to eat with me and Caleb? We were going to order takeout tonight because he's working until seven, but you're welcome to join us."

"Well, sure, since I walked all the way over here. And buying my dinner is really the least you can do."

"That's only going to get you so far."

"I'm still gonna milk it."

A couple of evenings later, Paige was still mulling over what she wanted. Being with Josh represented a big change in her life.

It was an odd thing to realize that bad dates were safe to her. Going on a date with some guy she met through an app was low stakes. If she didn't like him, she didn't have to go out with him again, and then she could go home to her safe apartment and enjoy life at her safe job and not worry about how any of it would affect her future.

But Josh represented something different. It meant letting someone else into her life, into her little bubble. It was something she'd *said* she'd wanted for a long time, but being faced with the reality of it made her nervous. Of course, if she did accept him into her life, they could be tremendously happy together.

Lauren walked out of the backroom and looked to be headed

to the front of the café, so Paige stopped her. "Can we talk for a sec?"

"Sure," said Lauren.

No one else was around, which made this easier. They were ready to close up for the day, once they finished the last few cleaning tasks, and Lauren had already sent the rest of the staff home. So they could have this out if needed.

Paige sighed. "Look," she said. "I just need to clarify something. We're friends, right?"

"Of course." Lauren looked confused by the question.

"I guess I just... I'm trying to decide if I should go for it with Josh."

Lauren frowned. "First of all, lord save me from people confronting *me* about why they shouldn't be together."

Paige wondered what Lauren meant by that but wanted an answer to her question more. "Well?"

"I told Josh I was stepping out of this. I'm not involved. You guys have to figure this one out on your own."

"Sorry. Not to retread old ground. I don't mean to drag you into this. But, like, advising me as my friend, let's say I'm not dating Josh, but instead, I'm dating some other guy whom you are not related to, and I'm not sure if I should stay with him or not."

Lauren looked at her lap for a long moment. "Okay. You're dating some guy named Mike or whatever, right? Then I'd ask, do you like him?"

"Yes. A lot."

"Okay. Then why don't you want to be with him?"

Paige balked. "What do you mean by that?"

"If you're thinking about breaking up with Jo...Mike, then there must be some reason, or something about him you don't like. I promise not to get offended or defensive. What's the problem?"

"There isn't really a problem. It's me. I put all this time and effort into my well-ordered life, my nice apartment and my job, and I guess I'd gotten used to my love life not working very well, and now that it is, I don't know what to do with it. Except now there's all this...stuff between us. I tried to break up with him, but I was wishy-washy about it, and he must have known I didn't feel good about it, because he didn't let me."

Lauren nodded. "Yeah. He mentioned that. I mean, *Mike* mentioned it." She winked.

Paige laughed despite herself.

"Okay. I think I see what's going on here. You, Paige, are one of my favorite people. I asked you to work here because you're good at this job. Hell, you're overqualified. You should be planning celebrity weddings, not kids craft events at a cat café. But I also asked you because I like having you around. I love working with you. Having you here means I get to see you more. So your job, it's going well, right?"

Paige tried not to smile at that and failed. "Right."

"And you saved up your money from your evil corporate job to pay for that tiny but very nice apartment I know you're really proud of."

"Also true."

"It's that whole New York triad. Home, career, love. We all want all three, but at any given time, one of those things is not working out. Until it all totally does."

"Like with you and Caleb."

"Exactly." Lauren grinned. "I count myself extraordinarily lucky. But you deserve that same happiness." She sighed. "I'm sorry I freaked when I first found out about you and Josh. It seemed too weird for you two to be dating. I mean, he's *Josh*. He's my baby brother. He doesn't have a dating or sex life."

Paige laughed, despite herself. She sat on one of the sofas. "That's not even the issue anymore. I'm still worried about what happens if things don't work out. I think the issue is really, it's a risk, and do I want to take it or stick with my nice, safe regular life?"

"Is the guy you're dating Josh again?"

"Sure, okay."

"Well, he works all the time, you know. I've hardly seen him at all since he moved to Brooklyn three months ago, and he only lives, like, eight blocks from here."

"Yeah. Finding time to see each other was a challenge."

"You should have a conversation with him about what you really want. Maybe he doesn't want to settle down right now, at least not at this point in his career."

"Did he say that?"

"No, I'm just speaking hypothetically. You asked for my help. I'm probably giving it badly. Feel free to tell me to shut up."

Paige shook her head. "We'd only been dating for a hot minute when I broke it off. We hadn't gotten as far as thinking about anything long-term." But she also knew Lauren was wrong. Josh seemed content to settle down romantically. He wasn't the kind of guy who felt the need to sow a lot of wild oats.

Lauren looked at her hands again. "I really don't want to get between you."

"I know."

"He came in here a couple of days ago and yelled at me for talking you into ending things with him. It was your decision, right? I know I said some things."

"It was my decision. It was getting complicated. I don't know. I mean, if anything happened between me and Josh, like if we had a fight or we hurt each other in some way, you'd take his side, and then where would I be?"

"I'm not sure that's true."

"Come on, Lauren. He's your brother."

"He's also not always right."

Paige sighed. "Well, I think it's over now, so it doesn't matter."

They were both quiet for a long time. One of the cats, a chubby striped cat named Anne Elliot, hopped up on the sofa and rubbed her head against Paige's thigh. Paige reached over to pet her.

Lauren said, "I only want the best for you. You are one of the smartest, most caring people I know. I love working with you. I love getting drinks after work with you. I love all the programs you're doing for the café. I don't want you to ever think that I don't value that. It was just, I don't know. Temporary insanity. Okay?"

Paige decided to believe Lauren. It didn't solve the central issue, which was that Paige wanted to run to Josh now to talk about this conversation. Nor was it a green light to go date Josh again, because Paige had some things to work out in her own mind and heart. But if she and Josh were the sort of people who were friendly at parties but otherwise didn't see each other much, then there was no tension between Paige and Lauren. And if Lauren really did care about and value Paige, that was pretty important.

Lauren stood. "Come here."

So Paige hugged Lauren and felt like they'd overcome whatever conflict was here. That was, her friendship with Lauren was good, but she still felt uneasy about Josh and all of it. She was on solid footing with Lauren again but more confused than ever about what she wanted with Josh.

As she walked home that night, she pulled out her phone and saw Josh had texted her again. He had a few times over the weekend, as well, and she hadn't felt up to responding. Paige responded.

I talked things out with Lauren, but I don't know what I want with you. I need more time to think. Let's take a break. Don't contact me for a while.

She hovered her thumb over the Send button and paused for a moment. She could easily picture the look on Josh's face when he got the text. The idea of it broke her heart. She hit Send anyway.

He responded right away. She deleted the text without reading it.

CHAPTER 20

PAIGE STOOD BEHIND EVAN IN the entryway to a large event space.

"The decor leaves something to be desired," said Paige.

"Picky, picky."

"They barely tried. The red velour curtains are a cliché, there are no rugs or anything to keep our feet from aching on this concrete floor, and there is nothing like enough seating."

"Sweetheart, the goal of an event like this is to mingle, not to sit. I thought you were an event planner. Now, come, I think I see the bar."

Paige was coming to resent Lindsay for letting them all know over drinks a few nights before that a friend of hers was helping to plan a singles mixer in Greenpoint. Since things were all but over with Josh, she'd let Evan and Lindsay talk her into coming, because she figured it couldn't hurt to meet someone new. But now she had regrets.

First, getting here had proved to be a trial. She'd met Evan at his place and they'd gotten on a wrong train and ended up lost in the subway system before Evan gave up yanked Paige back up to street level so they could get a cab the rest of the way. The space was done up to look like a cheap boudoir, everything red and black and tacky as hell. The vast majority of the people here were women, which was not a good sign for either Evan's or Paige's prospects.

"Lindsay promised there would be guys here," Paige said as she and Evan walked up to the bar.

Evan looked around. "The one over by the pillar at two o'clock bats for my team. So does the pink shirt with glasses talking to the girl with curly hair to the left. But I think the flannel shirt and skinny jeans by the curtain over there is one of yours."

"Why did we come?"

"It's fun. What are you drinking?"

Once Paige had a glass of mediocre white wine in-hand, she and Evan walked around. There was going to be some kind of cooking class/demonstration in about twenty minutes to encourage the singles to socialize with one another, so a group of staff people in black T-shirts were setting up an area with cloth-covered tables and electric hot plates.

"Something is going to catch on fire," said Evan.

"Why isn't Lindsay here again? She's also single, last I checked."

Evan laughed. "She may secretly hate us. Or it's like that episode of *Friends* when everyone forgets to tell Chandler they're going to a party and he ends up at a one-woman theater show that traumatizes him."

"You can't watch *Friends* anymore. I'm taking it away."

"Lindsay *claims* she got tickets to a TV show taping because that beardy celebrity chef she has a crush on is going to be a contestant, but I think she got those tickets so she wouldn't have to come here. Or she punked us. That's also possible."

"You were just saying this was fun!"

"I didn't realize how slim the pickings were. Oh, well. I hope we make something edible."

As the actual cooking demonstration approached, more men showed up, which was encouraging. Evan made her talk to a few of them. The first guy was good-looking but could only talk about cars.

"Are you a mechanic?" she asked.

"Oh, no. I mean, I worked for a mechanic for a bit when I was in my twenties, but now I work for GM in one of their corporate offices. What kind of car do you drive?"

"I don't. I live in New York City."

So that was the end of that.

The second guy was a young adjunct college professor who dressed the part in a tweed blazer and button-down shirt open at the collar. He taught freshman English at three different schools in the city to make ends meet. Paige had a mental image of him constantly in motion to make it to all these classes.

"You're not far off the mark," he said when she explained that. "On Tuesdays and Thursdays I teach at Cooper Union and City College. That's a solid half hour on the subway."

Paige laughed. "You ever see that episode of *Friends* when Ross has to teach classes across town from each other and ends up getting roller skates?" Then she silently cursed herself for spending too much time with Evan.

The guy frowned at her. "Is that a show? I don't own a TV."

The next guy was a foodie, and they did have an interesting

conversation about a new Manhattan restaurant Paige had eaten at the month before. "Best gnocchi I've ever had," she said.

"I love Italian. My sister is a chef, actually. She's the executive chef at Acre in the Village."

"Oh, cool. I've never eaten there. What kind of food is it?"

"New American, I guess? The menu is pretty eclectic. And it's all organic, farm-to-table with a large vegetarian and vegan selection."

"Sounds great. A friend and I ate at a place like that in Brooklyn about a month ago…" But she stopped talking because she'd been thinking about Josh and the day she'd taken him to brunch before they'd walked to the Brooklyn Bridge. That had been… Well, it had been one of the best days of her life, if she was honest. Remembering it made her wonder why she was *here* and not with Josh.

"You okay?" the foodie asked.

"Yeah, sorry, I was thinking about something unimportant." Paige smiled.

"Brooklyn has a *great* food scene," the guy went on. "A lot of new places are opening in neighborhoods where you wouldn't expect."

She managed to learn that the foodie's name was Gabe and she invited him to be her partner when the chef organizing the event called for them to do so. Paige saw Evan approach the guy who'd been holding up a pillar. As they approached the table in the middle, Paige looked around and saw a lot of mixed-up gender pairings, same and opposite sex and a few nonbinary couples, which made her smile.

The chef assigned each couple to a hot plate and quickly explained the instructions. All they really had to do was dump the pre-measured ingredients in a bowl when instructed to do so, then they'd be tossing vegetables in this spice mix and frying them in a pan with tofu or chicken, depending on the couple's preference. Easy enough.

It turned down that Gabe liked to eat but cooking was not really something in his wheelhouse, so Paige ended up doing most of the work. They opted for chicken *and* tofu and tossed them both with the veggies in the wok. The chef walked around to check on them as they cooked and deposited a little Styrofoam container of rice for them to add to their meal.

The meal came out pretty well and Gabe praised Paige's skill at cooking.

"They did a lot of the work for us," said Paige.

"Sure, but I don't know if I could have done that much. I can barely boil eggs."

"How do you eat?"

"A lot of takeout."

Paige and Gabe exchanged phone numbers before Gabe's friends pulled him away to go get drinks at a bar down the street. Gabe invited Paige, but Paige begged off to find Evan, who was shamelessly flirting with the pillar guy. Evan put his phone number in the guy's phone before the guy wandered away.

"Well?" said Evan.

"Gabe was nice, but I don't think he's very good at life."

Evan let out a surprised burst of laughter. "What makes you say that?"

"He can't cook. Like, at all. And yet I learned that he's thirty-three and lives alone."

"I don't know if that's a character flaw, but the fact that this is a cooking-related event does make him seem suspect."

Paige sighed. "How about you?"

"Will is a mid-level editor at a publishing company and was here because he's working on a cookbook by Chef André and felt obligated. He does at least know his way around a set of premeasured ingredients."

"You gonna see him again?"

"If he calls me, I will die of shock."

Paige laughed. "Aw, why?"

"It's pretty clear that Will has a huge unrequited crush on a guy in his office. He would *not* stop talking about that guy. Brian says this, Brian says that, ugh."

"Oh, I'm sorry." Paige looked around the room. Now that the cooking and eating were done, the crowd was thinning rapidly. "Remind me of the point of this again?"

"Worth a shot, I guess," said Evan. "I need to move on from Darius and Pablo and all the unavailable men in my life, and you need to move on from Josh, but good lord, dating in the twenty-first century sure is gimmicky."

Paige laughed.

"There's a fantastic pizza place a couple of blocks from here, and I could sure use something to eat after Will ate all my vegetables. Wanna get out of here?"

Paige linked her arm with Evan's. "Yes, let's."

Josh walked into the conference room reluctantly. Randolph's whole appearance was off-putting. He looked like a mob boss out of Central Casting, in a sleek gray suit with his hair slicked back and a day's worth of silvery stubble on his jaw. He sat across from Josh at the conference table and passed him a piece of paper.

"There's an issue with one of my buildings in Chicago," Randolph said. "That's the name of my lawyer there. She can fill you in. Mr. Provost said I should ask you to get in touch."

"Oh." Josh unfolded the piece of paper. It said *Megan Stanhope* and a phone number.

Of fucking course.

"What's the issue?" Josh asked.

"A tenant claims she slipped on ice in front of the building, but it's a garbage claim. It wasn't even cold enough to be icy the day she slipped. Call Ms. Stanhope. She'll fill you in." Randolph glanced at the phone number. "She also went to Georgetown. Do you know her?"

"Yep," said Josh. "She was in my class."

"Great! Then she can get you up to speed."

Josh's desire to call Megan ranked alongside his desire to jump into a tank full of sharks. "Why do you think I should call her? This seems like a local matter."

Randolph waved his hand dismissively. "Let's just say, I need to move some money around. Talk to Megan. She'll explain."

Josh walked back to his office wanting to kick something. He interpreted Randolph's comment about needing to move money around as needing to get out of the lawsuit in Chicago, so he could put some of those funds toward his various potential real estate holdings in New York. Josh was no accountant, but that seemed shady.

But worse than that, now Josh had to call Megan, of all people. The only reason he was reasonably functional was that he'd put Megan very firmly in a box labeled *past* and had no intention of ever speaking to her again. The last thing he wanted, especially given the situation with Paige, was to open that box and relive the memories.

He figured he should rip off the Band-Aid, though. His stomach flopped as he picked up his office phone. He was glad Randolph had given him a phone number because he'd taken Megan's out of his cell phone. He'd wanted a clean break so he could get on with his life. And he thought he had moved on but having to think about talking to Megan was bringing it all back.

He took a deep breath and dialed.

"Stanhope," she answered.

"Hi, Megan, it's Josh."

There was a long, drawn-out pause. "Josh."

"Just so you know, this isn't a social call. I'm calling on behalf of my boss, who is representing David Randolph. Mr. Randolph asked that I call you about the lawsuit regarding his building in Chicago."

"Ah, of course. A cosmic coincidence."

"Honestly, if someone else were telling me this story, I would not believe them."

Megan laughed softly. "Well, there's not much to the suit. Randolph owns three buildings in Chicago, one in the Loop and two in Lakeview."

"Sure." That job interview had been Josh's one and only time in Chicago.

"This was at one of the buildings in Lakeview. The situation is basically that a group of tenants claimed they slipped and fell on ice in front of the building and suffered various injuries, including broken limbs, but the super of that building was religious about salting the stairs and sidewalk in front of the building. We're pretty confident we'd win at trial, but my boss wants to offer them a settlement to go away first. I think the claim is bullshit, but I just worked a case where the plaintiff showed up in court in a neck brace and the jury awarded her three million in damages. But, like, this woman was in a Volvo that she claimed was rear ended by a semi. Josh, there wasn't even a broken taillight. If that semi had really hit the Volvo, it would have crumbled up like a tin can."

Josh sighed. He realized that this was the world in which Megan thrived. She was full steam ahead on representing her shitty client. She likely did not go home at night and lay in bed having any kind of existential crisis about what she was doing with her life.

Okay, that was dramatic, but Josh didn't think he was well-suited to being this sleazy.

"So, you think the plaintiffs are lying?"

"Yes. However, they've hired this real shark of a lawyer who is demanding a massive settlement and is threatening to show evidence in court that Randolph is a slumlord with a pattern of mistreating his tenants. None of that is true, but you know how juries are."

Perhaps proving Megan's point, Josh was starting to

sympathize with the tenants. "Okay. Why would this affect his business in New York?"

"I've drafted up a settlement agreement with a pretty big payout and I think they'll bite, but the catch is that Randolph wants to use that money to buy out the last remaining tenant in that building in Brooklyn he intends to tear down. Apparently that tenant *also* has a good lawyer and keeps jacking up the amount of money she'll settle for."

"Ah, okay." Well, that all made sense now. "So he probably wants me to talk you out of settling."

"You know that's terrible advice, right?"

"I'm not real jazzed about kicking a nice lady out of the apartment she's lived in for almost fifty years, so I'm the wrong person to ask here."

"You always were a Boy Scout."

"What's that supposed to mean?"

Josh rolled his eyes. He shouldn't let Megan rile him up. He'd really thought this woman was the one he'd wanted to spend his life with once, but somehow he'd never seen this side of her. She'd been a serious law student, she studied hard, and they'd had a lot of fun together in their downtime. But now she was a shark.

"I'm legit surprised you're still at DCL, frankly," Megan said. "I always figured you'd end up at the ACLU."

"Yeah, well. I'm a sellout, I guess."

"Don't be like that. That's not what I said."

"I'm paying my dues. Maybe I will quit to go work for the ACLU one of these days, but I'm here for now, so let's figure out how to handle Randolph."

"Of course. Remember to represent your client zealously. I think we can find a compromise here. Maybe I can lower the settlement offer so Randolph still has the money he wants to buy out that tenant. I'll email you, all right?"

"Sure." Josh dictated his email address to Megan and then decided he should really put the lid back on this box.

He didn't think she'd always been this way, but it wasn't a great color on her now. So really, it was just as well. If he'd followed her to that job, they would have broken up by now anyway, or still been living together and been utterly miserable.

So, fine. He'd work out the rest of this Randolph situation and then he'd close the box again, because he was well and truly done with Megan.

CHAPTER 21

JOSH SAT AT HIS DESK as he ate a sandwich and used his brief reprieve to pay his student loan bill. It *was* nice to be able to make a big payment, but he didn't know how much longer he could do this. He knew from asking around that about a third of DCL's associates quit before their first year was up. He was reluctant to become one of those casualties, but he felt a little dirty making a nice salary to defend these terrible clients.

I'm quitting, he texted Lauren.

You are not.

They'd been having this conversation over text for three days. He'd finally broken down and told her that Provost was representing Randolph. She'd been surprisingly rational about it, pointing out that, although she loathed Randolph with fiery fury, it wasn't like Josh had chosen him as a client. But now that he knew full well that he was helping out a client who could have done real damage to his sister's and his not-girlfriend's business, his ambivalence about this job was almost tangible.

End of the year, Lauren texted.

That was what she'd talked Josh into: waiting until September, his first anniversary at DCL, to make any decisions. She wasn't exactly happy that Josh was doing work for the man who had tried to shut down the Cat Café, nor did she like that Josh would likely help him shut down other perfectly good businesses in the city in the name of replacing them with ugly condos, but she understood he had bills to pay.

Still, it was one thing to take a sleazy corporate job for a paycheck. It was quite another to work at a job that could have a direct negative impact on people he cared about.

Fine, Josh responded.

Provost appeared by his door with a woman he didn't know. "I've got an interesting new case," he said.

Josh nodded and tried to look placid, even though inside he thought, *Oh no, now what?* "I'm glad to hear that."

Provost smiled like he knew Josh was kidding; after all, half a sandwich and an open can of diet soda sat on Josh's desk as clear evidence that Josh was working through lunch. An interesting case meant more work. Provost smiled. "Come with me to the conference room and I'll explain."

Josh grabbed a pen and a pad of paper and followed his boss down the hall.

As they sat, Provost said, "Let me introduce you to Penny Kincaid from the DA's office."

Josh shook her hand before he settled into his chair.

"Penny used to be an associate here. She asked my advice on a case, so I've decided to give the DA's office a little help pro bono. I know you've got a lot on your plate right now, but we have two new paralegals starting Monday who can take on some of the busy work so that you can focus on this."

"What's the case?" Josh asked.

He looked over at Penny. She was a strikingly beautiful woman in her mid-thirties, with long dark hair and bright blue eyes. He hated thinking about her that way and pushed it aside to focus on what she was saying.

She said, "Well, long story short, the state is pursuing a case against a medical supply manufacturer. They make artificial joints, primarily. We think they've been cutting corners, though, and we now have several reports of injuries and at least two deaths that we think can be directly linked back to bad parts that caused severe infections."

That definitely got Josh's attention. "Are you bringing severe charges against the manufacturer?"

"Perhaps. We haven't decided yet. I came here today to ask Mr. Provost's advice. He was a great mentor to me before I went to the DA's office. My boss thinks this is criminally negligent homicide, but that's an awfully difficult thing to prove against a corporation."

Josh murmured something in the affirmative, but he was distracted by how much this case excited him. It was terrible that people had died, but helping out with something like this was a great way to do good work; the outcome of this case had the potential to make people safer and healthier.

"We're asking you to help with research," said Provost. "You did such a great job on the Giardino case, and even though that didn't go the way we wanted, perhaps you were able to find some old case law that supported the argument I wanted to make. I think you can do that here. I know of some civil cases that are relevant here, but usually the victims sue the doctors and not the equipment manufacturer."

"There was a case in the nineties where a pacemaker manufacturer was sued," said Penny. "The judge dismissed the case, however, because there wasn't enough evidence to show the manufacturer was knowingly selling a faulty product, and in that case, it was only one pacemaker that stopped working. In *this* case, we've got a dozen patients who were injured by bad parts, and that sure looks like a pattern. So I'm working with the NYPD to investigate the manufacturer, but I *could* use some help finding precedents in the case law."

"All right," said Josh. "I'd be happy to help with that." And he wasn't even lying or being polite.

Penny smiled, which made some things stir in Josh, but again, he pushed it aside. A part of him was still determined to make things work out with Paige, and lusting after another woman, and one he was about to work with at that, seemed like a bad way to do that.

"Excellent," said Penny. She then launched into an explanation of the particulars of the case and the arguments she was hoping Josh could find case law to support. One thing Josh had learned on the job here was that, even when a case seemed completely unprecedented, there was likely some precedent set somewhere that would lend some credence to whatever argument the litigator wanted to make. In the Giardino case, for example, the plaintiff had wanted to include a video of someone smashing a defective window from Bobby's shop, and Josh had managed to find a similar case from fifteen years ago in which the judge had ruled against the plaintiff because there was no way to trace the chain of custody of what had, in that case, been furniture sold with faulty parts. In other words, the video could have shown any chair—or any window—and there was no way to demonstrate that the faulty item had come from the defendant's store. The judge, unfortunately, had ruled against Provost in that case because the plaintiff had produced receipts showing her lawyer had purchased a window a few days before the video was made. Josh didn't think that had been all that persuasive—they still couldn't prove the window in the video was the one purchased from the store—but the judge had disagreed.

He took notes now about Penny's case, scribbling down the major arguments she was looking to make. Her boss had been hopeful they could find an example of a case where a corporation had been held responsible for one or more deaths. No one in the conference room was that optimistic, but Josh promised to try.

"Great," said Penny. "Let's reconvene next week to discuss what you've found."

"I still need your help with the Randolph cases," said Provost, "but that's why I'm bringing in the paralegals. What I really need are your research and writing skills. Anything else can be delegated."

"Okay," said Josh, excited now. He wanted to find ways the law could help and protect people, not defend the Randolphs of the world. Hearing that he could delegate some of his work was a relief. He smiled at his boss.

"That's the spirit," said Provost.

Penny handed a folder to Josh. "All right, let me go over what we've found so far on this."

After the meeting broke, Josh headed back to his office feeling newly buoyed. He checked his phone and saw he had a text from Lauren inviting him to dinner over the weekend. I have some news, she wrote ominously.

He texted back: You can't tell me the news over text?

She responded, No, this is in-person news.

Yikes. Bad news? he asked.

No, it's good news. Stop being a jerk and come to dinner.

Fine, fine.

He sighed, wondering what the news was. There were a dozen possibilities, and he briefly wondered if any was Paige-related, but he decided probably not. In fact, he'd bet cash money Lauren spent much less of her day thinking about Paige than Josh did.

He wondered what Paige was up to now. Was she running new events at the café? Was she getting better at working with kids? She'd told him not to contact her for a while, so he was honoring that, but he missed her palpably. He wanted to see her, talk to her, hold her. He'd worked actively not to feel that pain in his chest, but he was starting to realize that maybe he had fallen in love with her. She hadn't dumped him, merely asked him for more time, so it was possible she'd come to her senses and recognize that, actually, they belonged together.

Because it couldn't be possible for him to have gotten a taste of life with Paige only for her to leave him. He could not accept that.

But he would respect her wishes, so he would bide his time for now. But as Provost had just told him, he was on his way to becoming a great litigator, and as such, surely he could craft the argument that would win Paige back. He just had to find that argument.

CHAPTER 22

PAIGE HAD OFTEN THOUGHT OF her time as a single person as a kind of baseline. A relationship might pull her away from that baseline for a time, but she always reverted back when that relationship ended.

Only this time, she didn't seem to be reverting. Something had definitely changed when she went out with Josh.

Oh, the routine was the same. Her home was the same—she went to work every day, and she spent time with her friends. Walking into Pop to meet the usual gang one evening felt routine; Paige said hello to the bartender by name on the way in. But it was different, too, because Paige couldn't help but think about Josh being here with her.

She'd never regretted her decisions where men had been concerned before. Oh, a few breakups had left her feeling sad for a few days. But for the last couple of years, no one had made it past the second date, so she'd moved on without much thought. With Josh, she'd told him not to contact her, and he hadn't, but part of her still kept checking her phone to see if he'd texted or hoped it was him whenever her phone rang. She couldn't sit at the corner table in the Cat Café without thinking about him sitting at the table with her. She couldn't cook at home without wishing he was sitting at the island, making witty banter while she finished dinner.

This was love, wasn't it? Or it was the end of it, maybe. This ache she felt in her chest whenever she thought of Josh, wondering if she'd done the right thing, this sure felt like heartbreak.

She looked at her friends gathered around their usual table and thought that she had done the right thing, because she couldn't possibly lose this. Was there some universe where she could have both? She didn't know, but it hadn't seemed that way.

She sat at the table with Caleb, Lauren, Evan, and Lindsay and ordered her usual and listened to them gossip about whatever had happened that day. And she couldn't help but imagine if Josh were here to add a joke about something insane that had happened with one of his less savory clients. He'd never come to drink night, but she'd hoped to invite him once Lauren knew about their relationship. Instead, everything had fallen apart.

"Brace yourselves, guys," said Evan after everyone's drinks arrived. "I was wrong about something."

"I am *shocked*," said Lauren.

"That has never happened before," said Paige.

"Dogs and cats living together! Mass hysteria!" said Lindsay.

Evan turned to Caleb. "You see the abuse I put up with?"

"What happened, Ev?" asked Lauren.

"Will the cookbook editor from that dumb singles thing Lindsay tricked me and Paige into attending actually called me. We're going out Friday."

"What, really?" said Lauren.

"What happened to Darius?" asked Caleb.

Evan pursed his lips and shook his head, his expression reading as though something unfortunate had happened to him.

"They broke up a couple of weeks ago," Lauren stage-whispered.

"Wait, I thought you said that the cookbook editor was hung up on another guy," said Paige.

"And so I thought, so I confronted him about it, and apparently this Brian guy he has a crush on is married and works in his office, and so is very off-limits, and he promised to work on not talking about him so much." Evan shrugged. "Time will tell, I guess."

"Good luck," said Lindsay. "And what about you, Paige?"

"The guy I met at the single's thing has *not* called, and I don't think he will. Which is fine, because I don't think we're very compatible."

"Yeah, I had an eye on you." To the rest of the table, Evan added, "When we started the cooking portion of the event, he made Paige do all the work."

"Oof," said Lauren.

"He's the first foodie I've met who doesn't know how to cook," said Paige.

"They're out there," said Lindsay. "Remember when I dated Matt Petroff?"

Everyone groaned. The Petroff family was well known in New York for being culinary giants. They'd run a food-related magazine empire before selling it off to the highest bidder for an absurd profit, and now Matt's parents owned several of the city's hottest restaurants. Matt Petroff had all the privilege of the sort of white guy who grew up with very wealthy parents and zero self-awareness.

"I don't know if that counts," said Paige. "Matt was like the one person in that whole family who did not care about food."

Lindsay frowned. "Well, his wife's social media is wall-to-wall pictures of food, so I guess he's eating. Oh. I didn't tell you? He married a photogenic home chef last year."

"Story checks out," said Evan.

Lindsay sighed. "You're right, Paige, men suck."

"I didn't say anything," said Paige.

"No, but that's the subtext. I have been unimpressed by Brooklyn's offerings of late."

"And yet you skipped the singles event of the year," said Evan.

"Something good came out of it, didn't it?" said Lindsay.

Evan narrowed his eyes at her. "Sure. I hope that taping you went to was better."

Lindsay mock swooned. "Chef Campanello is so dreamy. He's like if Superman grew a beard and became a chef."

"What was the taping?" asked Lauren.

"It's a new reality show called *Chef Gauntlet*. Four contestants have to get through three rounds of grueling cooking challenges, and whoever is left standing wins. Chef Campanello won, by the way."

"What is a grueling cooking challenge?" asked Paige.

"Oh, like, make an appetizer with this really gross ingredient, like an obscure fruit from Southeast Asia that smells like dirty diapers. Make an entree, but the only tool you're allowed is this one big knife. And the last challenge was to repurpose a birthday cake into an entirely different dessert. It was really fun to watch. I'm writing it up for *Dine Out New York*."

There'd been a time when these little gatherings had felt more like girls' nights, plus Evan. Caleb's presence was throwing Paige off a little. Not that she didn't feel free to talk openly in front of him, but he was often quiet and made her wonder if he and Lauren talked over everything they said when they got home.

But apparently this was just Paige feeling nervous; Lindsay said, "How about you, Caleb? How is the veterinary biz?"

Caleb smiled. "Fine. A poodle gave birth on my watch today, so that was unexpected."

Evan gasped. "Are the owners keeping the puppies?"

"Are you going to adopt one?" asked Lauren.

"My cat would probably disapprove."

"I think they are keeping the puppies. There were only three. The mama poodle is a retired show dog and I kind of got the vibe the owners want to show the puppies when they're big enough."

"Dog shows are so weird," said Lindsay. "I've always wanted to go to one. Actually, now that I write for an animal website, I wonder if I can finagle a press pass for the one they do at Chelsea Piers every year."

"You *have* to take me," said Evan.

Maybe the thing bugging Paige was how normal all this felt. Tonight could have been interchangeable with any other night that her friends met for drinks over the last couple of years. Except Paige felt out of sorts. Her gut churned, her chest ached, and she missed Josh so much that she was tempted to text him under the table, though she wouldn't.

She could so easily picture Josh here with his arm casually draped around Paige's shoulders the way that Caleb's was around Lauren. Josh would probably tease Lauren and make jokes with Evan and talk about food with Lindsay.

Paige had never really been able to picture any of the guys she'd gone out with fitting into her friend group so easily. Usually the guys she went out with were radically different from her friends. And that was probably why they'd never worked out; she thought she should date someone different and interesting but what she really wanted was a friend. She'd heard couples say that about each other, that they'd each married their best friend. That's what Paige wanted. Not some whirlwind romance. Not some impressive guy with an oddball hobby. She wanted to fall in love with a friend.

Which is what had happened. And she'd pushed him away.

"You okay?" asked Evan, who was sitting next to Paige. "You're a little quiet this evening."

"I'm okay. Sorry. Mind wandered off."

"Split a plate of mac and cheese bites with me?"

"Sure."

Evan leaned over and whispered in Paige's ear, "It's okay to miss him."

"Did I do the right thing?" she asked.

Evan pressed his lips together. "Honestly? I don't know. Does it feel like the right thing?"

"No. I think I've made a terrible mistake."

"Is it too late to fix it?"

Paige shrugged. "I don't know."

"If you kids are passing notes, you have to share with the class," said Lindsay.

"We were just discussing appetizers," said Evan. "Ever since Pop expanded their menu, I have struggled with what to order, but maybe we should get the mac and cheese bites *and* the cheeseburger sliders."

Paige almost groaned when Evan's talk of appetizers reminded her of Josh and his appetite. Would everything remind her of Josh?

"Ladies' room," Paige said, grabbing her handbag and running to the back of the bar.

She locked herself in a stall and let herself cry. She couldn't remember crying about a boy since she'd been a teenager, but she cried now because she'd started to fall in love with Josh and couldn't have him. Because even if she could find some way to reconcile what she wanted with her friends, even if Lauren gave them the green light, the longer she persisted in not talking to Josh, the less likely it was he'd come back. That was the lesson Lauren had been trying to give her when she'd talked about Josh's ex Megan. Megan hadn't been committed to making things work with Josh, but Josh deserved someone who was.

And she was afraid. She should let herself be happy, but instead, she'd let her doubts rule the day, and now here she was, alone in a bathroom stall with black marker graffiti on the door saying, *Liz + Jared*, as if to rub it in that less pathetic people had once been here.

Relationships ended. She'd been operating on the assumption

that her relationship with Josh would end at some point, no matter if they fell in love, and it was the fallout from the end of that relationship that she couldn't face because she knew that if they fell in love and he left her, she would be wrecked. *That* was the real risk. They would be happy together...until they weren't. Every relationship ended.

Until one didn't.

The safer option had always been to end it before they got too involved and retreat back to her comfort zone, but that zone wasn't so comfortable anymore now that Josh wasn't in it. There was no going back, not to how things had been before she met Josh.

It was too soon to know if she and Josh could be together for the long haul. And finding out was a risk. And she was a coward.

She let herself feel everything as she stood in the stall and cried. Her thoughts were all over the place and contradicted each other and didn't completely make sense, but that's how this whole situation was. She cried until she'd worked through all of it, then she sighed and exited the stall. She grabbed a tissue and wiped her eyes, then she fixed her makeup and hoped her eyes didn't look so bloodshot that her friends would notice. Once she felt like she looked normal and not like someone who had just sobbed in a bathroom stall, she rejoined her friends, who appeared to be laughing at one of Evan's stories.

She loved these people, and she'd sacrificed Josh so that she could keep loving them, but she wondered now if she'd given up too easily.

"Oh, Paige," said Lauren, "did I tell you? We have a customer who is interested in adopting Mr. Darcy and Mr. Bingley."

"Oh, that's wonderful," said Paige. "Also sad. I've grown kind of attached to those cats."

"It's not a done deal, but do you know that couple that comes in on Thursday evenings sometimes? They're both kind of frumpy and wear big hipster glasses. They always sit in the middle of the cat room."

Paige couldn't picture who Lauren was talking about, but she said, "Sure."

"They want both cats."

"It's fitting," said Evan. "I read an excellent bit of fanfic last year in which Darcy fell in love with Bingley instead of Lizzy Bennet."

"You read *Pride and Prejudice* fanfic?" asked Lindsay.

Evan shrugged. "I would have paired Darcy with Wickham, personally. I bet they'd have a lot of angry sex."

"How are we talking about gay sex in Jane Austen?" asked Lauren.

"Look, I reread the book last month, it gave me ideas," said Evan. "It totally holds up, by the way. If you haven't read it since high school, I recommend giving it another look."

Paige laughed, glad for a distracting conversation.

Josh watched the sunset from the conference room window, but he wasn't even that mad about it.

In the five days since Penny had first presented the medical manufacturer case to Josh, he'd dug up a number of old cases that generally showed courts ruled in favor of the manufacturer more often than not. He'd worked out that the key to holding the company accountable was to prove the company knowingly sold a bad product or had at least knowingly cut corners.

Penny had managed to find some examples of negligence, including the factory floor being monitored by company flunkies who didn't understand manufacturing and parts being purchased from overseas on the cheap without anyone bothering to verify that the parts were safe to use.

"We're standing on solid ground," Josh told her. "I found this case in Pennsylvania in which several patients sued a medical manufacturer because there had been electrical issues with a sleep monitoring device. The court found for the prosecution in that case because they managed to prove that the manufacturer had been using cheap parts to save money, but the wires were corroded. I think the fact that all of the people who worked for that manufacturer were making exorbitant salaries and the company was using cheap parts out of sheer greed also helped convince the jury that the manufacturer was at fault."

Penny nodded. "Good work. I agree, there's definitely a case here. Criminally negligent homicide will be hard to prove, but I think we should go for it. I don't believe these guys wanted anyone to die, but they had to know that using cheap parts in medical devices could lead to injuries. I don't know about you, but if I had to get a hip replaced, I'd want the highest quality replacement parts, you know?"

"Yeah, definitely."

Penny wrote some notes while Josh looked on. Then he said, "Can I ask you a weird question?"

"Shoot."

He took a deep breath. "What made you leave DCL and go to the DA's office?"

Penny looked up and smiled. "Honestly, a lot of it was that I hated most of the sleazes Provost represents."

Josh nodded. "I've only been working here a few months, but I have to say, my first experience in court was defending a guy who deserves to be out of business. And we're currently representing a real estate developer who I kind of want to punch in the face. Is that a bad thing to say?"

Penny laughed. "No. My first year, we defended both an insider trader and a politician who got caught using campaign money to buy presents for his mistress. They're not all winners."

Josh pointed to his notes. "This case, this is more what I was looking to do when I studied law."

Penny nodded. "When I worked here, Provost had another associate who was whipsmart, but it quickly became clear she hated the actual practice of law. I think she actually only went to law school because she wanted to get into politics. She quit after six months to go work for the mayor's reelection campaign. Which, you know, good for her, but she's drowning in law school debt. I always tell people, don't go to law school unless you want to be a lawyer. It's not worth it otherwise."

Josh laughed. "I went to law school with a few of those, too. And that's excellent advice. But why the DA's office?"

"It was a big pay cut, but the work is so much more rewarding. I got to be second chair on the Saperstein case last year."

Josh whistled. That case had made big headlines. Saperstein

was a television producer and serial rapist who had preyed on young starlets for decades before anyone found the guts to prosecute him. He'd been found guilty and was currently serving a twenty-year sentence upstate. "That's amazing. It must have been rewarding to put him away."

"It was. I was proud of my work on that case." She glanced at her notes. "Are you thinking about switching teams and becoming a prosecutor?"

"The thought crossed my mind. I want to stick this out for at least a year, but I have days when I want to quit. It's a lot of hours and, yeah, Provost defends some sleazy people. But this case is really interesting and, you know, I like being able to pay down my debt every month."

Penny smiled. "Well, just know that we could use someone with your research skills at the DA's office. And Provost says you write a mean brief."

Josh laughed. "I suppose that's true."

"Your help here has been invaluable. If you ever want to join the dark side, I'd be happy to put in a word for you with the DA. He is usually not a part of the hiring process directly, but he likes to have final say. And you'd have to work your way up. I work in major crimes now, but I was stuck in misdemeanors for a while, mostly issuing fines to kids who stayed in the parks after they closed. So it's not all glitz and glamour."

Josh laughed. "I was going to make an argument like, 'Well at least you're helping people,' but I didn't know until just now that the parks ever closed, so probably you weren't doing a lot to help people in those cases."

"Yeah, no, not really. Every now and then a trafficking case would get thrown my way, and those were kind of interesting. One of my law school classmates works for the Department of Labor and mostly prosecutes people who defraud the unemployment benefits system, but even then, a lot of the defendants in her cases are people who filled out a form incorrectly and aren't actually guilty of fraud. So I'm not saying working for the city is the best job in the world. And the hours are just as bad most of the time. And there's less money in it. But I do get to go after bad guys sometimes, and that is very rewarding."

"And, see, this is why I haven't quit this job yet. There is no perfect job, is there?"

"In law? Probably not." But Penny smiled. It was clear from talking to her that she loved her job.

And so did Paige. Why that thought popped into Josh's head *now* was a mystery. But Josh knew she loved working at the Cat Café. An easy solution to their relationship strife might have been to talk her into leaving her job so she didn't work for Lauren anymore, but Josh hadn't even offered it up because he knew Paige loved that job. Josh didn't really love working for Provost and DCL, but he thought it was a stepping stone to a job he would love. Maybe the DA's office wasn't the right place for him either, but if he paid his dues and got enough experience, there was a potential future in which he started his own firm and had complete discretion over which cases he took.

"You've given me a lot to think about," he said to Penny.

She smiled. "Can I confess something?"

"Please do."

"I find you really attractive. Maybe it's just proximity and the fact that you're the first guy I've worked with in a while under the age of fifty."

Josh met Penny's gaze. She really was gorgeous. And Paige still hadn't reached out, so that seemed to be over. There wasn't any reason why he couldn't...

He leaned forward and so did Penny. But just as their lips were about to touch, an image of Paige popped into his head. No, he wasn't done with Paige yet. He still wanted her, was still willing to try to win her over.

He jerked back. "I'm so sorry," he said. "You're smart and beautiful and I really appreciate you talking to me about jobs, but my heart is tied up with someone else. I can't do this to you or to her."

Penny smiled ruefully. "Yeah. I figured you were too good to be true."

"I mean, really, any other time...but I've got this 'it's complicated' situation with a really wonderful woman, and well..."

"You don't have to explain. I hate that your honesty makes you more likable, though."

"I'll try to lie more, if it makes you feel better."

She laughed. "Nah, that's fine. Let's get back to the case."

CHAPTER 23

PAIGE HAD A HABIT OF looking around as she locked up the café, which is how she saw Josh coming. He was clearly lost in thought, a bulky pair of headphones covering his ears. She probably could have slipped into one of the stores on the block and avoided him entirely. Instead, she paused with her hand on the door handle for a long moment, and when she moved again, he was right there.

He said her name.

"Hi," she said. "I was just locking up."

"I'm having dinner with Lauren and Caleb." He glanced at his watch. "I'm early for a change."

For days, Paige had been wallowing in her regrets and wondering if a moment like this would ever come to pass and what she would say. It was inevitable they'd run into each other again, she just hadn't expected it to happen so soon. Part of her wanted to plead with him to take her back, but she refrained. "How are you?"

"Fine. Busy. The same. You?" Josh's body was stiff, his shoulders raised.

"I'm all right."

Josh suddenly laughed and shook his head. "Can we, I don't know, call a truce? Given that you and my sister are close friends, I think the odds of us running into each other remain high, and as much fun as this awkwardness is, I'd really rather we can talk to each other like people who aren't creepy strangers."

Paige felt some of the tension seep out of her body. "Yes, all right."

"Cool. So, like, how are you, really?"

Not really sure what he wanted to hear, Paige said, "I *am* fine. We did another edition of Crafts and Cats on Sunday that ended up being a big hit."

"Cool, cool. I'm on a case at work that I actually find interesting. I'm helping the city go after an evil corporation instead of defending one this time."

"That's great."

"And Caleb is making some Middle Eastern dish tonight with a name I can't remember or likely pronounce, but that's still pretty exciting." Josh smiled.

Paige was surprised to find her heart pounding. Being this close to Josh and having what amounted to a fairly normal conversation was like the worst temptation. But instead of dropping to her knees and begging him to take her back, she said, "I lived in Dubai for a while."

"Oh, right. They probably have a lot of Middle Eastern food there."

"They do, but there are a lot of American expats in Dubai, so they have pretty much anything you'd want."

They both stood there silently for a while, so clearly they had not found the key to unlocking the awkwardness.

She sighed. "I'm so sorry about...everything. I miss you, for what it's worth."

"Yeah," he said. "I miss you, too."

And then she decided to be honest. "I'm still thinking through some things. I just... I realized that I have some things I have to figure out for myself. But I hope that you and I can be friends."

He slid his headphones into the tote bag he had around his shoulder, probably for something to do with his hands. "Breakup still on, in other words." He looked up and had a rueful smile on his face.

"Yeah. I'm sorry. Again."

"It's okay. Some things were not meant to be."

In that moment, Paige could think of no good reason for that to be the case, except that something just...didn't feel quite right. She was being a coward, she knew.

"It's good to know, though," said Josh, "that when Lauren throws her annual New Year's party, something I've been hearing about for many years but never been able to attend, that I'll at least be able to say hi to you and ask about work."

"Sure."

"So you'll tell me some story about a cat named after some literary heroine, and it will be unspeakably adorable, and I'll laugh. And I'll complain about work to you, because even though I know it's not one of my more endearing traits, it's what I think about most of the time. And we'll have some wine and smile like our hearts aren't breaking and give each other a peck at midnight, and everything will be fine."

"Josh." Lord. Her heart was breaking now. The sadness in Josh's voice was hard to reconcile.

This was on Paige and she knew it. He still cared about her, but she knew, given what he went through with Megan, that he needed someone willing to fight for him, willing to stick with him through challenging times, he needed someone willing to go all in on the relationship, and she was not convinced she was that person, not when the idea of giving herself to another person, of shaking up her life so much, made her nauseous.

He shot her a lopsided smile. "It'll get easier with time. And, hey, it's probably for the best, right? I don't know why I thought I had any business trying to maintain a relationship during my first year as an associate."

"That's not..." But Paige didn't want to get into a whole discussion right now. "Is it too much of a cliché to say it's not you, it's me?"

Josh barked out a laugh. "Well, look. If you think things through and you decide that maybe you'd be willing to give it a go with me again, you know where to find me."

Why did he have to be so charming and cute? "You'll be my first call."

He laughed again. "I hope so. I better get to this big Middle Eastern dish before it gets cold. I'll see you around, Paige." Then he pulled out a key and went into the residential part of the building.

Once he was gone, Paige leaned against the Cat Café's front window.

What was she doing?

Her whole life, Paige had always been the practical one. The one who had her shit together. She'd gotten good grades in school, she'd played two sports, she'd gotten into a good college. When she'd gotten that first job out of college, she'd been so good at it that she could retire now if she really wanted to.

But she *didn't* have her shit together. Not really. She applied logic and reason to work, and she'd tried to impose them on love, too.

Business wasn't even entirely rational. If she needed to put on a conference, she toured hotels and convention centers and let the staff wine and dine her and offer her anything she could possibly want for her event. When she found the right place, she got this gut feeling. There was nothing rational about a gut feeling, but in a moment, she could see exactly how everything would play out. She knew she was in control. And she'd been assuming that if she let enough guys wine and dine her, she'd get a similar gut feeling about one, and that would be the guy she married.

She was good at work but not at love. She kept looking at romantic relationships like a problem to be solved, like she could just collect data and put it in a spreadsheet and some back-end code would tell her the answer.

Behind everything Paige was feeling was some old vision she had of how her life would play out. When she'd settled back in New York, she'd expected to find Mr. Right. But now she wondered if she'd ever given any of her internet dates a chance. Some of them had been wrong for her, but some had been perfectly nice guys that she just hadn't connected with. None of them had ever given her that gut feeling she'd expected. And because of that, she'd never judged any of them fit to weave into her well-ordered life where she didn't have to compromise or change anything. She'd imagined they would fit together and everything would be comfortable and perfect. But maybe that wasn't how love worked.

And Josh, sweet, funny Josh, had thrown all of her ideas about what her life should be on their head. He made her feel things she'd never felt before. And she'd wasted a lot of time coming up with reasons why they *shouldn't* be together without letting herself think about all the reasons that they *should*.

———

The inside of Lauren's apartment smelled delicious. Lauren led him over to the little table off the kitchen. A huge cast-iron skillet sat in the middle of the table. It looked to be filled with poached eggs laying on a bed of chunky tomato sauce.

"It's called shakshuka," Caleb said. "Poached eggs in a tomato-based sauce with lots of vegetables. I added feta, too."

"They taught you how to make this in cooking class?" Josh sat at the table and let the spices in the sauce tickle his nose.

"No, actually, Lindsay sent me the recipe. I asked for her suggestions for some more challenging meals. This actually wasn't that hard. It's mostly throwing stuff in a skillet and letting it simmer for a bit."

"It smells great."

As Lauren sat at the table, she said, "Is everything okay? You look weird."

"What does that mean?"

She shrugged. "I don't know. I can't read your face."

"I just ran into Paige."

Understanding dawned. "Ah. How was that?"

"Okay. Awkward. But we called a truce and agreed to be friends. So I guess that's it."

Lauren frowned. "I don't understand."

Josh glanced at Caleb, who busied himself with dishing out portions of his shakshuka to everyone. Then he turned back to Lauren. "What don't you understand?"

"I will admit to being weirded out by you and Paige at first, but the more I thought about it, the more it made sense to me. I figured you kids had what it took to make it. I mean, she's crazy about you."

"Apparently not."

"How do you feel about that?"

Josh was tempted to snap at her—*What are you, my shrink?*—but he thought better of it. She was just trying to help. "I mean, it's fine. Gives me time to focus back on work, I guess."

"Doesn't all work and no play do something to a man?" Caleb said as he settled into his chair.

"I tried," Josh said. "I told her how I felt. I told her I wanted to be with her. But I can't be the only one willing to put myself out there."

Caleb nodded. "No, I know." He tasted a spoonful of sauce. "Oh, man. That's good. I'm a great cook."

Lauren laughed. "Thanks, honey. It's good that you impress yourself."

"Do you not like it?"

"No, it's great. You *are* a good cook."

Caleb looked a little smug as he ate another spoonful. Then he said, "Josh, I know we're not, like, super close friends of anything, but can I give you a little advice?"

"Sure." Josh respected Caleb and knew he'd been divorced shortly before he met Lauren. If anyone could understand what Josh was currently going through, it was Caleb.

"Don't repeat my mistakes. My first marriage ended because I was so self-absorbed I didn't notice my ex was unhappy. I was trying to get a business off the ground at the time, so I completely understand work taking over your life. And it's not really worth it in the long run. Not that I wish I was still married to my first wife." He looked at Lauren. "What I meant to say was…"

"Caleb, it's fine," said Lauren, taking his hand where it sat on the table.

"Anyway. Work is important, and if you've got a career you're passionate about, that's awesome. But don't let it be at the expense of a well-rounded life. I honestly think that working more reasonable hours in a shared practice and marrying Lauren are the two smartest decisions I ever made."

Lauren smiled, her cheeks going pink.

"Gross," said Josh, though he laughed.

Lauren stuck out her tongue at Josh.

"My point," Caleb said, "is that finding someone to share your life with makes everything else in your life better. Which, yeah, that's pretty cheesy, but I'm serious."

"I know. And I miss Paige. But I'm not going to chase after her if she's not that into me."

"Fair," said Caleb.

"But I take your point. Actually, part of why I'm able to have dinner with you tonight is that we hired a bunch of new paralegals, so I'm able to delegate some of my work. Including anything related to your real estate developer friend, which only makes me feel slightly less guilty."

"That's something. I recognize that you have to pay your dues. My intern year right out of vet school was brutal. I worked the night shift a lot and we got a lot of hard-luck cases at odd hours of the morning. But it got easier after that first year. So, don't base decision on what's going on now, but on what you think the future will look like."

Josh nodded, knowing that was good advice.

Caleb's big yellow dog Hank jogged over and started sniffing around the table with his tail wagging excitedly. As he nosed around Josh's shoes, Josh said, "I don't think dogs like spicy tomato sauce."

"He won't be satisfied with that until he's able to assess it for himself," said Caleb.

Molly the cat seemed to take a cue from Hank and started winding her way around chair legs. Then both animals seemed to decide that, not only was there nothing worth eating on the floor, but that the spices from the shakshuka did not smell so edible after all. Both retreated to the rug near the sofa. Hank flopped over to lie down, and Molly curled up near his belly.

"I can't get over that they're friends," said Josh.

"I know. I figured they'd grudgingly tolerate each other. But they nap together like that all the time." Lauren shrugged. "How's George?"

"He's good. Caught a bug the other day."

"Sure," said Lauren.

"A housefly got into my apartment. George saw it and jumped in the air and chomped down on it."

"See that? You did need a cat. He saved you from that nefarious insect."

Josh laughed. "Yes. Saved my life, that cat did."

CHAPTER 24

THE LOOK ON JOSH'S FACE as he'd walked away from the Cat Café the last time they'd seen each other had seared itself on Paige's mind. He'd looked so disappointed. She deeply regretted not saying anything about how she really felt. She should have been willing to take the risk, especially after she realized that Josh was exactly the man she should be with. Instead, she'd let him leave thinking she didn't care enough to fight for him. She did care, but she hadn't been able to say anything.

Maybe it would be better to just not date for a while, she reasoned. She was clearly terrible at it.

She tried to move on with her life over the next few days. She hosted another Cats and Crafts to great acclaim that weekend. The Cat Café finally received the T-shirts Evan had designed to sell in the store, and the café had sold so many Lauren would have to buy more soon, which was exciting. She'd had drinks with her friends one night and they'd whined about being single and then made fun of Lauren for her happy marriage.

As Paige and Lauren closed down the café one evening, Lauren ran a vacuum over one of the sofas and then stood up with a sigh. "I wonder if I could hire someone just to clean out the litter boxes."

Paige wiped down a table and glanced at Lauren. "That seems like a terrible job."

"I've been reluctant to ask the counter staff to do it. And don't feel like this is me asking you either. Maybe we could get, like, a cat maintenance person or something. I don't know what you'd call the position."

"I don't want to handle cat poop either, but is there a reason you suddenly don't want to do it anymore?"

"Caleb tells me pregnant women shouldn't handle litter boxes because of the possibility of toxoplasmosis. Really, I should just make him come over here and take care of the boxes."

Paige almost couldn't believe what she was hearing. "Oh my god. You're pregnant?"

Lauren closed her eyes for a moment. "I mean...yes."

Paige squealed.

"Only like twelve weeks. We weren't going to tell anyone for another month. But I keep forgetting that my immediate family members are the only ones who know. And our doctor, I guess, but—"

Paige cut Lauren off with a hug. "I'm so happy for you."

Lauren laughed softly and hugged Paige back. "Thank you. I mean, we planned it, and I'm still kind of adjusting to the news."

"I didn't know you even wanted kids."

"Turns out I do. It was a surprise to me as well, but once Caleb and I started talking about it, suddenly I really wanted a baby. I can't explain it."

"Well, I'm thrilled for you, then."

"Thanks. Don't tell anyone. I want to do it myself."

"Of course. And I can clean the cat boxes, or the staff and I can make some kind of schedule."

"Okay. I mean, it's a different scale than just cleaning out Bianca's box and you have to do it twice a day here. I didn't like having anyone do it because it is a fairly gross job. But if you guys divide it up, it's not so bad."

"Have you been doing it yourself the last few weeks?"

"No. Caleb does it whenever he comes over here, but he's getting grumpy about it and keeps mumbling about not being on my payroll." Lauren grinned. "I told him the staff could take care of it." She looked at the sofa. "Well, this is as hair-free as it will get. You want to close this down and then split the last muffin with me?"

"Sure."

As they finished cleaning, Mr. Willoughby tried to make a break for it, but Paige deftly caught him. After giving him a few extra pets and watching him settle in for a nap on the sofa, she and Lauren closed down the cat room. Then Lauren grabbed a paper bag from the counter, which had already been cleaned. The bag turned out to hold the lone blueberry muffin that was the only pastry leftover from the day.

"The cinnamon chip muffins from Pierre's have been a big hit lately," Lauren said. "And the carrot cream cheese ones, although those are basically just carrot cake."

The blueberry ones were good, too, so Paige dove in.

"Can I ask you something?" Lauren said.

"Sure."

"How are you doing with what happened with you and Josh? He said you broke up for good."

"What did he tell you?" Paige asked warily.

"Not much. You guys ran into each other before he came over for dinner the other night, right? He said it was awkward."

Paige nodded. She didn't want to talk about this, but she thought maybe it would be good. "He... Well, you know."

Lauren smiled. "I don't know. That's why I asked. I don't need a lot of detail or anything. I just wanted to make sure you're okay."

"I will be." Paige took a deep breath. "Honestly? It sucks."

"Yeah?"

"I don't know what's wrong with me. But you were totally right that Josh deserves someone who is all the way there for him, and I wasn't sure I could be that person. I probably overthought everything. In some ways, he's perfect for me. But falling in love with someone... It really shakes up your life."

Lauren laughed softly. "Yeah. I know a little bit about that." Lauren ate a bite of her muffin. "So what now?"

"I don't know." Paige sighed. She knew this was on her now. Josh had made his feelings clear. "Well, I've been wondering if breaking up was a terrible mistake. He keeps reminding me his present work situation is not forever. It's not great that he's working for the evil real estate developer, but I know his heart is in the right place."

"Okay."

"What was a huge deal was that he's your brother. And I love you. And I didn't want to do anything to jeopardize my friendship with you. Sisters before misters, right? And I worried that if there was tension between me and you, that it could drive a wedge between me and everyone. Evan told me not to worry about that, but, like, you and Evan and Lindsay have these long histories, and I just... I didn't want to jeopardize any of that. I didn't want any fallout to make me leave this job. I love this job. I love you. I didn't want to lose any of it."

Lauren nodded slowly. "I know. I never meant to make you think that anything I felt about you and Josh would impact your place here or as my friend. Josh yelled at me for making you think that, so I tried to tell you that it would all work out, but I guess I wasn't very clear."

"No, you were. I believe you."

"At first, it just hit me very strangely. I don't know how to explain it. In my head, Josh is still, like, fifteen, and I couldn't picture the two of you together. And I worried about him. I didn't think he was ready for a relationship again, but maybe I was wrong about that."

Paige nodded. She didn't have siblings, but she tried to imagine how she would feel if she did and one of them dated one of her best friends. It would probably be weird. And she knew Lauren was trying to protect her brother from further heartache.

"It's not even that, though. The problem is me. *I'm* the one who ended it because suddenly it was all too much and I freaked out. Being with someone in a real relationship requires schedule shifts, requires letting someone into your home, into your life, in a way that I wasn't ready for. And I thought I could just go back to my regularly scheduled life, but it turns out I can't. Josh shook everything up, but now I can't figure out how to put it all back."

Lauren was quiet for a moment, like she was turning that all over. "I'm certainly no expert, but one thing I've learned in the last couple of years is that, although I don't really believe in fate or there being one perfect person in the world for everyone, I do think that once you've met someone really amazing, your life is never the same. I mean, Caleb and I hated each other when we first met, and he still managed to change my life entirely."

"You think that's what happened with me and Josh?"

"I don't know. Only you can answer that. But I saw how upset Josh was when you two broke up, and I've seen how sad you have been over the last few days, which is why I asked this question to begin with. If you guys are happy together, then that's all that matters."

That did go a long way toward making Paige feel better. "But what about you and our friends and everything? What if things get weird?"

"I mean, say you do get together," Lauren said after popping another bit of muffin into her mouth. "You'll have fights. You'll probably pull me into them a few times because I'm the only one who knows you both really well. Or, you know, you'll have a fight and I'll side with one or the other of you and it will get awkward. And, yeah, you might even break up. But if there's a chance you won't? Please don't let me be the thing that keeps you from trying."

Paige nodded. "I don't like not knowing what the future holds."

"I know."

"I don't like that he's working for the real estate developer who tried to close the Cat Café, nor that it seems like he kind of hates his job. That's a lot to deal with."

Lauren nodded.

Paige looked off into the distance, hoping the answer would make itself clear. "If I could know that Josh and I will be fine, it'd go a long way toward making the decision about what to do easier."

"Unfortunately, you can't know that. There are no guarantees in life. If you had asked me two years ago, I never would have expected to be married and expecting my first baby now. But that's kind of the beauty of it, don't you think? We don't know what will happen, so we have to take each experience as it comes."

"Spoken like a smug married."

Lauren laughed. "You sound like Evan."

Paige smiled, but she felt sad now. She'd really bungled her last conversation with Josh, and she completely understood why he was mad. "You know, I realized when Josh and I were having that last talk, he's kind of perfect for me."

Lauren tilted her head. "He might just be, but I still haven't reconciled that he's gone through puberty. He's still that annoying kid who pulled my hair and fought with me over the TV remote."

"He's a grown-up now, you know."

"I don't need the details."

Paige laughed. "Okay. But what do I do now? Do you think it's too late? Should I try to win him back or...?"

"I don't think it's too late. What is it you truly want?"

"I want him back. I want for us to be together." Paige didn't even hesitate. She knew in her gut that was the right answer. She could date a hundred guys she met through her phone and never find a guy she connected with like she did with Josh, a guy she loved like she did Josh.

"And you're all in? You're willing to fight for him? Because it might be hard to get him to trust you now."

"Yes. One hundred percent. I'm all in." And Paige meant it. Josh had shaken up her life, but she welcomed it. She wanted things to be shaken up. She wanted to fall in love and she wanted to have a partner in life and she wanted to find some great apartment for the two of them and their cats and she wanted to break right out of her comfort zone and find the kind of happiness that Lauren and Caleb found. The kind of happiness she knew she and Josh could find together.

"Okay." Lauren nodded and grinned. "Let's make a plan, then. What do you think you need to do to get him back?"

"Are you serious?"

"Yeah. I want both of you to be happy. So let's make a plan to make that happen."

Paige nodded and thought about it for a moment. "He needs to know that I would risk something to be with him."

Lauren nodded. "In other words, you need to show him you're all in."

"Yeah. But things were really awkward between us, and I know I've jerked him around a little. How do I even get him to talk to me?"

"Regardless of what happens, you are my friend and he is my brother and you will definitely be invited to things together. So you'll have to get used to seeing each other either way."

"Might one of these events be coming up soon?"

"Caleb mentioned maybe wanting to get some friends together to celebrate his birthday. We celebrated plenty when we went out of town last week, but I could put together a dinner party or something."

"That seems reasonable."

"You have to promise not to make a scene, of course."

"I would never."

"Right." Lauren laughed. "I mean, I don't want to give you the key to figuring out how to get back in my brother's pants or anything, because gross, but I think if you really want him? You have to be totally honest about how you feel. So what do you want to do? I mean, I guess you could just go over to his place and tell him how you feel, but—"

"No, it has to be bigger than that. I need to prove myself." Paige thought for a moment. "I have an idea."

The only question now was whether Josh would be willing to listen to her.

Aisha, another associate at DCL whom Josh had been working with, stuck her head in his door.

"Hey, kid, I just wanted to let you know in person that I've given notice and my last day is next Friday."

"Oh, I'm sorry to hear that," said Josh. "It's been great working with you. What are you doing next?"

"I got a job at the ACLU! It's a bit of a pay cut, but it's my dream job. I'll be working mostly on women's rights issues."

Josh nodded, feeling like that was familiar. "Congratulations! I'm thrilled for you." He smiled. "Can I ask why you came to work here if the ACLU was your first choice?"

Aisha smiled and walked into Josh's office. She dropped into one of his chairs. "I'd been thinking about going to work for a nonprofit when I graduated, but I also wanted to pay off my loans."

"I hear you."

"I've learned a ton from Provost, but I don't think this is the right place for me. I got into law to help people. My last case? I helped defend a grocery store chain against accusations of price gouging. And honestly? They were gouging on some items. Six bucks for a box of cereal is insane."

"How did you even defend that?"

"Well, it didn't end up in court, but the defense we were working on when the chain finally came up with a deal the attorney general could live with was that the store had to increase prices because of supply chain issues. And it is true that distributors charge more to deliver to stores in the city and that there was an interruption in the dairy supply chain after some kind of bovine illness broke out at a huge dairy farm upstate. But the chain was mostly just greedy. And I'm tired of defending greedy people in court."

Josh nodded. "Oh, man. I so agree. I actually have a couple of cases in the queue that I'm excited about, but my very first time in court was on the Giardino case."

Aisha winced. "That was a doozy. Giardino should be in jail."

"I know. And now Provost is representing a real estate

developer who wants to kick people out of their homes so he can build luxury condos."

"Well, listen, if you ever want to break free from this place, give me a call. I'll send you my personal email and cell phone before I leave. Provost actually said you were one of the better associates who has come along in a while."

"Wow, really? He said that?"

"Yeah. I remember because I was a little offended." Aisha laughed. "It's all good, though. I can't be mad because this new job is going to be amazing."

After Aisha left, Josh thought about Penny at the DA's office and the medical manufacturer case. He'd enjoyed working on that case mostly because he knew the outcome had the potential to make people's lives better. And he was about to start work on a new case in which DCL was representing a group of local businesses who were suing a big cable company for not honoring their advertising contracts, and though it was still early in the discovery process, it sure was starting to look like the cable company had been suppressing some of the ads because of racism in the ad department. So he was actually looking forward to bringing that suit against the cable company.

Josh had studied criminal law in law school, probably because he watched too much *Law & Order* in college, but he'd long pictured himself working as a prosecutor. Through circumstances—and a little nepotism; he had an uncle who had gone to law school with one of the DCL partners—he'd ended up with this job at a huge, prestigious firm with a great reputation. Some of his law school classmates would have walked over their own mothers to get this job. But Josh knew deep down that this was not a good fit for him. He was a little jealous of Aisha's job at the ACLU.

But the good news was that he had options. He'd finish this year at DCL and pay those dues, and then maybe he'd cash in a favor. He'd had a professor in law school who had said once that defense attorneys made the best prosecutors because they understood how the defense thought.

The point was, his career was just starting and the possibilities were endless.

He nodded to himself, happy to have decided something.

He still missed Paige, though. He'd gotten takeout from the Italian place near the office for lunch that day, and the mere sight of the restaurant's logo on the takeout bag was enough to remind him of her sitting at the corner of his desk, eating and chatting and laughing with him, looking gorgeous and happy. Sometimes he still imagined a future where she snuck dinner into him on nights when he had to work late and they stole kisses in his office, and after, they'd go home together.

He shook his head. That was nothing more than a dream. It was over. She'd made her feelings clear.

He finished work for the day at a reasonable hour, took the subway home, and pet George as he reheated some leftovers for dinner. He was trying to discourage George from getting onto the kitchen counters—George seemed to in particular like licking the kitchen faucet, which was weird—but right now he needed some friendly comfort more than he wanted to shoo George away.

Now that he knew Paige would probably never be coming here again, this apartment felt empty.

A few minutes later as Josh sat on his sofa and twirled noodles around his fork, George hopped up on the sofa and settled against Josh's thigh.

"It's just you and me, buddy. What do you think of that?"

George yawned and fell asleep, which wasn't much of an answer.

Josh sighed and turned on the TV.

CHAPTER 25

CALEB'S BIRTHDAY PARTY WAS AT a barbecue place in Gowanus tucked into a side street. Josh found it easily enough. A huge mural of a pig wearing sunglasses and riding a motorcycle took up an otherwise blank wall next to the restaurant entrance.

He was surprised to see Paige waiting at the entrance.

"Hi," he said as he approached. She had on a pair of cat-eye sunglasses that were cute but obscured her eyes and made it hard for him to read her expression. "Is everyone else inside, or..."

"Actually, I asked Lauren to invite you here a little early so that I could talk to you."

What was all this about? "Oh-kay."

"Take a walk with me."

"Okay."

Josh didn't know whether to hope. Part of him dared to, because he'd missed her from somewhere deep in his soul. He'd known they'd see each other here—Lauren had warned him of that in advance—but he figured it would just be like the last time they saw each other. It'd be awkward, he'd make jokes to deflect from how uncomfortable it was to be around her without being *with* her, he'd pine for her but pretend he didn't, then they'd retreat to their separate homes.

"Did I just see you get out of a cab?" Paige asked.

"Yeah. This neighborhood is all new territory to me, and I didn't trust myself not to get lost if I took the subway."

Paige laughed. "All right. You probably missed this, then. Let me introduce you to another Brooklyn landmark." Paige led Josh down the block and paused when they stepped onto a short bridge. "This, my friend, is the Gowanus Canal."

"Oh." The canal itself was almost picturesque. Most of the buildings beside it were industrial, old warehouses, most of which had likely been converted into apartments. The water was quiet, placid. But the smell was... something else. "It's...pungent."

"Yeah. I can't even argue like this is something we Brooklynites are proud of. It's polluted as hell."

"If it didn't smell like eggs someone left to bake in the sun, this spot might even be pretty." There was something out of time about this spot, but wow, that smell. "Nope, it smells to gross. I hope this was not where you wanted to go."

"No. There's a *great* ice cream parlor just up the block. Are you gonna ruin your dinner if you have a little ice cream now?"

"No. There's always room for ice cream."

It wasn't that Josh didn't appreciate this little tour of Brooklyn, but he wanted Paige to cut to the chase. His patience wore thinner as they walked up the block.

The line at the ice cream parlor wasn't too long, but there were enough people in front of them that Josh had plenty of time to peruse the lengthy menu. Today, there were sixteen flavors available, plus two nondairy options. "Maple bacon ice cream?" he said.

"I don't recommend. I mean, ask for a taste so you can have the experience, but it works better theoretically than it does in practice. The bacon isn't crispy enough and ends up with this weird leathery texture."

Josh grimaced. "Hmm, okay. How much of this menu have you tried?"

"A lot. They have another location near my apartment."

"Okay. I guess I'm just going to have to sample some things."

Choosing an ice cream flavor was an important task, and Josh tried half the flavors before settling on the Fluffernutter. Paige ordered what she said was her favorite, a blue cotton candy ice cream. The ice cream parlor had a crowded seating area inside, but their backyard was nearly empty, probably because it was so hot. But this moment seemed to call for quiet more than air conditioning, and there was a breeze that made the heat tolerable.

Once they were seated, Paige said, "See, I know the way to your heart is through your stomach."

Josh ate a heaping spoonful of ice cream and nodded. "This is so good."

"So, I brought you here because I wanted to tell you that we should be doing *this* a lot more."

"I agree. You want to take me to eat my way across Brooklyn, I'm on board."

Paige laughed. "I meant, we should go out with each other."

Josh paused with the spoon halfway to his mouth. "What?"

"I don't know about you, but I've been miserable these last few weeks. But I knew that what you needed, what you deserved, was to have someone in your life who was all in. You need someone who wants to be by your side, who is willing to fight for you. After Lauren told me about Megan, I couldn't get out of my head that you needed a girlfriend who wouldn't bail at the first sign of difficulty. But then that's exactly what I did. So I get if you don't trust me."

Josh was having trouble parsing what he was hearing. His heart started to pound. He'd been missing Paige something awful, and he'd almost gone over to her place a dozen times to ask for forgiveness. But he'd also known that he couldn't put himself through what happened with Megan again. Being with Paige was magic in a way being with Megan never quite had been, so he'd been willing to give her a chance to prove that she wasn't Megan, but then she'd bailed.

"I don't understand," he said.

"I made a mistake in letting you go. I'm all in now, if you still are."

And there it was. "Are you sure?"

"Yes. I've thought about it almost nonstop for three weeks. If you're still in, I am. And I knew I had to come up with a way to show you that I was. So I took a risk. I told Lauren to tell you the party started an hour earlier than it did. You are surprisingly punctual, you know that?"

Josh shook his head and laughed. "What?"

"I wasn't sure if you'd talk to me if it was just me, so this was a little bit of an ambush, but I wanted to show you I was for real.

I mean, it's just been me in charge of my life for such a long time, and I didn't realize how much I've been guarding that space. You coming into my life shook up all of my ideas of what I wanted and how I lived. I thought that I could go back to how things were before I met you, but I couldn't. You were too much a part of my life. So I'm telling you, I am here for you 100 percent, if you'll still have me."

Was this what Josh wanted? Yes, if he was honest. He'd wanted her to come to him and tell him that it had all been a mistake. And he needed Paige to tell him that whatever hang-ups she had were behind her. They'd probably have issues and struggles in the future, but if she was willing to fight for and with him, they could get through them.

"Are you sure?" Josh asked.

"Yes, absolutely. I was trying to come up with some big romantic gesture to convince you I was being honest and this was what I wanted, but all I could think of was food and Brooklyn and... I don't know. Am I screwing this up?"

Josh smiled. "No."

She smiled back. "Oh. Okay."

"All I ever wanted, Paige, was for you to be honest about how you felt. I wanted you to push past all those excuses and dig into what you really wanted. If you want to be with me, then that's great. I still want to be with you. But only if you're all in."

"I am. I'm all in. And you? Are you still all in?"

Josh grinned. "I am still all in."

Paige smiled and then surprised the hell out of him by leaning across the table and planting a kiss on his lips. He loved that she was sometimes shy and unsure of herself when it came to physical affection, but there was no hesitation now. They kissed, and Josh reached up to cup her cheek.

And it was like coming home.

"If you think about it," Paige said after they parted, "you and I did break up. That was pretty much the worst thing that could have happened. And everything else in my life survived. I still have a job. Lauren and I are closer than ever. But I don't have you. That's really the greatest loss in all this. And you know what? That's the part I may not survive. I mean, I'll live, obviously, but my life has a lot less...joy in it, if you're not a part of it."

Josh reached across the table with his free hand and grabbed hers. "I mean, as love confessions go, I give that a B minus."

Paige laughed. "What I'm saying is that breaking up with you was a huge mistake and I've regretted it every moment since I did it and I love you and will you please take me back?"

"Yes. But only because you asked nicely."

Paige reached across the table and ruffled his hair. "You're a jerk sometimes, you know that?"

He grinned. "Lauren tells me that a few times a week." Then he took a deep breath. "I didn't want to break up, but I couldn't go on feeling like I was the only one who cared enough to be in the relationship. I'm glad you changed your mind, and I hope this means that we will live happily ever after and all of that. I love you, too, and I've missed you every day since the last time we spoke."

Paige let out a little squeal and leaned across the table to kiss Josh again. He laughed as she did it, and it made his lips vibrate, but then he sank into the kiss with her. He felt giddy. She loved him! They loved each other! And now they were kissing in an ice cream parlor like a couple of teenagers on a first date, but he didn't care about that. What he cared about was that Paige was here. Everything felt lighter than it had in weeks.

"We should probably eat our ice cream before it melts," she said.

He laughed. "Fair enough."

"So, uh, how are things?"

He smiled and ate some ice cream. Then he said, "It's been an interesting few weeks at work, which I say not because I want to talk about it, but that it...put some things in perspective. I mean, this is not all going to be easy going forward. I've got two parale-gals doing some of my busywork now, but mostly because my boss put me on a pro bono project that, actually, I'm enjoying in a perverse way? We're going after an evil corporation instead of defending it, basically. But that's not..." He stopped talking and shook his head. "My point is, I'm going to have to work late nights, probably for the foreseeable future, because I think odds are good that when I finish my first year at DCL, I'm going to find a new job. I've got offers already, even."

"Really?"

"Yeah. We can get into it later. I have a *lot* to tell you. But now we have all the time in the world, right? I can tell you the rest later, so let's set work aside. I only brought it up to demonstrate, you know, there will be late nights and canceled plans, but I will do my best. And probably there will be weirdness with Lauren, but she's got her own stuff going on, too. Hopefully that will distract her."

Paige smiled. "Okay. I take your point. Probably not all smooth sailing. But I think if we talk to each other and stay honest, we'll be okay."

"Yes. I promise to be honest and tell you how I feel, if you do the same. If we hold up this bargain, this might just work out."

"I certainly hope so."

"How's your ice cream?"

Paige had nearly finished hers, so she scooped the last bit onto her spoon. "Excellent. How is yours?"

Josh looked into his cup. "Fantastic. Sneaky of you to feed me to butter me up and then mold me to your will."

Paige reached across the table and took the hand he hadn't been using to eat his ice cream. "You liked all of it, didn't you?"

"Immensely."

"So you want to go join this party now?" Paige glanced at her watch.

"When does it *actually* start?"

"Five minutes ago."

"Cool. We'll be fashionably late. And you can smell that pork being smoked from here. I can't wait."

———

When they walked through the entrance of the BBQ restaurant, they found a nondescript space full of picnic tables. The entire back of the restaurant was a series of glass doors that were pushed open to a back area with more picnic tables. The place was mobbed and smelled like pork.

Paige got out her phone to text Lauren to ask if they'd arrived yet, but she spotted Caleb's head above the crowd in the outdoor area.

They were more than five minutes late. Once they had noticed that they were totally alone in the ice cream parlor's backseat area, Josh had insisted on kissing Paige again, some more, and they'd lost track of time until Josh's stomach rumbled. They'd had a good laugh about it and then walked hand in hand back to the BBQ place. So by the time they got to Caleb and Lauren's table, Evan, Lindsay, and a couple of guys Paige didn't recognize but who must have been Caleb's friends were all there.

"This was a choice," Josh said as they joined the group.

Paige couldn't disagree. The crowd was one thing, but the fact that it was a steamy mid-August day and this place was not air conditioned was something else. There were huge fans positioned all over the dining area, but they were mostly just pushing hot air around. Apparently Paige was the only one bothered by this.

Lauren took one look at the two of them and let out a little squeal. "So what happened?"

"Oh, right, you were a coconspirator," said Josh. "That was tricky of you, making me show up an hour early."

"And yet you're still late," said Caleb, with a raised eyebrow.

Evan looked between everyone. "What's going on?"

Josh shrugged. "Paige used subterfuge to feed me ice cream and talk me into taking her back."

"And?" Lauren said.

Josh, still acting casual, said, "I took her back."

Everyone let out a little cheer.

"Anyway," said Caleb. "Thanks for coming, everyone. We didn't think it would be this crowded."

"You really should have known better," said Lindsay. "A Brooklyn barbecue joint on a nice summer day? I'm surprised it's not *more* crowded."

"It's casual and summery," said Lauren, sounding defensive.

"Oh, guys, this is Will," said Evan. "He's my date for this shindig. He's a cookbook editor."

"Nice to meet you," said Josh, shaking Will's hand.

Paige almost laughed, surprised she hadn't recognized Will from their disastrous singles event. Will was a cute blond guy with glasses. "Nice to see you again."

"Josh is Lauren's brother, right?" Will asked.

"Yes, and he and Paige are now dating again, by the sounds of it."

"Accurate," said Paige.

The setup at the restaurant was that diners ordered food and drinks from one of a few different counters and then were given a buzzer that lit up when their food was ready. After ascertaining what Paige wanted, Josh got up to go order their food.

When Will left to pick up his and Evan's food, Paige leaned over and said, "So that's going well."

"Yeah, so far, so good. He's cute, he's smart, and he's a great home cook."

"And you know this because you've been to his home?"

"Maybe. Also, his boss is this apparently famous, award-winning cookbook editor. Like, she was on an episode of *Top Chef* as a judge. So he's gotten to meet all these celebrity chefs. You'd be surprised which ones are cool and which ones are assholes."

"I bet I wouldn't."

Evan laughed. "But, yeah, I like him, hence inviting him to meet my friends."

"I'm happy for you, Ev."

"And how are things with you and Josh, really? Did you talk to him?"

"Yes, just before we came over here." Explaining all that she was feeling and everything they'd said too each other was too much in a loud restaurant, so she summed it up by saying, "We're gonna give it a go."

"Excellent. I was rooting for you kids."

"Yeah?"

Evan shrugged. "What can I say? I'm a hopeless romantic."

As the sun set, Lauren banged a fork against Caleb's beer glass and said, "Hey, guys, Caleb and I have some news, and since you're all here, now is as good a time as any to tell you."

They had everyone's attention. Since Paige already knew the news, she sat back and watched everyone else's reactions.

Caleb put an arm around Lauren and said, "You tell them."

"Okay. Well, we're having a baby!"

Josh apparently already knew, too, because he didn't look even a little surprised, though he smiled. Everyone else clapped and cheered and congratulated them. For the next half hour, everyone peppered them with questions. Did they know the sex? No, they'd decided to wait. How did Lauren feel? Good now, but her morning sickness during the first trimester had been a bitch, which is why she'd changed the schedule so she wouldn't have to open the Cat Café for a few weeks. Paige had noticed that but hadn't said anything at the time, figuring Lauren had her reasons for not wanting to open. Were they excited? Immensely. Caleb had, in fact, already started measuring their guest room to convert it into a nursery.

Guests started to leave as it got darker. Once Lauren announced she was tired and ready to go home, the party was basically over. That left Paige and Josh behind at the restaurant as stars started to appear in the sky.

"So you want to get another drink or try that peach cobbler, or what do you want to do?" Josh asked.

"Let's get out of here," she said. She raised an eyebrow.

Josh grinned. "Your place or mine?"

EPILOGUE

A NEW HIGH-PROFILE RESTAURANT HAD opened on Whitman Street about a month ago, and it was a mere three blocks from Josh's new office near Brooklyn Borough Hall, so Paige thought it would be a fabulous place to have an anniversary dinner.

She'd arrived first and spent a few minutes perusing the menu, which was mostly classic American dishes with Latin influences. The chef had three other well-regarded restaurants in Manhattan, but this was his first foray into Brooklyn. As the menu explained, the chef had also been a fixture on the Food Network and a contestant on several cooking-related TV competitions. Where did he find the time?

She was saved from having to worry about that too much when Josh arrived, finally. When he sat across from Paige, he looked tired and a little disheveled, but happy.

"One week down," Paige said.

Josh grinned. "What a week! They threw me right into the deep end."

There had been an opening in the Law Enforcement Assistance

Unit of the Brooklyn DA's office, so Josh's new job involved the kind of investigation he found really exciting, plus he got to prepare subpoenas and warrants to help bring in the bad guys. The unit helped with a wide range of cases, but Josh's first was a homicide. He hadn't told Paige much about the particulars of the case, but he had told her that he was working with a pair of detectives he really liked. He also hoped that, eventually, he'd get promoted into the trial division, but for now he was content to work on investigations. Either way, Paige hoped he was much happier at this job than he had been at DCL.

Paige admired Josh's ambition and ability to look toward the future. And she knew that the last few months at DCL had been a slog for him as he'd worked on a series of cases that left a bad taste in his mouth, ultimately pushing him to start job searching in earnest. His dream of being a prosecutor was finally being realized, although he'd spent a fair amount of time fretting about the pay cut. Paige had assured him it was fine. After all, she knew all about leaving a lucrative job for something one found more fulfilling. They both had money in savings, and two months ago, they'd moved into a new apartment where they were splitting the rent, so already Josh's monthly expenses had gone down.

They were happy. And Paige had some ideas for the future, too.

They ordered, and then Josh settled into his chair and smiled. "Sorry I was late, by the way."

"It's fine. They let you leave before sundown."

"True! I mean, I'm on call in case something develops in the investigation this weekend, but otherwise, I am all yours for the next two days."

"I got the weekend off from the Cat Café."

"Wow, really? No Sunday events? No crafts?"

"Nope. Somehow we have a weekend with nothing on the schedule. Not even a private event."

"So we really do have the whole weekend to ourselves." Josh lowered his eyelids. "I wonder what trouble we could get into."

Paige laughed, and their drinks and the appetizers Josh had, of course, ordered arrived.

When they were halfway through their dinner, Paige said, "There was something I wanted to ask you."

"Yeah? This steak is really good, by the way. I've never had skirt steak this tender."

Paige laughed. "Josh? I love you."

He grinned. "I love you, too. More than I love food, even."

"That's a lot." She reached over and pat his hand. "But anyway, I've been thinking lately that, you know, we're in a committed relationship, we love each other, maybe it's time to take the next step."

Josh stopped eating and stared at her. "Next step? Paige, are you—"

"I think we should get married."

Josh pressed his lips together, but Paige could see the mirth in his eyes. "I'm supposed to ask you, you know."

"That's sexist. I don't see any reason why whoever wants to can't propose to their significant other."

She felt pretty strongly that she had to keep showing Josh

that she wanted to be with him, even though she knew he believed she did. Things between them had been really good these last several months. Paige had even mentioned her plan for tonight to Evan, Lauren, and Lindsay over drinks. All three had been on board, although Evan had bet that she'd chicken out. He reminded her of the time when Monica proposed to Chandler on *Friends* and how Chandler had to take over. Paige had pointed out that Monica had set up all the candles and everything. She'd done the work. That was the important part. They'd shared a laugh over that.

Josh sat across from her now and raised an eyebrow. "Do you have a ring?"

"Well, no. Men don't wear engagement rings. Which I also think is sexist, by the way. I mean, who cares about the rings? If you say yes, we'll tell people we're engaged, or I'll buy you a watch or something. That's a thing people do, I've heard. Why haven't you said yes?"

"Because I win."

Paige frowned. What had he won?

Josh reached into his pocket and pulled something out, which he placed on the table. It was a ring box. Paige was surprised to find her heart starting to pound. She'd thought this through carefully and rationally. They loved each other, they already lived together, and they often talked as though they had a long future together. Josh was ambitious and forward-looking and had big plans for his life and career, and for the last few months, he'd been talking as if it was a given that Paige would be part of those plans. And Paige had thought that, in order to really show Josh what he meant to her and that she was completely committed to their relationship, she should be the one to propose. But all she'd said was, "I think we should get married." She hadn't even asked him.

And there was a ring on the table.

"You may have asked first, but I bought a ring," Josh said. He sounded smug.

Paige reached for the ring box and picked it up. She opened it. Tears sprung to her eyes. She couldn't believe he had done this. It was a simple but beautiful ring, a diamond set in the middle with tiny diamonds on either side on what looked like a platinum band. Something likely absurdly expensive. Something he couldn't afford now that he was working for the DA.

"*Bought* is maybe overselling it," Josh said. "You're looking at the diamonds from my grandmother's wedding ring. But the band was damaged, so I had them reset in a new band."

"Are you serious?"

"Yep. My grandparents were happily married for almost sixty years. That seemed like a good omen. My mom told me when Grandma died that she had intended for the ring to go to my future bride, so I figured it was time to call that in."

"What I hear you saying is that you and I are so on the same wavelength that we both had the idea to propose tonight."

Josh smiled. "I mean, *technically*, I had the idea first. I had to get the ring from my mom and then take it to a jeweler and all that."

"Well, now you're just showing off. When did you get the ring from your mom?"

"Uh, when Mom flew out here for Lauren's baby shower."

"But that was four months ago!"

Josh shrugged. "When you know you know."

"What took you so long? You haven't been walking around with a ring in your pocket in case I bring it up, have you?"

"Oh, no. The ring happened to be ready to pick up from the jeweler's today. That's why I was late. I went to pick it up. Then they gave me this fancy bag and blah, blah, but I figured that would be a giveaway, so I took the ring out and ditched the bag. It's just a tremendous coincidence that you decided to mention it today. Or fate! I prefer to think it was fate."

Paige laughed. "Fine, it's fate."

"You should put the ring on."

Paige took the ring, which really was quite beautiful, out of the box and slid it on her finger. It fit perfectly, which meant Josh had probably had the forethought to get the right size from one of Paige's other rings. "You're too thoughtful." The words came out watery because Paige was really crying now. How had she ever ended up with a guy this amazing?

"*Too* thoughtful?"

"I was trying to make this big gesture to make it clear that I love you and I'm committed to you, and you have to go and upstage me."

"It's not a contest." Josh reached over and grabbed her hand to admire the ring. "That does look really spectacular. I take it that's a yes."

"Neither of us technically asked."

Josh titled his head. "Oh, true. You're totally right."

"But I'll marry you if you marry me."

"Deal." He reached over and wiped the tears from her face. "I think we should seal it with a kiss."

She smiled. She marveled again at how lucky she was and then she leaned across the table and kissed Josh.

KEEP READING FOR A PEEK AT
LIKE CATS AND DOGS

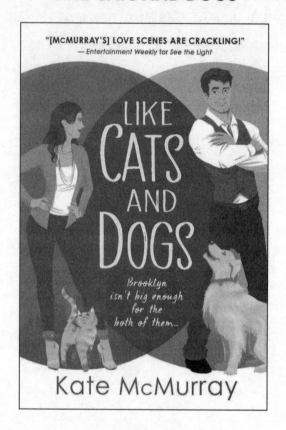

Available now.

CHAPTER 1

SADIE THE OFFICE MANAGER YOWLED.

"I hear ya," Lauren said absently as she leaned against the counter and looked at her phone. There was an unusually long line of people waiting for their morning coffee. Lauren was a bit of a spy in her own kingdom as she waited for her own coffee, letting customers go ahead of her as she kept an eye on her staff.

She glanced at her phone and refreshed the page one more time. The photos were still right there on top. Derek and Joanna's wedding. Derek smiling like he hadn't in years, Joanna looking ridiculously beautiful, and Lauren wondering how Derek was happy and married now when she was single and surrounded by cats.

Literally. Sadie walked up and rubbed against her leg. The little butterball of a cat had the loudest purr Lauren had ever heard, and she deployed it now, sounding like dice being rolled across a wooden table.

Lauren had read recently that cats likely purred not to display happiness but rather to lure prey into a false sense of security. She leaned down and pet Sadie's head anyway.

Evan walked into the Whitman Street Cat Café, pushing through the second door and grinning at Lauren like he'd already had three cups of coffee.

"Derek got married this weekend," Lauren said by way of greeting.

"Aw, honey, I'm sorry," said Evan. "Anything I can do?"

"Drive to New Hampshire and punch him in the face?"

Evan tilted his head and seemed to consider doing just that. "As fun as that sounds, Derek is kind of a big guy. He might punch back, and I bruise like a peach."

Lauren laughed despite herself. She shoved her phone in her pocket. "I'm over it. So my ex got married? It's fine. I'm fine."

"Attagirl." Evan looked up at the menu like he didn't get coffee here nearly every morning.

"Not that I'm sad for the business," said Lauren, "but where did all these people come from?"

"Didn't you hear? The Star Café closed last week."

The Star Café was a great independent coffee shop that had, apparently until last week, been right across the street from the Cat Café. If it had closed, that explained all the people here, the last place that served coffee between Henry Street and the subway entrance on the next block.

"I'm devastated," Evan continued.

Lauren raised an eyebrow at him. "If anything, this is probably better for your health. There are only so many cups of coffee you can drink per day because you think the barista is cute before the caffeine gives you heart palpitations."

Evan sighed and leaned against the counter next to Lauren. "Pablo gave me heart palpitations."

"Any idea what he's up to now?"

"When I got my caramel vanilla latte on Friday, he told me he'd applied to work at that little indie bookstore a few doors down. Hope springs."

"Crazy idea, but you could, like, ask him out."

Evan gasped dramatically. "Where's the romance in that? We're performing an elaborate dance."

"Right." Lauren glanced behind the counter, where Monique looked panicked as she took another order. "Maybe I should hire him."

"He makes a mean caramel vanilla latte."

A bewildered man with light brown hair walked into the café then. Lauren had never seen him before, and she would have noticed. He was so handsome, Evan sucked in a sharp breath.

Lauren had sworn off men ever since Derek had announced his engagement, because she was tired of getting her heart stomped on, but that didn't mean she couldn't look. Because this man was pretty foxy. He was tall and fit with neatly trimmed hair, a square jaw, and blue eyes that sparkled even from behind the dark-rimmed glasses he wore.

"Hello," said Evan.

The man looked around. When Sadie trotted over to investigate him, he looked a little startled by her presence.

"Oh," he said, catching Lauren's eye. "I've heard about places like this, but I guess it didn't occur to me that the cats would just be...out."

"Only Sadie has free rein in the café," said Lauren. "She's in charge. She's also terrified of cars, so she doesn't try to escape. The rest of the cats are through that door." She pointed.

"Ah."

Lauren wasn't really sure what to say next. Evan elbowed her, though, so she said, "Did you want to see the cats, or—"

"I just need a cup of coffee for now. This place is hopping."

"Go on," Lauren said. "I'm not in line, and you look like you're in a hurry."

The man pulled a phone from his pocket and glanced at the time. "Yeah, a little." He slid forward. "Thank you."

"Are you new to the neighborhood?"

"Yeah. Just moved to Brooklyn a week ago, actually."

"Welcome!"

He shot her a bashful half smile and nodded. "Thanks."

Monique said, "Next!"

The brown-haired man nodded at Lauren and then walked to the register.

Victor, the other barista, must have noticed this guy was a little twitchy, probably with a job to get to—he was wearing a blue oxford shirt tucked into navy-blue slacks, the uniform of the Midtown office worker—so he grabbed the pot and poured a cup of coffee right away. Once the man paid, Victor handed him the cup and said, "Milk and sugar are at the end of the counter."

"Great." The man took his cup.

"The usual," Lauren said to Monique now that the line had dissipated. Then she walked over to the man as he shook a sugar packet. "I'm Lauren, by the way."

The man gave her a genuine smile this time. "Caleb. Maybe

I'll see you around, Lauren." Sadie meowed and sat at his feet. "And you, too, Sadie."

Handsome, and he liked the cats. No wedding ring. This had some potential.

Oh, except for the part where Lauren was not dating in order to concentrate on making a fulfilling life for herself without a man.

Caleb walked back outside.

"Girl," said Evan. "He was totally checking you out."

Warm excitement spread through Lauren's chest. It had been a while since she'd met anyone who made her pulse race like this. She wondered if Caleb would come back.

"Boss, your coffee's ready," said Monique.

Lauren took it gratefully. "All right. Do you have to work today, Ev, or do you want to meet our newest resident? We've got a gorgeous new calico named Lucy."

"I'm meeting a client at ten, so I gotta go, but you can tell me all about Miss Lucy and report back on that tall guy over drinks tonight."

"Pop at seven?"

"Perfect."

Monique handed Evan his coffee, which he took with a grin. He blew Lauren a kiss with his free hand and then walked out the door.

"Come on, Sadie," said Lauren. "Let's get to work."

———————

Caleb walked out of the Cat Café, wondering what he'd just seen. For some reason, he hadn't expected actual cats. When his new boss had recommended it as a place to grab coffee, he'd expected beatniks or something. There was a bar on his block called the Salty Dog that contained zero dogs, after all. But, no, the Whitman Street Cat Café was a place people went to get coffee and pastries and hang out with actual cats.

The woman had been pretty nice to look at. Lauren, she'd said her name was. A little tall, with long, straight brown hair, a fringe of bangs across her forehead, and a dusting of freckles across her nose. Pretty smile. And, okay, he'd noticed her figure, too. After his recent and very messy divorce, it was nice to know that part of him hadn't died along with his belief in happily ever after.

She'd been so comfortable in the space that he figured she worked there or was at least a regular, so maybe he'd run into her again.

In the meantime, though, he had to cope with his first day at the new job. Caleb strolled all ten feet from the café door to the main entrance of the Whitman Street Veterinary Clinic. A little bell rang over the door, catching the attention of the cat perched on the lap of a woman sitting in the waiting area.

"Dr. Fitch!" said the vet tech at the reception desk as Caleb approached. He couldn't remember her name at first, but then noticed she had a name tag on her scrubs identifying her as Rachel. Olivia's weird insistence on name tags would pay off after all, because Caleb was terrible with names.

Although he'd remember Lauren.

No, not the time. He smiled at Rachel. "Good morning."

"I see you got coffee from the Cat Café," she said, pointing to his cup. "The Star Café made better lattes, but they're closed now."

Caleb took a sip of his coffee. It was pretty standard drip coffee, stronger than the stuff those dumb little pods at his old job made, so he was happy enough with it.

"Welcome to Whitman Street," Rachel said. "Olivia's in her office. She told me to send you there when you came in."

"Right. And that is…"

"Oh!" Rachel hopped up and led Caleb to a swinging door that he remembered led to the exam rooms and administrative offices. She held the door open and said, "Go left here, then right at the end of the hall, and Olivia's office is right there."

"Thanks."

Olivia Ling was indeed in her office when Caleb found it. She seemed absorbed in something on her computer screen, so Caleb knocked on the doorframe. She looked up and seemed confused for a moment, but then recognition dawned. "Caleb! Please come in."

He'd already taken care of the new-hire paperwork, so the main thing would be to work out scheduling and procedures. Caleb would be the fifth veterinarian on staff at a fairly busy clinic, but he was happy to work in a big office. The clinic he'd come from had been run by two people and constantly felt short-staffed.

"I see you got coffee from the Cat Café."

"Oh. Yeah, you said it was the best coffee on the block." Also the only coffee on the block, from what he could tell.

"Did you talk to the manager?"

"No. I got coffee."

Olivia smiled. "Well, just so you know, we have a partnership. We're the official vet of the Cat Café, and they help us find forever homes for any cats who end up here."

That made sense. "Do they do pet adoptions?"

"Yeah, that's the Cat Café's secret mission. They lure people in with coffee and pastries in hopes the customers fall in love with one of the cats and take it home."

"Sneaky."

"Anyway, scheduling."

Olivia had already explained when she expected the vets in her clinic to work—including at least one overnight per week, because this was the only animal clinic in Brooklyn that kept emergency hours. A whiteboard on the wall showed which vets were scheduled on which days. Then she took him on a chatty tour through the exam rooms.

"Remind me where you worked before this?" she asked, sounding like she was trying to make conversation but probably gauging whether she could leave him alone with patients or if she needed to keep an eye on him until he adapted to her preferred procedures.

"The Animal Care Clinic on 110th Street in Morningside Heights. It closed a few weeks ago." Well, it closed because Kara had divorced Caleb, shut down the clinic, and moved to LA with her new boyfriend, but this was not information Olivia needed.

"Let's do the first patient together," Olivia said. She grabbed a chart from the plastic holder on the door to Exam Room 1, then popped her head into the waiting room and said, "Jingles?"

The woman, who'd been holding the cat in her lap when Caleb had walked in, kicked a cat carrier under the seat and carried her surprisingly placid-looking gray cat into the exam room.

All right, that was how this would play out. Caleb plastered his best animal-loving smile on his face and prepared to examine this cat under Olivia's watchful eye.

About the Author

Kate McMurray writes smart, savvy romantic fiction. She likes creating stories that are brainy, funny, and, of course, sexy, with regular guy characters and urban sensibilities. She advocates for romance stories by and for everyone. When she's not writing, Kate edits textbooks, watches baseball, plays violin, crafts things out of yarn, and wears a lot of cute dresses. Kate's gay romances have won or finaled several times in the Rainbow Awards for LGBT fiction and nonfiction. She also served in the leadership of Romance Writers of America. Kate lives in Brooklyn, New York, with two cats and too many books.

Website: katemcmurray.com

Facebook: facebook.com/katemcmurraywriter

Twitter: @katemcmwriter

Pinterest: pinterest.com/katem1738

Instagram: @katemcmurraygram

MOOSE SPRINGS, ALASKA

Welcome to Moose Springs, Alaska,
a small town with a big heart, and the only world-class
resort where black bears hang out to look at *you*.

The Tourist Attraction

There's a line carved into the dirt between the tiny town of Moose Springs, Alaska, and the luxury resort up the mountain. Until tourist Zoey Caldwell came to town, Graham Barnett knew better than to cross it. But when Graham and Zoey's worlds collide, not even the neighborhood moose can hold them back...

Mistletoe and Mr. Right

She's Rick Harding's dream girl. Unfortunately, socialite Lana Montgomery has angered locals with her good intentions. When a rare (and spiteful) white moose starts destroying the holiday decorations every night, Lana, Rick, and all of Moose Springs must work together to save Christmas, the town...and each other.

Enjoy the View

Hollywood starlet River Lane is struggling to remake herself as a documentary filmmaker. When mountaineer and staunch Moose Springs local Easton Lockett takes River and her film crew into the wild...what could possibly go wrong?

**"A unique voice and a
grumptastic hero! I'm sold."**

—*Sarina Bowen, USA Today* bestselling author

For more info about Sourcebooks's books and authors, visit:

sourcebooks.com

HAPPY SINGLES DAY

A funny and fresh romance by author Ann Marie
Walker is something to celebrate!

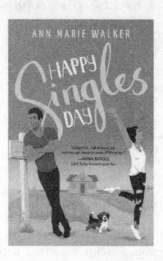

As a Certified Professional Organizer, everything in Paige Parker's world is as it should be. Perfect apartment, perfect office, perfect life. And now, the perfect vacation planned to celebrate Singles Day at an adorable B and B.

As the owner of a now-dormant bed-and-breakfast, Lucas Croft's life is simple and quiet. It's only him and his five-year-old daughter, which is just the way he likes it. But when Paige books a room that Lucas' well-intentioned sister listed without his knowledge, their two worlds collide. If they can survive the week together, they just might discover exactly what they've both been missing.

"A positively delightful romance full of heart, joy, and enough charm to jump off of the page."

—Nina Bocci, *USA Today* bestselling author